That's My Baby!

"Married? This is a joke, right?"

Lydia gawked at the lawyer who had summoned her and Powell to her office.

"Surely there is a family better suited to care for two small children," Powell said.

He shifted, a subtle movement that brought him so close, Lydia could feel him, smell him, react to him with every fiber of her being. *She'd thought she was over him.*

"Did the two of you not agree to be godparents to Dan and Susan's children?"

Lydia glanced at Powell. "Ms. St. Ives, those arrangements were made a long time ago, when Powell and I were, uh, well…"

Lovers. The unspoken word shuddered in the silence.

"Involved," Powell finished for her.

Ms. St. Ives closed the file on her desk. "Well, it seems to me that having been *involved* is a good thing for two people about to become husband and wife. And parents."

Dear Reader,

As you head for your favorite vacation hideaway, don't forget to bring along some Special Edition novels for sensational summertime reading!

This month's THAT'S MY BABY! title commemorates Diana Whitney's twenty-fifth Silhouette novel! *I Now Pronounce You Mom & Dad*, which also launches her FOR THE CHILDREN miniseries, is a poignant story about two former flames who conveniently wed for the sake of their beloved godchildren. Look for book two, *A Dad of His Own*, in September in the Silhouette Romance line, and book three, *The Fatherhood Factor*, in Special Edition in October.

Bestselling author Joan Elliott Pickart wraps up her captivating THE BACHELOR BET series with a heart-stirring love story between an amnesiac beauty and a brooding doctor in *The Most Eligible M.D.* The excitement continues with *Beth and the Bachelor* by reader favorite Susan Mallery—a romantic tale about a suburban mom who is swept off her feet by her very own Prince Charming. And fall in love with a virile *Secret Agent Groom*, book two in Andrea Edwards's THE BRIDAL CIRCLE series, about a shy Plain Jane who is powerfully drawn to her mesmerizing new neighbor.

Rounding out this month, Jennifer Mikels delivers an emotional reunion romance that features a rodeo champ who returns to his hometown to make up for lost time with the woman he loves… and the son he never knew existed, in *Forever Mine*. And family secrets are unveiled when a sophisticated lady melts a gruff cowboy's heart in *A Family Secret* by Jean Brashear.

I hope you enjoy each of these romances—where dreams come true!

Best,

Karen Taylor Richman
Senior Editor

Please address questions and book requests to:
Silhouette Reader Service
U.S.: 3010 Walden Ave., P.O. Box 1325, Buffalo, NY 14269
Canadian: P.O. Box 609, Fort Erie, Ont. L2A 5X3

DIANA WHITNEY

I NOW PRONOUNCE
YOU MOM & DAD

Published by Silhouette Books

America's Publisher of Contemporary Romance

To my wonderful son, Neil, and his beautiful wife, Lisa.
Not that the title of this book is a hint, but you'd both
make terrific parents. Really. Terrific.
Hmm...maybe it IS a hint. *grin*

SILHOUETTE BOOKS

ISBN 0-373-24261-1

I NOW PRONOUNCE YOU MOM & DAD

Visit us at www.romance.net

Printed in U.S.A.

Books by Diana Whitney

DIANA WHITNEY

A three-time Romance Writers of America RITA finalist, *Romantic Times Magazine* Reviewers' Choice nominee and finalist for Colorado Romance Writer's Award of Excellence, Diana Whitney has published more than two dozen romance and suspense novels since her first Silhouette title in 1989. A popular speaker, Diana has conducted writing workshops, and has published several articles on the craft of fiction writing for various trade magazines and newsletters. She is a member of Authors Guild, Novelists, Inc., Published Authors Network and Romance Writers of America. She and her husband live in rural Northern California, with a beloved menagerie of furred creatures, domestic and wild. She loves to hear from readers. You can write to her c/o Silhouette Books, 300 East 42nd Street, 6th Floor, New York, NY 10017.

Dear Reader,

Children are so precious, so dear. I'm a mom, and I adore children. Babies have a particular hold on my heart, though, with their sweet powdery scent and infectious, high-pitched giggles. But babies, and all children, need the nurture of family, the love of parents who treasure them and cherish each other. That's what THAT'S MY BABY! is all about. And my new miniseries, FOR THE CHILDREN, also celebrates the joys of children, as Clementine, a crafty, white-haired matchmaker, creates kinship out of chaos, brings romance to the lonely and heals splintered families with love, warmth and a devious touch of blarney!

In *I Now Pronounce You Mom & Dad,* it's a rollicking battle of wills when Powell Greer and Lydia Farnsworth, once star-crossed lovers, are reunited to care for their orphaned godchildren, a bewildered four-year-old and his precious baby sister. The catch? Powell and Lydia have to get married. The problem? Neither of them knows the slightest thing about children, but both know all too much about each other.

Or do they?

Since children are so dear to my heart, this is a very special series for me, and *I Now Pronounce You Mom & Dad,* my twenty-fifth Silhouette novel, is a very special story. I hope you enjoy reading it as much as I enjoyed writing it for you.

All the best,

Chapter One

"Married? You can't be serious." Lydia Farnsworth jolted forward, sloshing tea from the bone china cup balanced on her knee.

After a stunned moment Powell Greer set aside a cup too frail for his large, callused hand, wiped his palms on his worn jeans and spoke to the grandmotherly woman seated in a rocking chair across the room. "This is a joke, right?"

Without disrupting the rocker's rhythmic creak, Clementine Allister St. Ives glanced up from the fat file in her lap, allowing magnifying granny glasses to slip from her nose and bounce at her matronly bosom on a pair of pearl bungees. "Don't bedevil yourself, lad, 'tis nothing to fear. Young folks nowadays step in and out of matrimony as if trying on slippers. Now in my time…" Her bright gaze flitted to Lydia, who was absently rubbing at a spreading stain on the skirt of her ivory linen suit. "Oh, gracious, we can't have that."

Lydia blinked, startled when the woman rose from her chair to snatch a fine linen napkin from a nearby refreshment buffet. "It's nothing, really."

Ignoring the protest, Clementine scuttled across the room at a spritely clip for a woman who was rumored to be in her seventies, with arthritic knees. Before Lydia could say another word, Clementine hunched over her lap, dabbing at the moisture and chattering madly. "Most folks think it's the tea that stains, but my sainted mother swore 'twas the milk." She straightened, frowned, dropped the napkin on Lydia's lap and *tsked* under her breath. "A bit of club soda should put things right. Dierdre?"

"Please, don't bother—"

"Pish, child, 'tis not a bit of it." Dismissing the concern with a flick of her gnarled fingers, Clementine brightened as a demure, dark-haired woman appeared in the doorway. "Ah. Dierdre, my sweet, there's been a wee accident. Would you please be a love and bring Ms. Farnsworth a bit of seltzer?"

As the smiling young woman hurried off, Lydia could practically feel Powell's smug grin, but wouldn't allow herself to look at him. He was no doubt enjoying her embarrassment at having committed such a social breach. Her own parents would have been mortified. Farnsworths simply did not slop refreshments upon themselves, nor did they use the wrong eating utensil or incorrectly fold a napkin after use. Throughout Lydia's childhood, the social graces had been rigidly taught, scrupulously enforced. Since Powell knew that, she wasn't surprised that he was enjoying her discomfort.

The moment Clementine stepped out of hearing range, he leaned over to whisper, "How terribly uncouth and common of you. Mama—'' he stressed the final syllable in the pretentious pronunciation upon which Lydia's mother insisted ''—would not be pleased.''

Balling the napkin in her fist, Lydia responded with a tight smile and a loose shrug. "At least I don't eat spaghetti with my fingers."

He chuckled. "It got your attention, didn't it?"

Despite her determination not to smile, the corner of her mouth twitched upward. The memory was too humorous, too dear to her. The incident had occurred the first time she'd laid eyes on Powell Greer and realized that life as she'd known it would never be the same. Powell had always made her laugh, sometimes by exaggerating life's serious moments with an unexpected absurdity, sometimes simply by teasing her out of a churlish mood until she could no longer stifle a giggle.

She'd always loved that about him. Loved it too much, it seemed.

Her attention refocused on Clementine, who had returned to offer a silver platter heaped with cookies and scones. "Would you fancy a biscuit, Mr. Greer? A big strapping man like yourself needs his nourishment. My sainted da believed it bad luck for a man to conduct business on an empty stomach."

Powell's eyes glazed at the word *business* as if he was just recalling the solemn occasion for which they were gathered. He refused the proffered refreshment, nervously cleared his throat. "Now, about this agreement—"

"All in good time, Mr. Greer, all in good time." With a swish of lavender scent, the tray was poised in front of Lydia's startled face. "Dierdre makes the finest shortbread this side of the big pond," Clementine purred, referring to the Atlantic Ocean with the affectionate brogue of her homeland. "Melts on the tongue like sweet cream in sunshine. Do try some, dear."

With her nerves stretched raw, Lydia found her stomach knotting at the thought of food. "Perhaps later."

Clementine issued a worried cluck, but returned the platter to the buffet and hobbled back toward her rocking chair without further comment.

Powell shifted, a subtle movement that moved him closer, so close Lydia could feel him, smell him, react to him with every fiber of her being. Her pulse raced as a familiar throb ached its way from heart to belly in the blink of an eye. It had been so long, so terribly long.

She'd thought she was over him.

Maybe not.

A blur from the doorway caught Lydia's attention. Dierdre strode into the room, smiling and radiant, to hand over an open bottle of club soda. She accepted Lydia's thanks with a cheery nod, then disappeared again, closing the massive carved doors behind her.

"Now," Clementine murmured, settling back into her rocker. "Let's see what we have." She retrieved the file as a gray tabby appeared from behind a teakwood étagère to leap effortlessly into her lap. Trilling softly, the cat rubbed its chin on one corner of the open file. Clementine absently stroked the animal, but was otherwise preoccupied studying a document in the file, presumably the last will and testament that had brought them here today, and would change their lives forever.

Lydia shuddered, shifted, forced her focus away from that somber document to regard the woman who had summoned her and Powell. Clementine St. Ives was a bona fide eccentric, a baffling amalgam of wrinkled wisdom blended with a brilliant and crafty mind. With degrees from Harvard, Stanford and Berkeley, Clementine practiced family law, was a professor of genealogy and used her credentials as a licensed psychologist to conduct counseling sessions inside the stately Victorian manor where she'd purportedly resided for over fifty years.

The house was an extension of the woman herself, a blend of old-world elegance and modern technology. A Tiffany-style lamp twinkled from a gleaming antique sideboard that complimented a decor more appropriate to a turn-of-the-century parlor than a law office. Doilies, Irish lace window sheers and tapestry cushions were used generously, and cut-crystal vases were filled with fresh flowers that lent their own distinctive fragrance to the scents of potpourri and sweet lavender. An old-fashioned grandeur surrounded them and reminded Lydia of her great-grandmama's sitting room.

Except there had been no laptop computer winking on great-grandmama's cherry-wood desk, nor had her delicate floral wallpaper been studded with framed university degrees, service awards and at least one honorary doctorate.

Clementine, too, was a dichotomy, one minute a fussy hostess serving shortbread and tea biscuits, and the next a consummate professional from the top of her neatly coiffed silver hair to the soles of her no-nonsense, chunky-heeled business pumps.

She spoke without looking up from the file. "Now then, Mr. Greer, what part of the agreement puzzles you?"

Startled, Powell shifted, shrugged, absently adjusted the open collar of a plaid work shirt that clung to his muscular chest like a second skin. "The, uh, guardianship itself. Surely Dan and Susan have…" He hesitated, and a flash of pain dulled his eyes as he corrected himself. "Had family members better suited to care for two small children."

"Sadly, no." Clementine closed the file without disturbing the snoozing cat. "Danny, rest his soul, was an orphan himself, just as his own wee ones are now. Susan's mother would love to care for her grandbabies, bless her, but she's too ill to care for a pair of feisty young ones on her own. She's a widow, you know.''

"Yes, I know, but still there must be someone—"

"Ah, but there is," Clementine agreed brightly. "Says so right here in Dan and Susan's will. Shall I read it to you?"

"No." Powell heaved a miserable sigh and leaned back against the red velvet cushion. He coughed, squirmed, scrupulously avoided Lydia's gaze. "This has all been a terrible mistake."

"Mistake, is it?" Clementine pursed her lips, glanced from Powell to Lydia and back again. "Did the two of you not stand up at Dan and Susan's wedding and agree to be godparents to their future children?"

"Yes, but—"

"And do they not have two such children?" She referred to the file. "Kenneth, not yet five, and dear little Tami Lynn, just turned one, bless her wee heart."

Powell's eyes darted sideways. "They do, but—"

"Well, there you have it." Clementine closed the file, flashed him a gloating grin. "'Twas no mistake at all."

He flinched. "I never thought…I mean, who'd have believed…" He looked away, pain etched on his face, the loss of a friend reflected in eyes so sad that Lydia's heart ached in response.

Clementine, too, softened in sympathy, leaning forward in the rocker until her bosom pressed against, but didn't disturb, the dozing feline in her lap. "Aye, 'tis a terrible thing when two young people are struck down in the prime of their lives." A silent moment passed, then Clementine again referred to the document she held. "Dan and Susan were good parents. A trust has been established for the children's care, and they clearly wanted you and Ms. Farnsworth to raise their little ones together.''

Powell opened his mouth to speak, closed it, then slanted a wary glance at Lydia. He sighed, licked his lips. ''Like I said, Ms. St. Ives, those arrangements were made a long time ago, when Lydia and I were, uh, well…''

Lovers.

The unspoken word shuddered in the silence. Lydia looked away, furious with the sudden rush of moisture fogging her gaze, the sudden ache twisting through her heart.

''Involved,'' Powell finished lamely.

Clementine chuckled. ''Involved, is it? That should make things easier, don't you think? Knowing each other so well and all.''

Lydia managed not to moan. Powell simply stiffened. ''Look, I promised Dan and Susan I'd make sure their kids were taken care of. I never said anything about marriage.''

''It won't be forever,'' Clementine said with a dismissive flick of her hand. ''Just long enough to convince the court that the children will be in a stable, loving home. Judges have a nasty habit of tossing babies into foster care at the slightest provocation, they do, but once the guardianship papers are finalized, the two of you can draw up your own custody agreement and go on about your lives.''

If Powell's frown was any clue, he was not convinced. Nor was Lydia, who cleared her throat to venture a question. ''But marriage? That does seem rather extreme.''

''Aye, but it's for the children, lass.'' A sly gleam danced in the old woman's eyes. '''Tis always for the children.''

Shrouded by fog, whipped by blustery winds, a choppy sea lapped at barnacled pylons under the pier. Lydia turned her face away from the wind, tucked her icy hands in her coat pockets. A few feet away Powell tossed a French fry over the seawall toward a hungry flock of gulls. One dived from the group to snap up the treat. It settled on a pier post to enjoy its meal, while the losers circled the wharf, screeching in protest.

Powell tossed a final tidbit into the air. When he pitched the wadded bag into a trash can, the squawking gulls shifted en masse to seek out another amiable tourist for harassment.

Zipping a thick nylon jacket, Powell turned away from the ocean, ignoring the frigid wind whipping through his hair. He regarded Lydia thoughtfully, then nodded toward one of the open-air seafood establishments strung along San Francisco's Fisherman's Wharf. "How about some steamed crab legs?"

"No, thanks. I'm fine."

A hesitant smile touched the corner of his mouth. "You're fine, all right. But are you hungry?" His eyes gleamed with that odd blend of admiration and amusement that was uniquely his own.

It had been a long time since Lydia had felt the freeing laughter in her heart, that unexpected giggle in response to a teasing twinkle in his eyes. There was a manner about him, a way of making whomever he was with feel like the only person on earth capable of understanding the joke. He'd always made Lydia feel that way. He'd always made her feel special.

Perhaps that's why losing him had hurt so much.

The memory evoked a pang of regret, not unexpected, but sharp enough to be surprising. Her lower lip quivered. She caught it between her teeth and turned away.

The wharf, usually bright and humming with activity, was nearly abandoned on this dreary day. Gray fog clung to the city, along with a drizzle annoying enough to keep all but the hardiest tourists away. That suited Lydia, suited her reflective mood.

Behind her, sand crunched on concrete, as if Powell had shifted his stance. "Do you remember the last time we were here?"

Lydia remembered.

"I still have that hat."

She peered over her shoulder. "The whale cap?" She laughed. "Do you ever wear it?"

"All the time." He cocked his head in that endearing way of his and tried for a stung expression that didn't quite come off. "I told you I would, didn't I?"

Lydia didn't bother mentioning that he'd told her a lot of things back then. "I still have the necklace, too." A tiny golden starfish on a fragile golden chain. Lydia had always cherished it and the memories it evoked.

"Do you?" He gave her a wistful smile. "I wondered." He crossed his arms, tucking his hands under his armpits, and squinted into the wind.

Tall, muscular, with lean hips poured into denim work pants so tight they ought to be illegal, Powell Greer was by any standard an incredibly sexy man. It wasn't just the strength of a body honed to perfection hoisting fifty-pound rolls of phone cable up thirty-foot poles, nor was it the rugged planes of an angular face too sharp to be pretty, too appealing to be ignored. The secret of Powell's allure was in his eyes, hypnotic eyes reflecting his mood evocatively, like mirrors. Those eyes could gleam bright as polished silver, or growl dark as a winter storm.

Now they were the color of a cool ocean mist, obscure, nebulous, gentle but a little wary. "You look good, Lyddie. Real good."

A lump wedged in her throat. She whispered around it. "So do you."

"I hear you got a promotion last year."

"Dan told you?"

"He mentioned it." Powell's gaze skittered out to sea. "I always figured you'd make a name for yourself. Congratulations."

Lydia took a cleansing breath, held it and exhaled slowly. "It wasn't that big a deal, actually. I just moved up one very short rung on a very tall ladder. When I become the first female offered a partnership in the largest investment banking firm on the West Coast, then I'll celebrate."

He offered a limp smile. "Still thinking in terms of when rather than if?"

She flushed at the reminder that her ambition and his lack of it had always been a sticking point between them. His teasing had taken a resistant turn then. He'd used it to push her away, instead of drawing her closer. It had been subtle, so delicately evolved that she couldn't even remember when the change had taken place. She only knew things between them had suddenly been different. She still didn't know why.

Her shrug was indifferent enough to conceal the turmoil in her heart. "If we don't know where we're going, how can we possibly know when we've arrived? Besides, the future is never assured. Just because I want something doesn't mean I'll get it."

"You will." Powell pursed his lips, pushed a broken seashell with the toe of his boot. "You've always been too smart to settle for second best."

If there was an edge to his voice, Lydia didn't notice. It didn't occur to her that after six years Powell, too, might be reliving the past with ambivalence. Perhaps even a sense of loss.

As college sweethearts, they'd been star-crossed lovers

from separate worlds. Powell had been the middle-class issue of a blue-collar family, a young man who'd craved excitement and adventure over the daily drudgery his father had endured raising a family. Lydia, born privileged and raised to believe that no dream was beyond reach, had harbored grand ambitions for her own future, ambitions Powell hadn't shared and couldn't understand.

Their breakup hadn't been amicable, but it had been civil enough. Powell had left to see the world; Lydia had shored up a broken heart and headed off to grab the world by the tail.

Now their lives had collided again, and both were struggling to cope with that, and with the tragic loss that had brought them to this point.

As if reading her mind, Powell said, "I can't believe they're gone."

"I know."

For a moment, Powell studied the broken seashell beside his toe, then, without warning, he crushed it under his boot. "They say the other driver was drunk. Came out of it without a scratch."

"Yes." The pain hit again, sharp enough to make her suck in a breath. "Thank God the children weren't in the car."

"Yeah." There was no bitterness in his voice, only resignation. "Lydia?"

She glanced up, saw the lost look in his eyes.

"What are we going to do?"

"I don't know." She chewed her lip a moment. "What do you think we should do?"

He gave a helpless shrug. "Do you know anything about raising kids?"

"Not really."

"Me, neither." He stuffed his hands in his pockets and

studied the clouds. "I won't let them go into foster care. Dan spent his whole life bouncing from one family to another. He'd haunt me forever if I let that happen to his kids."

"Foster care isn't an option," Lydia agreed. That pesky knot in her stomach tightened again. Her head was spinning; her heart ached. A voice whispered through the mist, raw, choked with emotion. It was the sound of her heart, words uttered without thought, without permission. "I wish I'd spent more time with Susan."

Powell nodded. There was no reproach in his eyes, only understanding. Lydia presumed he was thinking back, remembering happier times, when the four of them had been inseparable. But that had been a long time ago, not long after Dan and Susan had married. Then Lydia and Powell had broken up, and their lives had taken different directions.

As Lydia's career had consumed more and more of her time, Susan's world had centered solely around her family. Phone calls between them became less frequent, visits even scarcer. They'd joked about how hectic their lives had become, but it hadn't concerned them. There was always tomorrow, or the next day, or maybe next month. It hadn't occurred to either of them that tomorrow might never come.

"I went fishing without him," Powell said suddenly.

Lydia blinked, saw a brief flash of regret in his eyes before he turned to lean on the pier railing with folded arms.

"We used to try and get away two or three times a year. Just the guys, you know?" He glanced over his shoulder, then looked away again. "But Dan was always worrying about something. Either Susan was pregnant, or one of the kids had a cough, or he couldn't scrape together enough money for the trip. When he did go, he could never relax, was always uptight, always looking for a damned phone to check on things at home. It made me crazy.''

Because she couldn't help herself, she reached out to touch his arm, then caught herself and stuffed her hand back into her coat pocket.

Powell's voice was wistful, a little sad. "Last summer, a bunch of us drove up to Clearlake to do some bass fishing. I was supposed to ask Dan to come along.'' His sleeve vibrated as if a tremor had run down his arm. He shook it off and ran his fingers through his wind-whipped hair. "I figured, why bother? He'd just spend the whole day showing off pictures and worrying about Kenny's runny nose. I told the guys he couldn't make it.''

"You can't blame yourself for that.''

He shrugged. "Who can I blame?''

"Nobody, because it's nobody's fault. You were right about Dan. He hated those fishing trips. He only went because he knew how much you loved them, and he didn't want to disappoint you.''

Although clearly surprised, Powell quickly rearranged his features into the emotionless mask Lydia recognized as his favored defense mechanism. "Dan told you that?''

"Susan mentioned it.''

He nodded, regarded her with enough intensity to make her squirm. "You and Susan talked about me?''

Now it was her turn to don the expressionless mask. "Occasionally.'' The reply was airy, nonchalant, tossed out as if she hadn't made it a point to ask about Powell each and every time she and Susan spoke. "Since you knew about my promotion, I presume you and Dan talked about me, too.''

Other than a rapid dilation of his pupils, his expression remained unchanged. "Occasionally.''

She brushed a flapping strand of smoky-blond hair from

her eyes and tipped her face into the wind, smiling. "Okay, okay. So we've kept up with each other's lives through our friends. That's not a crime."

A laugh line at the corner of his mouth deepened. "Speak for yourself. I plan to sue."

"California's a joint property state. Suing your wife is like suing yourself."

He stepped sideways, leaned against the railing with a startled expression. "So you think we should go through with it?"

Puffing her cheeks, Lydia blew out a breath. "According to Clementine, there's not much choice if we want to keep the children from being raised by the state."

"But *marriage*..." He had the grace to look embarrassed when his voice cracked. He coughed, shrugged, took a deep breath. "I mean, that's heavy-duty."

Lydia angled a look at him. "The children and I will try not to infringe on your precious freedom." The minute the words were out she regretted them. Powell's eyes darkened like a thundercloud. She reached for his arm as he turned away. "I'm sorry. Sniping at each other won't help the situation."

He nodded, slid a glance at the small hand resting on his sleeve. "So, you think it could work?"

"Yes, I do. The way Clementine explained things, we'd only have to share the house for a few months, then we'd terminate the marriage, draw up a joint custody agreement."

"How would that work?"

"I'm not sure, but I do know it wouldn't be good to move the children from your place to mine every six months."

He flinched. "No, that wouldn't be good."

"Perhaps," she said slowly, "it would be best if one of us maintained physical custody."

A wave of relief lightened his gaze. "Yeah, that would probably be best."

There wasn't much doubt that Lydia would be the full-time parent. She'd expected to be. After all, she knew Powell Greer better than anyone else. To him, parenthood would be like prison. "Title to the new house Clementine plans to purchase will be held by the children's trust." The condominium the children had shared with their parents was in the San Francisco area, much too far from Sacramento for Powell and Lydia to commute. "If we pay rent directly to the trustee, that should give the kids a nice nest egg for their education."

"Isn't it a little early to be thinking about how we'll put them through college?"

"It's never too soon to think about the future."

Powell's smile was slow, not particularly pleasant. "Yeah, that's right. Why live for the moment when there's a future to worry about?"

"What's that supposed to mean?" Lydia snapped, bristling at the implication that she didn't know how to live.

"Nothing." He sighed. "Look, Lydia, this isn't going to work. Those kids need real parents, not two people who can't spend five minutes together without arguing."

"We're not arguing, we're discussing. Not that I'd expect anyone who dropped out of college to dig irrigation canals in Central America to understand the difference."

"It was the Peace Corps."

She tossed her head, tapped her foot. "Whatever."

Powell laughed. "God, I love it when you're haughty."

"I am not haughty."

"Your eyes flash, and your nose kind of wrinkles at the edges. I like that stiff-upper-lip thing, too. Reminds me of the look your mother gave your dad on Thanksgiving, when he got tipsy and put his elbow in the mashed potatoes.''

"That was your fault."

"My fault?"

"You're the one who brought that godawful bottle of peppermint schnapps."

"I don't recall pouring it down his throat."

"My father would never be rude enough to refuse a guest's offering, no matter how disgustingly inappropriate."

"Hey, I wanted to bring a six-pack of beer. You're the one who freaked out and told me to bring a bottle of vintage white."

Lydia tossed up her hands. "I meant *wine,* and you knew it. You deliberately embarrassed me in front of my family."

He regarded her for a moment. "You're right, I did. I felt like you were ashamed of me because my pedigree couldn't be traced back to the *Mayflower,* and my folks were the kind of people your folks hired to cut their lawns."

The admission knocked the wind out of her anger. She started to protest, but realized there was more than a grain of truth in what he said. Teasing had always been a double-edged sword for Powell, part affection, part protection. "I'm sorry you felt that way."

"I got over it," he said, although the tiny twitch beneath his ear indicated otherwise. "The thing is, I didn't expect to like your parents. I didn't want to like them. But I did."

Lydia smiled. "They liked you, too."

"I know." He stuffed his hands back into his pockets. "Do you think they'll come to the wedding?"

For some odd reason, the teasing question made her blush. "Under the circumstances, I doubt it."

"I was kidding."

He wasn't, of course, and Lydia knew it. She saw the pain in his eyes, the same pain as six years ago. She hadn't understood it then. Now she did, and it touched her deeply.

Before she could consider the consequence of her action, she reached up and laid her palm on his cheek. His breath caught. Their eyes met. Suddenly, it was as if those six years hadn't existed, as if the two of them were young again and desperately in love. In the space of a heartbeat Powell had gathered her into his arms, lifted her off the ground and pressed his lips to hers in a kiss that shook her to her toes.

The surf roared in her ears, the wind whistled through her hair and her blood boiled with a need she hadn't felt since the last time she'd been in Powell's arms. She was spinning, spinning, moaning into his mouth as the kiss deepened, then flinging her arms around his neck to pull him closer, and closer still.

The kiss ended slowly, gently, their lips parting with a sad reverence that brought tears to her eyes. She took a shaky step back, bewildered by the sudden surge of emotion.

As she studied Powell's face, he studied hers.

Lydia was still beautiful, he decided, perhaps even more appealing in confident womanhood than she'd been as a fresh-faced, radiant girl. The years had been more than kind to her. He wasn't surprised by that, but he was surprised by his reaction after all these years. When she'd walked into the St. Ives law office this morning, Powell had felt gut-kicked. He hadn't expected that. It had disturbed him.

It still did. There was something about this woman that haunted him, although he hadn't realized it until now. Oh, he'd thought about her over the years, even dreamed about her on occasion, but had dismissed such images as the random wanderings of a weary mind. Now he realized that it was more than that. Much more.

A stunned silence stretched between them. It was Lydia who broke it. "Well." She licked her lips. "This won't do, will it?"

She gazed up at him with eyes the color of warm bourbon, eyes that had once sucked his breath away with the merest flick in his direction. As if reading his thoughts, she refocused her gaze on a neutral spot in the middle of his chest.

Somehow Powell found his voice. "No, I suppose not."

"We are discussing a business arrangement."

"Yeah, business."

"I mean, we're both adults, after all. Surely we've matured enough to conduct ourselves appropriately and control our little, um, urges."

"Urges. Right." Powell's head wobbled, which Lydia apparently mistook for an affirmative nod.

"Then it's settled. We'll be roommates, nothing more."

"Sure. Roommates. No problem."

But when she gazed up with a breathless smile, Powell's belly tightened like a vice, and he felt like he had a blowtorch in his pants.

He'd thought he was over her.

Maybe not.

Chapter Two

The preacher's fly was open. One witness sneezed his dentures onto the dingy chapel carpet; the other, a withered old woman with a face like a dry creekbed, dozed off, clutching a cheap tape recorder. When elbowed by her toothless colleague, she grunted, poked the Play button and drowned out the rest of the ceremony with a rousing rendition of Mendelssohn's ''Wedding March'' bellowed by a bass sousaphone.

Afterward, signatures were duly affixed, money changed hands, the witnesses shuffled away and the preacher tucked his ragged note cards in the pocket of his coffee-stained shirt, then sat in the front pew to read his morning newspaper. His fly was still open.

All in all, it was not the most elegant wedding Lydia had ever attended. Too bad it had been her own.

Now Lydia gazed out the car window at the bustling sidewalks along Reno's busy casino row, offering silent thanks that her parents had moved from San Francisco to Connecticut. Eventually she'd have to tell them about her arranged marriage and the reason behind it, but at least they hadn't suffered the indignity of attending the tawdry event. She wished she could say the same for herself.

As for Powell, well, he'd been his usual stoic self, muttering his vows with a distinct lack of enthusiasm. Lydia couldn't fault his reluctance, particularly since she shared it, but now the deed was done. They were officially wed.

"So what do we do now?" Powell suddenly asked.

Lydia replied automatically, without shifting her distracted gaze. "I'll fax a copy of the license and certificate to Clementine when we get back to Sacramento. I suppose she'll attach them to the custody petition."

An irritable sigh caught her attention. "I meant which way do I turn?"

"Hmm?" Lydia blinked up, realized the car had stopped at an intersection. "Oh. Left, I think. No...wait." She retrieved the handwritten map she'd used as a bookmark in the child care manual that had been her constant companion for the past two weeks. "Yes, turn left here, then right at the third stop sign and right again into the apartment house parking lot."

He grunted, eased into the right lane and made the first turn. She angled a glance, noted his white-knuckled grip on the steering wheel. Something squeezed her heart. Instinctively she touched his wrist, felt the fine hairs dust her palm. A shiver worked up her arm, into her voice. "Are you okay?"

"Sure, why not?" His gaze darted toward her, then back to the road. Beneath her fingers, his wrist flexed, his grip loosened. "Are you?"

"I'm fine, thanks." She folded her hands in her lap. They were feigning the forced courtesy of strangers, trying to convince each other they weren't haunted by the past, frightened of the future. Pretending they weren't torn up inside.

Lydia was torn up inside. Powell's presence affected her, seeped into every fiber of her being. She remembered how it had been between them, the secret whispers, the longing looks, the way he'd stroke the inside of her arm with his thumb and all the worries of the world would dissipate in a wave of sheer, sensual pleasure. God, she had loved him.

"Good. That's, er…" He frowned, crimped his fingers around the steering wheel. "Good," he repeated lamely. They drove in silence, while Lydia returned her attention to the chapter on dealing with childhood abandonment.

Except for the hum of the engine and muffled sounds of traffic, the car was silent as a tomb. At the first stop sign, Powell shifted to look at the woman beside him. A swing of honey-colored hair slipped forward to dangle along her sleek jaw. Too engrossed in her book to notice his scrutiny, she flipped a page, then tucked the errant strand behind her ear and continued to read with a calmness that irritated him. After all, they'd just been forced into a shotgun wedding, and were preparing to embark on a charade that would seriously screw up a serious hunk of their lives. It was bothersome that she didn't seem concerned about that.

It was more bothersome that she didn't seem concerned about him. There had been a time when they hadn't been able to bear being apart, even for a few hours, a time when the tilt of her lips into the merest smile had made him feel as if he carried the world in the palm of his hand. There had been a time when he couldn't imagine his life if she wasn't a part of it. It had been glorious, magnificent, the happiest time of his life. There was a time when he'd realized that he was falling in love with her. That's when he'd driven her away.

Life after Lydia had been duller, more predictable, but it had been safe. Love was dangerous. It stole a man's freedom, captured his soul. Love and the commitment it represented were the only things Powell truly feared. Yet here he was, married to the one woman on earth who had ever found her way into his heart.

Swallowing a sigh, Powell eased the car forward, still wondering why he'd agreed to this silly masquerade in the first place. There was the guilt, of course, and a sense of duty to the man who'd once been his best friend. Maybe that should have been enough, but it wasn't.

Freedom was the most important thing in Powell's life. It always had been. Freedom to stay, freedom to go, freedom to work in fresh air instead of a stuffy office, freedom to quit and hit the road if the mood struck him, freedom to spend his last dollar on pizza and beer without worrying about kids needing milk, and most important of all, freedom to avoid becoming a miserable drudge like his father.

Hello marriage, goodbye life.

Nope, "I-do-forever-after" wasn't for Powell Greer. At least, not a real marriage, a real commitment. Even a fake one gave him the shivers.

There was no way on earth he'd have ever agreed to Clementine's cockamamie proposal if Lydia hadn't been a part of it. Lydia would take care of everything. She always did. She was brilliant, confident, ambitious. There was nothing she couldn't accomplish if she put her mind to it. Powell had always admired that about her.

And he'd admired so much more. Her dignity, her regal bearing, the way her shield of aristocracy crumbled when he took her in his arms and her soft breasts pressed against his chest, with nipples hard as—

Beside him, a page crinkled. "Did you know that a child's personality is fully formed by the age of three?"

Lydia shifted, tapped the open book with her fingertip. "That means a one-year-old would be reaching a vulnerable age for abandonment issues. We'll have to give Tami extra attention or she may be emotionally scarred and unable to enjoy a fulfilling marital relationship with her own husband."

Sweat beaded on his upper lip as he forced his wayward thoughts away from the passion of the past. "She's a baby." He cleared the annoying squeak from his voice, absently pressed the brake to slow for the next stop sign. "All she needs is a sweater when it's cold outside, a clean diaper and a bottle when she's hungry."

"Actually, at this age she should be ingesting toddler foods, cereals and other nutritional supplements to formula." Without glancing up from the book in her lap, Lydia continued to drone on as if delivering a thesis. "On the other hand, Kenny is old enough to understand the loss of his parents, but probably not mature enough to comprehend the reason behind it."

"There is no reason behind it," Powell said with surprising bitterness. "It was a stupid accident that never should have happened."

He felt rather than saw Lydia glance over at him. "I only meant that Kenny will be even more confused than his sister. He needs someone to care for his emotional needs."

The thought of being responsible for fulfilling so many needs tightened Powell's lungs and honed an irritable edge in his voice. "Kenny's just a kid. All a kid needs is someone to hand him the television remote and cut the crust off his peanut butter sandwiches."

If Lydia caught a whiff of his panic, she didn't comment, but nattered on with a confidence that both intrigued Powell and irked the hell out of him. "Television is a waste of time for blossoming young minds. Also, peanut butter is highly overrated. I've read several studies concluding that children raised on a high-fiber, low-fat diet have a lower risk of heart disease as adults. For example…''

Lydia continued to talk, but Powell wasn't listening. A gold flash on his left hand had caught his eye.

A wedding ring, one of the pair Clementine had sent to them by courier only yesterday. Good thing, too. Marital jewelry had been the least of Powell's concerns as he'd boxed up the last of his possessions and said a sad farewell to the bachelor-pad apartment with a balcony view of the pool. He dreaded moving, particularly into a boring, suburban track home that Clementine, in her capacity as executor, had purchased as part of the children's trust.

The place was okay, Powell supposed. Lydia had allowed him a quick walk-through last week, although he'd sulked through the tour with his hands jammed in his pockets and his heart wedged in his throat. Sure, the house was conveniently located halfway between Lydia's downtown-Sacramento office and the phone company maintenance yard where he received assignments before the crew headed out to the field. And yes, there was a nice fenced yard for the kids, too. Clementine had thought of everything. She'd even promised to furnish the place with the kids' own beds, and other special things from the home they'd shared with their parents. In theory that was supposed to make the kids more comfortable. Powell suspected it would just make them more homesick.

He could relate to that, because despite the indisputable amenities of the place, Powell didn't want to live there. He suspected the kids wouldn't want to live there, either.

Home was more than a convenient flophouse. It was an extension of personality, of comfort and style. Like his own cluttered apartment, with the worn lounger flattened in all the right spots to fit his body perfectly, and the stack of sports magazines piled within reach, along with the convenience of having his television remote tied to the armrest with a twist of leftover phone wire. It was all pretty tacky, he supposed, but it was nonetheless home. He missed it already.

It wouldn't be forever, of course. Powell would be back in a few months, as soon as the legal stuff was finished. Of course, he'd still have responsibilities—financial responsibilities along with occasional visits to provide support and a male role model.

Responsibilities. Even the word made him shudder. Which was why Lydia's presence was such an important part of the equation. They hadn't worked out the details yet, but Powell had no doubt that Lydia would take on the day-to-day child-raising chores, not only during their faux marriage, but afterward as well. He was willing to go along for the ride. That was all he was willing to do.

Lydia looked up from the book. "Turn here."

"It's only the second stop sign."

"No, it's the third. I've been counting."

"You've been reading."

"I can read and count at the same time."

"Sure you can. You can do everything." He didn't mean to sound so sharp, nor did he intend to slow the car quickly enough to force her to brace herself on the dash.

She straightened in the seat and gave him a stunned look. "Are we having a testosterone crisis?"

"Sorry," he said, and meant it even if his voice conveyed more amusement than repentance. A man never groveled, after all. If he made a mistake, he shrugged it off and went on. To do otherwise gave a woman the upper hand, made her think she was in charge. Watching his unhappy father give up everything he'd cared about for the sake of his family had provided valuable lessons on male-female relationships.

Not that Powell wanted to dominate women. He simply wanted to keep himself on an even footing to avoid being trampled. Of course, he'd also wanted to avoid being married. For all the good *that* had done.

Powell pulled into the apartment complex, parked the car and stared out the windshield. "Go ahead, say it."

Lydia knew perfectly well that he was waiting for her to point out that her directions had been accurate and she'd been correct about where to turn. Powell hated being wrong almost as much as Lydia loved being right. When they'd been a couple, she'd rarely missed an opportunity to crow about such small triumphs. Humility had never been one of her virtues.

In retrospect, she wasn't particularly proud of that. "We're here. That's all that matters."

Clearly startled, Powell shifted in his seat. The intensity of his gaze unnerved her. "You were right about the other thing, too. We should have stayed at the courthouse and waited for a magistrate."

To her surprise, he seemed genuinely distressed, although there had been at least thirty couples in line for a civil ceremony, a two-hour wait according to the bored clerk at the appointment desk. Since the children and their grandmother were waiting on the far side of town, neither of them had been in the mood to cool their heels that long. Besides, this was Reno, second only to Las Vegas in the number of wedding chapels per capita. "It doesn't matter. It's over and done with."

"Yeah, but if I'd known how disgusting that place was..." Powell suddenly chuckled. "I suppose it could have been worse."

Lydia shuddered. "I don't know how."

He chuckled again, slid her an amused glance. "Remember the guy whose teeth fell out?"

"Yes, unfortunately."

"Well, think about what might have happened if old drafty drawers had been the one who sneezed."

Lydia nearly choked at the thought. "You are truly twisted."

"Uh-huh." Grinning madly, Powell opened the car door, winked over his shoulder. "Isn't it fun?"

"What do you mean you're not coming?" Lydia braced herself on a rickety kitchen table stained with dried milk and heaped with breakfast dishes. The cramped apartment was crowded with scattered toys, children's clothing draped over every knob, heaped in every cranny. Soiled dishes spilled from sink to counter. The place was a riot of clutter and chaos, smelling of baby powder, stale sausages and exhaustion. "But we've already discussed it, everything has been arranged."

Rose Watson touched her forehead with the back of her palm. "The doctors won't let me, Lyddie. They say my blood pressure has gone back up again." The woman flinched as a childish squeal filtered from the living room, temporarily drowning out the screech of crowd noise from the blaring television. "I guess caring for little ones has taken more out of me than I thought."

Swallowing panic, Lydia perched on the edge of a vinyl chair with a torn seat. She focused on Rose, noting the shadows around her eyes, the taut skin stretched thinly over cheekbones that seemed much more prominent than they had two months earlier at her daughter and son-in-law's funeral. The woman was truly ill, Lydia realized, and her heart sank. "Oh, Rose, of course it has. You've been through so much these past few weeks. You need rest."

"But the kids…it'll be hard for them, moving to a new house, new surroundings. I'd hoped to be there with them for a few weeks, just to make things easier but…" Tears welled in eyes already reddened from grief and loss. "I'm so sorry. I feel like I've let you down, let my grandbabies down—"

"Nonsense." Lydia laid a compassionate hand on the woman's shoulder, was shocked at how thin she'd become. "If not for you, Kenny and Tami Lynn would have spent the past two months in foster care. You've done everything you could for them. Susan would want you to take care of yourself now. Everything will be fine."

With a stoic sniff, Rose dabbed her moist eyes with a wadded paper napkin. "Are you sure you can manage on your own?"

"Of course I can—" She flinched at a bloodcurdling screech. A moment later, a screaming, curly headed tot wobbled into the kitchen clutching a small metal truck.

The child shrieked again as her brother skidded into the kitchen and made a grab for the toy.

"Give it back!" the boy demanded.

Grunting madly, the baby toddled behind her grandmother's chair to glare at her frustrated brother.

To Lydia's shock, Rose seemed oblivious to the chaos. "I've packed all their things," she murmured with ludicrous calm. "Tami has a little ear infection, and there's some medicine in the bag. Directions are on the bottle."

"Gimme my truck!" Kenny shouted.

The tiny girl took a swipe at her sibling, dropped to her knees and crawled under the table while poor, tired Rose droned on without so much as a flinch. "I wrote up a schedule for naps and meals and such. You can call me if you have any questions.''

Lydia spun in her chair as a curly blond head popped up behind her. She stared down into somber blue eyes the same color as her mother's. Susan had been a wonderful parent, calm and rational in defining expectations and explaining consequences for inappropriate behavior. Lydia herself had little experience in these matters, but was fairly certain the children were exhibiting behavior of which their mother would not have approved.

Lydia cleared her throat. ''Ah, Tami, sweetheart, it's not nice to take your brother's toys.''

Clearly startled by the correction, the baby instantly stopped shrieking. Kenny, too, fell silent. Apparently sensing victory, he stood quietly, his gaze riveted on the precious truck in his sister's fat little hand.

Encouraged, Lydia offered praise, as her child-psychology books had suggested. ''Thank you, Tami. I really like it when you are quiet and attentive. I understand that you'd like to play with the truck, but it doesn't belong to you, so please give it back to your brother now.''

The baby's eyes narrowed as if she'd just spotted a peculiar bug and wasn't certain whether to squash it or run. She grunted, glared, shook her small head until the blond curls vibrated. Lydia took that as a no.

Puffing her cheeks, she blew out a breath. ''I'll tell you what. You give the truck to me, and I'll give it to Kenny. I'm sure if you ask your brother nicely, he'll be happy to share some of his other toys with you.''

Kenny's head snapped up. ''Huh?''

Tami hid the truck behind her back. Feathery blond brows wrinkled into the most ferocious frown Lydia had ever seen on such a tiny person. The toddler glared at Lydia as if wishing her dead, before wobbling back toward the living room screaming at the top of her lungs.

Exasperated, Kenny tossed up his hands. "Aw, geez, now you went and made her mad."

"She wasn't already mad?"

"Nah, we were just playing."

There was nothing in the psych books about this. "But I thought you wanted your truck back."

"Yeah," he muttered. "But now that you've got her all ticked off, she'll probably flush it." With that ominous prediction, the boy heaved a sigh of frustration and sprinted away.

Stunned, Lydia turned to Rose, who was staring into thin air and didn't even flinch when a muffled thump vibrated the walls.

"Got to get Tami's blankie out of the dryer," Rose mumbled. "She can't sleep without her blankie. And Kenny needs his ABC books. He loves those books." There was a crash, a screech, a yelp of pain. "He knows his alphabet. Susan taught him. Such a smart little boy, and he's not even in kindergarten yet."

"That's, er, wonderful, Rose." The noise was deafening. Unable to endure it another moment, Lydia excused herself, pushed away from the table and strode into the living room.

Both children were embroiled in a wrestling match on the floor not ten feet from where Powell sat on the sofa, engrossed in a basketball game on TV. It took a moment for her to find her voice. "Kenny, stop that at once."

Kenny hopped up, allowing the now-free baby to disappear into the hallway with her prize. The boy let out a yelp and dashed after her.

Lydia rounded on Powell. "The children were fighting."

He favored her with a glance. "Yep."

"Did it occur to you to stop them?"

"No."

"Why on earth not?"

"Kids fight. It's what they do." He jerked upright, stared at the screen and shot a fist into the air. "Yes! Look at that. Man, what a beautiful move."

Shrieks, howls and yelps continued to filter from the hallway, along with a few ominous thumps. Powell seemed as oblivious to it all as Rose had been. It was quite bewildering to Lydia, an only child who'd been raised in an environment so solemn and immaculate it had once been referred to as a cathedral with cushions.

Powell suddenly shouted at the screen. "Foul? Oh, get a clue— Hey!" He swung around as Lydia tugged the remote control out of his fist and muted the sound.

"Rose isn't coming with us," she announced.

Powell stared at her. "Okay."

"That doesn't concern you?"

"Should it?"

"Yes, it should." Lydia tossed the TV remote aside and rubbed her aching temples. "It will make the transition more difficult for the children, and it will certainly make it more difficult for us."

"Why?"

"Because having their grandmother with them would make moving to a strange place easier for them, that's why, and easier for us, too, considering we have no experience caring for children."

Genuine puzzlement clouded his gaze. "You feed them when they're hungry and don't let them run naked outside. How hard could it be?"

She slumped forward with a soft moan. "Don't you take anything seriously?"

"Sure I do."

"What?"

"Basketball." He retrieved the remote and flipped on the sound.

Lydia recognized the evasion tactic. She'd seen it before. Powell had an infuriating ability to remove himself from a situation he found unpleasant, and drown out his surroundings with an oblivion that Lydia found admirable under other circumstances. Now she simply found it annoying. Still, she knew how to break into his self-imposed reverie by appealing directly to his finely honed sense of masculine honor.

"I need your help, Powell." Instantly she had his complete attention. "Rose is exhausted and the place is a wreck. I can't leave her with all this work."

He glanced around as if just noticing that the room looked as if it had been bombed. "You want me to shovel some stuff into a corner?"

"What a magnanimous offer." Lydia favored him with her most appealing smile. "That's very sweet of you, but what I'd really love is for you to take the kids for a walk or something. Just for a little while, so I can clean up the kitchen and make certain all the children's things are packed."

He angled a longing glance at the television. "I don't know—"

"Please?" She touched his wrist, let her fingers linger a moment before tracing soft circles on the back of his hand. When his Adam's apple bobbed, she heaved a soft sigh. "I just don't think I can do it without you."

His arm quivered, his chest puffed and his voice deepened with the primitive pride of a caveman promising to drag a mastodon back for the little woman's stew pot. "Sure, why not?"

If she stretched her phony smile another millimeter, her face would crack. "Thank you so much, Powell. I can't tell you how much I appreciate this.'' She gritted her teeth and spoke through them. ''I really, really can't tell you.''

Powell grinned happily. ''No prob, Lyddie. Let me know if there's anything else you can't handle without me.''

Before she could reach for his throat, a soccer ball flew out of the hallway to knock a stack of books off the telephone table.

''Hey, buddy,'' Powell said as Kenny chased the ball into the room. ''Wanna go shoot some hoops?''

Kenny lit up like neon. ''You bet!''

Unfurling his lean body, Powell stood, stretched, then ruffled the boy's hair. ''Let's go get your sister.''

''Aww, does she have to come?''

''Yep, she does.'' Powell headed down the hallway. A few moments later he reappeared with the sweater-clad one-year-old in his arms. ''Wave bye-bye to Aunt Lyddie.''

Giggling sweetly, Tami opened and closed her baby fist. ''Ba-ba.''

Lydia couldn't help but smile back. Despite being stubborn and feisty, Tami Lynn was a precious child. Lydia had always adored her. ''Bye-bye, sweetie. Have fun.''

Kenny scooted into the room wearing a snazzy denim jacket and clutching a basketball. ''We're going to shoot hoops,'' he said importantly. ''Tami's just gonna watch, on account of her being a girl and stuff.''

Clearly amused, Powell met Lydia's narrowed gaze with a lazy shrug. Halfway out the front door, he paused to look over his shoulder. ''Hey, Lyddie? Keep an eye on the game for me, will you?''

She smiled sweetly. ''Why, certainly.''

As soon as the front door closed, she peevishly turned off the television, rolled up her sleeves and went to work.

* * *

Rose hovered at the front door, wringing her hands. "Are you sure you'll be all right?"

"We'll be fine." Lydia hugged her warmly. "You just take care of yourself and get lots of rest, you hear?"

The woman's gaze hovered in the distance, where Powell was struggling to buckle Tami's car seat in the back seat of Lydia's imported sedan, which was already weighted down with baby paraphernalia, including a playpen and high chair strapped to the roof. "You call me if you need anything."

"I will." One more hug, then Lydia stepped back to regard the woman who had been a mother to her throughout her college years. "We'll be back for a visit real soon."

Rose nodded, smiled and waved goodbye to Kenny, who returned her wave a moment before climbing into the back seat. After a moment's hesitation, Lydia crossed the parking lot and climbed into the passenger seat.

Powell revved the engine twice, then steered out of the parking lot. They'd barely reached the highway when Tami let out a bloodcurdling bellow. Lydia spun in her seat in time to see Kenny dancing an action figure in front of the baby's face. "Don't tease your sister, Kenny."

Kenny giggled. "She likes it."

Tami shrieked again, and pressed forward against the car seat harness to snatch the figure out of her brother's hand.

Now it was Kenny's turn to wail. "Aunt Lyddie, Aunt Lyddie, make her give it back."

Lydia's heart gave a palpable leap. "Tami, sweetie, that belongs to your brother."

The toddler howled and held the toy over her head, whereupon her brother promptly snatched it away. Tami screeched in fury, arched her back and kicked wildly. Her smirking brother, apparently unwilling to learn from prior mistakes, began dancing the action figure across his sister's car seat tray again, only to whip it away when the baby reached for it. Tami's frustrated wails escalated into a tantrum of major proportion.

Lydia was beside herself. She tried to entice the child with a stuffed monkey, a bottle of juice and a cookie, all to no avail. The baby's face was crimson, and she was shrieking so loudly that Lydia's ears rang.

And despite Lydia's pleas, Kenny just kept teasing his sister into a frenzy.

Powell suddenly cleared his throat, spoke without taking his eyes from the road. "Maybe we should just ignore them."

"That's ridiculous. Kenny's behaving like a bully and Tami will make herself sick."

He shrugged. "Well, short of tying the boy's hands together and taping the baby's mouth shut, I don't think there's much you can do."

There was enough truth in his observation to panic her. The one thing on earth Lydia feared was failure. No matter what the cause, no matter what the obstacles, success was the only option, and there was no way she could be a successful parent by ignoring a screaming child. "I don't understand," Lydia murmured, more to herself than to Powell, who probably couldn't hear anything beyond the baby's furious screams, anyway. "I've never seen Kenny deliberately tease his sister into a tantrum like this with Susan around, except when—"

She snapped her fingers, remembering a shopping trip when Tami had reacted to her brother's incessant tickling by flinging herself on the boutique floor and screeching until nearby customers covered their ears. Recalling how Susan had dealt with that situation, Lydia confidently turned in her seat and blurted, "If the two of you don't behave yourselves, we'll have to take a time-out."

To her surprise, Tami stopped screaming and Kenny's eyes popped wide-open in shock. Powell, too, seemed a bit stunned. "A time-out? What the devil is that?"

"It's, well…" She fidgeted, cleared her throat. "Child behavior specialists agree that the most appropriate reaction to a misbehaving youngster is, ah, separation."

"Separation," he repeated dully, staring at her as if she'd lost her mind.

"Yes, separation."

He shrugged, nodded, tightened his grip on the steering wheel. "Yeah, okay. The car roof is already full, but I guess we could strap one of them to the hood like a deer."

Face flaming, Lydia realized that threatening a time-out while inside a moving vehicle was not a particularly viable option. She turned around with a huff, rebuckled her safety belt and snatched up her child care book.

If there were windows in heaven, Susan must be laughing her head off.

This had been a terrible mistake, Lydia thought. There was no way she could be a proper parent to these beautiful children, and the realization terrified her. She'd always had this habit of biting off more than she could chew, of believing herself capable beyond her true abilities. Panic surged like bitter bile, burning her throat, bringing tears to her eyes.

Suddenly a soft warmth radiated from her shoulder. She turned, gazed into Powell's gentle eyes. He squeezed her shoulder, brushed her hair from her neck with his knuckles. "It'll be okay, Lyddie. You'll be a great mom, the best." As he spoke, his fingers slipped down to rest at her elbow, and he circled his thumb along the sensitive flesh of her inner arm. The familiar gesture soothed her, comforted her.

Tears spilled onto her cheeks, tears of relief that he understood, tears of gratitude that he still believed in her. Their eyes met, held, and the years melted away like magic.

To the world, Powell Greer was a man's man, quietly macho, uncompromisingly honest, loyal to the bone, admired, respected and emulated by his peers.

But Lydia knew a different side of him, the tender core he kept hidden away. The man she knew couldn't resist a mewing kitten, cried at sad movies, had once lived on canned soup for a week to replace a bicycle stolen from a sobbing child he'd never even met before. In his heart Powell was tender and caring, a man who had believed in her and who had the unique ability to make her believe in herself. It was that man Lydia remembered.

It was that man Lydia had loved.

Chapter Three

Apparently the time-out threat, ludicrous as it was, had done its job, and the two-hour trip from Reno to Sacramento was less chaotic than originally promised. Kenny ignored his baby sister, who dozed off in her car seat and slept most of the journey. Powell listened to the end of one basketball game and the beginning of another on the radio, while Lydia, one of those rarefied few able to read in a moving vehicle without experiencing queasy side effects, continued to study expert advice offered in one of the half-dozen child psychology books she'd scooped off bookstore shelves during the past week.

By the time they pulled into the driveway of the tidy suburban home Clementine had readied for them, an unseasonable September rain had slicked streets and freshened the air. Lydia was feeling cautiously optimistic.

"Wow!" Kenny exclaimed as he stepped through the front door. "Is this our house now, all ours?"

"Yes, all ours." Shifting the sleepy baby against her hip, Lydia entered the small tiled foyer. She held the door open for Powell, who struggled inside with a suitcase in each hand and one under his arm.

He dropped the luggage, shook his wet head and glanced around with vague interest. "It looks different than it did last week."

"That's because it has furniture in it." Since Tami had begun to grunt and squirm, Lydia put her down, but kept an eye on the toddler, who followed her brother toward the hallway leading to four compact bedrooms. "Kenny, please watch your sister," she called out. "And for goodness sake, be nice!"

At the boy's muffled "Okay," she returned her attention to Powell.

"The movers came yesterday." A hint of lavender wafted in the air. "And unless I'm very much mistaken, Clementine has been here as well."

"Clementine?" Frowning, Powell jammed his hands in his pockets. A damp tendril of dark hair stuck to his brow, giving him a rakish appeal that was strangely alluring.

Lydia wanted desperately to brush it aside. Mostly she just wanted to touch him, an urge she found annoying, if not surprising. Powell had always had that affect on her, had always evoked an overwhelming need to touch, to taste, to absorb every nuance of sight and scent and feel until passion erupted like an unquenchable thirst, and she thought she'd die if she couldn't have him inside her.

The power of those memories shook her to the marrow. Her mouth went dry; her knees trembled.

"I thought Clem was handling everything over the phone," he said. "Why would she drive all the way in from San Francisco?"

"Drive?" Yanking her gaze away, Lydia cleared her

throat, annoyed by her nervousness and the sensual direction of her thoughts. Her light laugh was uncharacteristically high-pitched, and irksome, forcing her to focus on a more professional tone. "Unless I miss my guess, Clementine probably hitched a ride in a governmental jet. I've heard she has connections from the state assembly to the Pentagon."

Following the fragrance, Lydia emerged into a cozy family room furnished by a collage of items blended from the Housemans' compact condominium and her own sleekly modern apartment. What wouldn't fit was in storage, including almost all of Powell's eclectic, flea-market decor.

He noticed the absence of his belongings as soon as he walked into the room. "Hey, where's all my stuff?"

"In your bedroom," Lydia murmured, preoccupied by the distinct impression that something in the room had been changed since her visit yesterday. Something was missing. Even worse, something had been added. Her horrified gaze settled on the ugliest hunk of patched plaid she'd ever had the misfortune to lay eyes on. "What in the world—?"

"All right!" Crowing happily, Powell strode past a polished oak tea table accented with Clementine's trademark fresh flowers, a sleekly upholstered modern sofa and two delicate Victorian armchairs to gaze lovingly at the green-and-brown monstrosity in the far corner of the room. A remote control device dangled from the chair's arm by a ragged twig of twisted telephone wire.

Powell caressed the lounger's frayed backrest as if greeting a long-lost friend. "Hey, buddy, am I glad to see you."

Before Lydia could so much as sputter a protest, he flopped into the chair, pulled a worn-out side lever to which only a few tenacious threads still clung, and heaved a grateful sigh as the leg rest shuddered upward. "Ah, heaven. And my magazines!"

As excited as a kid at Christmas, he bolted upright, reached down and plucked a tattered sports magazine from a crooked stack piled beside the chair. A cheap floor lamp tottered nearby, one of those dime-store models that boasted a flexible gooseneck light fixture sprouting from a metal tray-table covered with peeling, wood-grained adhesive paper. It gave an ominous flicker when Powell turned it on. He grinned at Lydia. "This is so cool. Thanks."

His childlike joy gave Lydia a moment's pause. Only a moment's. A determined rattle vibrated her chest. "There's been a mistake. That chair isn't supposed to be here."

"Why not?"

"Well, it's…" The words *ugly* and *unsanitary* teetered on her tongue. "It doesn't match the decor."

"It does now." Heaving a contented sigh, he stretched out like a cat in sunshine. "Good old Clementine. I owe her a steak."

Lydia moaned. "Look, Powell—"

A shriek of childish dismay emanated from the other side of the house. "Aunt Lyddie, Tami's in my room and won't get out!"

Heaving a sigh, Lydia called over her shoulder, "I'll be there in a minute." She refocused on a smiling, satisfied Powell, who had tucked his hands behind his head. "Now about the chair—"

He opened one eye. "If it goes, I go."

"We'll miss you."

"Fine with me. None of this was my idea."

"And you think it was mine?"

He shrugged. "I'm just saying that I never even heard of Clementine St. Ives until last week. You, on the other hand, seem to know her quite well."

"Are you suggesting this is some kind of conspiracy to force you back in my life? Of all the nerve." Fuming,

Lydia crossed her arms so tightly her shoulders ached. "Far be it from me to pop such a magnificently inflated ego, but—"

A high-pitched wail from the hall made her flinch. *"Don't touch that!"* Kenny hollered. "Aunt Lyddie!"

"I'm coming!" Lydia shouted back, startling herself by having raised her normally quiescent voice. She spun back to Powell. "If you'd ever used those funny flaps on the side of your head to actually listen when people spoke to you, you might have heard the part of our discussion about Clementine being the legal advocate who petitioned the court when Dan was just a child to keep him from being thrown into a group home full of ruffians and rowdy delinquents."

The red flush crawling up Powell's throat revealed that her point had hit home. "I knew that." The guilty dart of his gaze implied otherwise. "I just don't remember names and details about every conversation I ever had over the past ten years so I can club people over the head with them."

Since the pointed observation was accurate, Lydia felt her own cheeks heat. "I didn't ask for this any more than you did, Powell Greer. I could have happily gone the rest of my life without ever laying eyes on you again." The lie nearly choked her, but she wouldn't give him the satisfaction of knowing how much she had missed him.

He sat up, eyes somber.

"Furthermore, I am here in spite of your presence, not because of it, and if you believe otherwise—" she flinched at a sinister thump from the hallway "—then you're even more arrogant than I remember. Now if you will excuse me, I'm going to put Tami down for a nap, haul the playpen and high chair off the car roof and unpack all the suitcases you so kindly dumped in the foyer. No, no, don't get up," she snapped, although he'd made absolutely no attempt to do so. "I wouldn't want to inconvenience you."

She spun on her heel, strode purposefully across the room, only to be stopped by what she interpreted as a contrite plea.

"Lyddie, wait."

Sucking in a breath, she glanced over her shoulder to spear him with a frosty stare, which she charitably planned to soften in response to the apology she presumed was forthcoming. "Yes?"

A mischievous gleam in his eye belied an otherwise somber expression. "Would you bring me a sandwich first? I'm starving."

As Lydia's angry footsteps thundered down the hall, Powell leaned back in his beloved lounger, wondering why he'd deliberately aggravated her. Actually, he knew the answer. Self-preservation. Teasing was his pretense, the shield he used to turn back those who ventured too near. It's what men did, what Powell had been taught. Lydia understood that about him. He saw it in her eyes, in her disappointed expression when he used the technique to turn her away.

Experience had taught Powell exactly where her hot buttons were, and whenever he felt threatened, whenever his heart seemed vulnerable, he'd always used that knowledge to force her back a step and put a comfortable distance between them.

Besides, Lydia wore indignation well. It looked good on her. When she slipped into it, as other women might don diaphanous lingerie, sensual tension enveloped her like a silken shield. The angrier she became, the more appealing she was. There was just something about the way she hiked that sharp little chin of hers, and the fiery passion flashing in those whiskey-colored eyes that flat brought out the devil in him. Her voice got all husky and raw, trembling like bare skin beneath a lover's touch.

The image affected Powell like a punch to the heart. It always had.

In the past Lydia had accused him of being threatened by the premise of a strong, capable woman. Powell had denied it, still did. It was Lydia's independence, strength and intelligence that had drawn him to her in the first place. He admired the hell out of her. Always had, always would.

But his feelings for her went far beyond admiration. It was those feelings that threatened Powell, a terrifying, out-of-control sensation of wanting one person more than he wanted his next breath. Lydia had wormed her way into his heart like no other woman ever had or ever could. She'd gotten to him once. He had no intention of allowing her to do it again, and was determined to use every weapon in his male arsenal to keep her at arm's length.

Emotionally, that is. Physically, well, Powell was a man, after all, and Lydia was a woman. A gorgeous woman who had once roused him to heights of passion he'd never experienced before or since. If their close proximity happened to evoke a rekindling of physical amour, Powell would certainly be receptive. More than receptive, actually. His body tightened at the delicious thought, which was immediately disrupted as the scamper of small feet heralded Kenny's arrival.

The youngster skidded across the elongated family room, eyes wide, head whipping right then left, and finally settling on the large-screen television conveniently situated across from Powell's chair. "That's my daddy's TV!" the boy squeaked, then wiggled an excited finger at the matching wing chairs at the far end of the room. "And those are Mommy's favorite chairs."

Smiling, Powell lowered the lounger's footrest and

leaned forward, propping his elbows on his knees. "Your aunt Lyddie thought you'd like to have some familiar things around."

"Yeah, 'specially the TV." Kenny wandered over to finger the object of his affections and found himself standing beside a large sliding glass door. "Wow, a real backyard." He spun around, pressed his nose against the rain-splattered glass. "We never had a yard at my other house," he murmured, referring to the small condominium his parents had owned in the Bay Area. "Just a dinky little patio where Mommy grew flowers and stuff." A wistful frown crossed the boy's face. "Mommy bought Daddy a little grill so we could have barbecues, but all he did was burn stuff up. One day he even set one of Mommy's plants on fire. She was real mad."

Powell smiled. "Yeah, I remember. Your dad told me all about it."

"He did?" Kenny looked over his shoulder, huge blue eyes dominating a pale, pinched little face. "You liked my daddy a lot, didn't you?"

Pain knifed through Powell. "Yes."

The child considered that. "Do you miss him?"

"Yes, I do." More than he could ever express.

"Me, too." Kenny's eyes moistened. "Nana says Mommy and Daddy went to heaven."

Since Powell couldn't think of anything to say, he remained silent.

The boy issued a stoic sniff, rubbed his eyelids with the heel of his hands. After a moment, he stiffened his skinny little shoulders and tilted a head bristling with tousled, caramel-colored hair. "Uncle Powell?"

"Yeah, buddy?"

"How come they didn't take Tami and me to heaven, too?"

A lump wedged alongside Powell's Adam's apple, threatening to choke him. He swallowed hard, sucked in a ragged breath. Emotions swelled up, exploded inside him with nuclear force.

Powell could deal with anger; he could deal with danger; he could deal with loss. But he couldn't deal with other emotions. The gut-twisting pain that defied definition always left him panic-stricken and feeling out of control.

His preference was to defuse emotion with humor. It was his coping mechanism, the armor of his soul. Nothing was so serious that it couldn't be put in perspective by a witty remark or lightened by a well-timed joke.

Nothing except this.

A child was looking for answers. Powell didn't have those answers, nor did he have the courage to pose such questions in the first place. He couldn't tell this innocent child that he and his sister had been left behind because their lives mattered without implying that the lives of his parents hadn't mattered. Nor could he say that all things happened for a reason, because he didn't believe that. Tragedy had no reason.

As for the truth, Powell dismissed that without a second thought. There was no way he would tell a grieving child that his beloved parents had been snatched away by a fluke of fate, a drunk who'd turned a speeding vehicle into an instrument of death.

No, the truth would not set Kenny free, just as it had never set Powell free. It had imprisoned him, disillusioned him, broken his heart. It would do the same to Kenny someday. But not on this day. Not if Powell could help it.

"Uncle Powell?"

"Hmm?" He looked up to see Kenny standing beside the lounge chair, chewing his lip. Such a courageous little guy. A real man's man, that one. At least he would be someday. Right now he was just a bewildered youngster trying to make sense of a nonsensical world. Powell sat forward to ruffle the boy's thick hair. "What's on your mind, my man?"

"I was just wondering. Are you and Aunt Lyddie our new mom and dad?"

The question startled Powell, although he supposed it shouldn't have. A tense ball knotted inside his stomach, as it always did when serious issues confronted him. "Not exactly," he said carefully. "Lyddie and I are your guardians. That means we're going to take good care of you and your sister, and make sure that you always have everything you need."

"Oh." The child's eyes clouded with confusion, but he requested no further explanation, and Powell offered none.

Instead, he patted his lap and hauled up the wire on which the remote was tied. "Come here, buddy. Let's see if we can find something fun to watch on your daddy's TV."

Kenny hovered only a moment before clambering onto Powell's lap. When offered the TV control device, he grinned, turned on the set and flipped through the entire bank of channels three times before settling on an old Disney movie.

They were engrossed in watching it when Lydia appeared, her face red and eyes snapping amber fire.

Every warning alarm in Powell's brain went off. He sat up carefully, shifting Kenny in his lap. "Is something wrong?"

"It's Clementine," she said tightly. "This time she's gone too far."

"What's this?" Powell asked from the doorway.

"This," Lydia replied with a sweep of her arm, "is supposed to be your bedroom.'' The room was clearly set up as an office, containing her desk, computer and file cabinets, which only yesterday had been crowded in one corner of the family room.

''Then why's all your stuff in here?''

''That's what I'd like to know.''

If Powell noticed a distinct chill in her voice, he made no comment. Instead, he absently rubbed the back of his neck and gave every appearance of a sincerely baffled man. ''Where's my bed?'' His eyes widened. ''And my dresser? That dresser belonged to my grandma. It's been in my family for years. There's going to be hell to pay if someone lost it.''

Lydia skewered him with a gaze. ''You play the innocent so well.''

''Huh?''

''Oh, spare me. I'm wise to your tricks, remember?'' Ignoring his flicker of perplexed annoyance, she crooked a finger, spun around and strode across the hall, to the doorway of the master bedroom. After a flicker of hesitation, he followed. She shoved the door open and stepped inside with an aggravated huff. ''Your dresser, m'lord.''

The old cherry-wood armoire, arguably the only decent piece of furniture Powell owned, was displayed against a wall freshly papered with a romantic floral pattern. Powell's relieved grin flattened as he raked the rest of the room with an increasingly bewildered gaze. ''Hey, that's not mine.''

She followed his glance to the mirrored, claw-footed mahogany vanity on which a sparkling array of feminine products were tastefully displayed, along with a porcelain jewelry box in which a certain gold starfish necklace was lovingly stored. ''No, it's mine.''

''So why is it in my bedroom?''

''According to the agreement, this is my bedroom.''

Judging by the blank look in his eyes, the significance of that statement hadn't sunk in. Powell simply offered a bewildered frown and readjusted his gaze to the focal point of the room, a king-size canopy bed accented by fabric swags twisted into elegant knots at the apex of each carved post. The huge mattress was covered by a thick, forest-green comforter upon which a riot of pink and emerald pillows had been piled.

There was also a pair of nightstands in gleaming cherry to match the antique dresser, but constructed in a unique claw-foot design that also complimented Lydia's mahogany vanity table. One nightstand held a framed photograph of Powell and Lydia, taken years earlier at a college formal. The other held a greeting card, carefully propped against a small bronze lamp with a pleated mauve shade.

Clearly mystified, Powell rubbed his knuckles over his scalp. "I don't get it."

For a moment, Lydia almost believed him. Then she reminded herself that she was dealing with a man who'd once hoisted a disfavored college professor's automobile onto the science building roof as a prank, then denied it with such guileless ease that the incident was still considered unsolved. "You're in cahoots with her on this, aren't you?"

"Cahoots?"

His eyes widened rather deliberately, she thought.

"With who? About what?" he continued. "Have you always been this paranoid, or is it a relatively recent malady?"

"You are, aren't you?" She tossed up her hands. "I should have known. It's just the kind of thing your sick little mind would cook up simply to torment me."

"I'll admit that tormenting you is one of life's little

pleasures,'' Powell muttered, ''but at the moment I haven't a clue what you're talking about.''

''You don't, huh?'' Crossing the room, she flung open the closet door. ''What do you have to say about that?''

His gaze narrowed. ''Why are my shirts hanging next to your dresses?''

''That's exactly what I'd like to know.''

He did a double take, then hooked a thumb toward his own sternum. ''You're asking me? How the hell should I know? You're the one who was supposed to be here yesterday to show the movers where everything went.''

''I *was* here.''

''Well, I *wasn't,* so if anyone has some explaining to do, it's you.'' His head swiveled around. ''Where the devil is my bed, anyway?''

''You mean that undersize box spring with the lumpy mattress and bent frame?''

He looked stung. ''You always hated my bed.''

''It wasn't a bed, it was a torture chamber.'' Her face warmed at the reminder that only intimate acquaintance with the sleep unit in question allowed her to make such an informed statement. ''That's beside the point.''

''Yes, it certainly is. You had no right to throw it out.''

''I did not throw it out.''

''Then where is it?''

She regarded him thoughtfully. ''You really don't know?''

''And you accuse me of not listening.'' Frustrated now, he jammed his hands in his pockets and started to pout. Lydia had always loved that pout of his, an odd pursing of lips and bunching of brows that for some unknown reason managed to make him look brooding and sexy rather than childish and silly.

Although not completely convinced of his innocence,

Lydia decided to give him the benefit of the doubt. "I don't know where your bed went. I don't know where my bed went."

That clearly surprised him. "That isn't yours?"

"Of course not, I'm hardly the frou-frou canopy type. Besides, you know—" She broke off abruptly, before reminding him that he knew perfectly well what her bedroom ensemble looked like, since he'd spent a fair share of time in close proximity with it, just as she had with his. She huffed, snatched the greeting card from the nightstand. "Read this."

He hesitated, then took it. "'A gift for your wedding—'"

"Not out loud."

"Hmm? Oh." He opened the card, scanned it quickly, then paled before her eyes. "The bed is a wedding present from Clementine?"

"Apparently. Read the back." Since Lydia's tone brooked no argument, he flipped the card over and complied. To her horror, he burst out laughing. She drew her shoulders up. "I fail to see the humor in that."

Chuckling so hard he nearly choked, Powell wiped his eyes and handed the card back. "So, old Clem forgot to mention a few teensy details of the agreement, hmm? Like the fact that we're expected to share a bedroom to convince any court investigators that might drop by in the middle of the night. The bit about putting up a united front before the children was a nice touch, too. I mean, we can't have our phony marriage being discovered because Kenny tells a preschool teacher that his newly married legal guardians sleep in different rooms. That old woman, Clementine, is a real corker."

"I'm glad you're amused." Lydia shrugged with as

much nonchalance as she could muster. "I hope you'll be just as amused sleeping on the sofa."

"I'm sorry, you must have me confused with someone who enjoys taking orders." Powell's grin didn't fluctuate as he bent to lay his palms on the bed and jiggle it to test its firmness. "Half of this belongs to me, and I intend to use it."

"We are not sleeping in the same bed."

"Fine with me. You can sleep in the bathtub for all I care. I'm sleeping right—" he pivoted and flopped backward onto the mattress "—here."

She sucked in a breath, stared at him in utter disbelief. "We'll see about that," she muttered, hating the sensation that her carefully constructed world was spiraling totally out of control. "We'll just see about that."

Powell simply smiled. "Hey, Lyddie?"

She paused in the doorway, spun around with a huff. "What?"

"You didn't forget my sandwich, did you?"

The infuriating sound of his laughter followed as she stormed down the hall.

Swinging his legs from the king-size bed to the floor, Powell rose to investigate the rest of the house. Jamming his hands in his pockets, he sauntered out into the hallway. In the quick walk-through from last week he'd barely taken note of where the main rooms were located, but a brief peek into what was clearly Kenny's room proved that Lydia's request for his new room to be arranged as closely as possible to the old one had certainly been honored. A white dresser with crimson drawer knobs, a red-enameled bed complete with teddy bear comforter and matching curtains, and a white wicker toy box had all been arranged precisely as they'd been in his parents' condominium.

The wicker lid of the toy box had been lifted, as if Kenny had taken inventory of its contents. A few books lay askew on the floor, along with a couple of toy vehicles and a plastic squirt gun. It was good clutter, happy-child clutter.

Smiling to himself, Powell moved down the hall and peeked into another bedroom. The door squeaked a bit as he opened it to peer into the dimness. Ruffled curtains dotted with bows and balloons in soft baby pastels had been closed to block off the light. A white, slatted crib in the corner creaked, drawing Powell's attention. Inside the crib, the baby shifted, popped a tiny thumb in her mouth and suckled quietly for a moment before drifting into deeper slumber. A stuffed bunny sat in one corner of the crib. A faded pink blanket was twisted around her legs, its tattered corner clutched in one tiny fist.

There was also a changing table, a small dresser, a diaper pail and a shelving unit made up of white plastic crates that were piled with baby toys. But Powell's attention was riveted on the sleeping child. Pink cheeks chafed by slumber, blond ringlets clinging to her moist baby scalp, a twitching eyelid, a soft sigh—nothing escaped his scrutiny, because the sight touched him so deeply.

Something fluctuated inside his chest, a peculiar oscillating sensation that affected him profoundly, but which he couldn't identify and dared not examine too closely.

He didn't like the feeling. It was too intense, too close to the core. Backing out of the room, Powell closed the door softly. All sleeping children were appealing; all evoked a sense of parental protectiveness, of poignant awe. It was normal to experience such feelings for a child, any child. It didn't mean anything. He wouldn't allow it to mean anything.

None of this was real, he reminded himself, not the setting, not the fake feelings snaking through his gut. He was not a father. He was not a husband. He was simply a visitor to this house. A temporary visitor.

Very temporary.

Retreating to a more neutral area of the house, Powell set aside thoughts of his own precarious situation to focus on the sound of Lydia's voice, which seemed unusually high-pitched and more than a little intense.

"Yes, yes, I understand all that," she was saying, "but—"

Powell paused outside the kitchen, where she was engrossed in lively conversation with someone. He sidled closer, hovered outside the open door and chanced enough of a peek inside to confirm she was on the telephone. It didn't take long to figure out who was on the other end of the line.

"I never agreed to that, Clementine— Hmm?... All right, yes, Clem it is." There was a muffled thump, as if Lydia had leaned heavily against a cupboard. "As I was saying, Clem, sharing a house with Mr. Greer is acceptable. Sharing a bed is not— Excuse me?" Her voice quavered an octave higher. "The relationship Powell and I shared in the past has nothing to do with this."

He flattened against the wall and leaned toward the opening, straining to hear.

"Yes, I understand the marriage is legal—"

He issued a somber nod.

"Yes, I understand that married couples traditionally share the same bed, but this is hardly a traditional situa— *What?*" Her outraged gasp sent Powell back a step. "Of course I can control myself sexually!" She sputtered. "That's hardly the point."

He managed to slap a hand over his mouth to muffle a guffaw.

"I understand, however— Excuse me?"

Powell glanced toward the living room just as Kenny emerged, his eyes wide and curious. Powell held a finger to his lips, signaling that he should be very quiet, then motioned him over. The boy agreeably tiptoed toward him.

"Yes, I know about the home-check visits. Yes, I'm aware that they are quite thorough, but surely they don't count beds and paw through people's closets.... They do? But what about our— You had them put into storage? Oh. I see.... No, no, I just wish you'd discussed it with us—"

A soft moan was followed by the sound of utensils being forcefully placed on a counter. "Yes, we got the note. Yes, we understood it. I would have preferred the opportunity to discuss it in advance. I mean, you've made decisions, moved my computer— Hmm?"

Clearly confused, Kenny opened his mouth, then closed it quickly when Powell shushed him. The two males leaned toward the open door as Lydia lowered her voice.

"Ah, yes, of course I agree that the computer is safer in a separate room, but I'd planned to keep the equipment out of the baby's reach.... No, please...I don't mean to criticize, it's just that I presumed our privacy would be respected.... *I beg your pardon?*" Her voice rose to a disbelieving squeak. "Simply because we won't be exposed to anything we haven't seen before— Oh, please." A series of soft, muffled thumps sounded eerily like the echo of a skull making frustrated contact with a wall. When she spoke again, her voice was heavy, as if she'd become resigned to an awful fate. "Yes, I know. For the children. Of course. Hmm? Oh, no, I haven't."

The rhythmic thump was replaced by the shuffle of feet and the creak of the refrigerator door. "Yes, I see it. Uh-huh. Yes, it was very thoughtful of you. Three-hundred and fifty degrees for thirty minutes. I understand."

Powell chanced a peek, saw Lydia clamp the receiver

between her chin and shoulder while she struggled to retrieve a large, flat, foil-wrapped casserole from the fridge without being strangled by the phone cord.

As she turned, he straightened, grinning down at Kenny. He mouthed, *"Lasagna."*

Kenny mouthed, "Yay!" and yanked down a fistful of air.

In unison the two males leaned forward again, listening to the distinctive, spring-loaded whine of an oven door being lowered and the scrape of glass on metal grates. "Yes, it's in. I know. Thank you." The oven door sprang closed with a jarring slam. "In that case, please convey my appreciation to Dierdre. I can handle it from here— Yes?"

More footsteps sounded, more repetitive muffled thumps. "Uh-huh. Right. No, no, that won't be necessary. We'll, ah, work things out..." there was a pregnant pause "...somehow."

As the receiver was cradled with a forceful slam, Powell and Kenny sprang to attention. They were still standing there like a pair of military recruits when Lydia strode out of the kitchen.

She jerked to a stop, stared first at Powell's impassive expression, then down at Kenny's wide-eyed gaze. "Dinner in thirty minutes," she snapped, then spun on her heel and marched away.

As soon as the master bedroom door slammed, Powell and Kenny simultaneously exhaled, whirled to exchange a jubilant high five, then headed for the living room to watch the rest of the movie.

By the time the spicy tang of bubbling lasagna filled the air, Powell had decided that family life might not be so bad, after all. A warm meal, a warm bed and maybe even a warm body to snuggle up against. Yes, indeed, things could definitely be worse.

Chapter Four

"Here you go, sweetie," Lydia crooned, lowering the freshly scrubbed baby into the crib. "Nice clean sheets, a nice warm comforter and—" wrinkling her nose, Lydia plucked the crumpled pink flannel up between her thumb and forefinger as if it were contaminated "—your, ah, blankie."

From his vantage point at the doorway, Powell saw the toddler snatch her beloved hunk of cloth out of Lydia's hand, wad a flannel corner against a pink baby ear and pop a tiny thumb in her mouth. He'd studied both children through the tense evening, and although he felt out of his element Lydia seemed to have things all in hand. Now it was the children's bedtime. And Powell couldn't suppress his curiosity about the peculiar creatures for whom he was now at least partially responsible.

Sucking madly, Tami gazed up with suspicious little eyes. She was a somber baby, with a permanent frown

etched between feathery brows so blond they were almos
nonexistent. Powell didn't have much experience with ba
bies—none, in fact—but he didn't think a one-year-ol
should have eyes like a cynical politician. It bothered him
but he had no doubt Lydia could handle it.

Lydia could handle anything.

Refocusing his attention, he studied the woman wh
leaned over the crib-slats murmuring softly. With an ex
pression hovering between awe and adoration, she stroke
the baby's silky curls while her own gleaming hair swun;
forward like spun gold. The graceful sweep of Lydia's fin
gers drew his gaze like a magnet: lean, sensuous, with nat
urally buffed nails short enough to be practical, lon;
enough to be sexy.

Lord but she was a beautiful woman. Beautiful, capable
Extraordinary.

A burst of pride nearly suffocated him. Foolish pride
perhaps, and one he couldn't explain except that he stil
couldn't believe that a woman so bright and accomplishe
had once cared for him. Cared too much, actually. O
course, she'd been younger then, not exactly naive but cer
tainly inexperienced in the way things were. She'd though
the world would bend to her wishes, and had applied tha
theory to everyone in it. Powell Greer, however, was not
malleable man.

That had been Lydia's first lesson in reality. Teaching i
had given Powell no pleasure.

Not wanting her to catch him watching her, he backe
away from the doorway and moved quietly down the hall
As he passed Kenny's room, he saw the pajama-clad chil
sitting on the edge of his bed looking at a picture book.

Powell hesitated a moment. The boy contemplated th
pages with intense focus, moving his lips as if discussin;
the contents with himself just as his father had done. Powel

had always admired Dan's studious nature, his ability to eliminate extraneous distraction. Powell himself was the exact opposite, with a mind that skittered from one topic to another like a greedy honeybee in a rose garden.

If not for Dan's generosity in sharing notes for classes Powell found too boring to bother with, he wouldn't have made it through college. It wasn't that Powell was stupid or lazy; he simply had no tolerance for situations that didn't challenge him, and had a tendency to tune out lectures on subjects he already understood while his mind zipped along, dissecting more fascinating and difficult topics.

Like how to convince a certain golden-haired freshman with haughty eyes and a taunting smile that her life wouldn't really be complete unless she went out with him.

In retrospect Powell realized that his ruthless pursuit of Lydia had been motivated by the thrill of the chase. There had been an aloofness about her that intrigued him from the first moment he'd seen her in the college cafeteria, regally seated among the brilliant future business leaders whom she considered to be her peers.

Powell had been with his peers, too, a ragtag group of football players fueling up for afternoon practice. The entire team had snapped to attention when Lydia floated to a nearby table, smiling and chatting, yet holding that proud chin just a notch higher than she needed to. Powell had been instantly smitten, desperate to capture her attention. Her gaze had flicked over him once before settling on a geeky graduate student with horn-rimmed glasses and a predominant Adam's apple that bobbed like an escaped tennis ball.

Whatever the guy was saying seemed to fascinate Lydia, so much so that Powell decided desperate times required desperate measures. Outrageous acts garnered attention, and attention was what he'd wanted. So he'd spooled spaghetti around his index finger, then sensually sucked the pasta into his mouth while fixing her with an intense, smoldering gaze that left little to the imagination.

The ploy had worked. Her eyes snapped open; her cheeks glowed pink. And that evening they'd gone out on their first date.

Thinking back, Powell realized that Lydia's initial reluctance had fueled his determination. She'd been a challenge. Eventually she'd become more, so much more that the sheer power of his emotions had scared the spit out of him. It still did.

The crinkle of a turning page brought Powell's attention back to the small, stoic boy with footed pajamas waiting patiently to be tucked into bed by people he barely knew, people who were now responsible for the direction and quality of his young life. Taken aback by an unexpected surge of responsibility, Powell instinctively backed away from the door, swallowing a peculiar ache at the back of his throat and telling himself it would be best to let Lydia handle the tucking-in process. Powell would probably just screw it up.

Soft footsteps startled him. He stepped quickly into the darkened master bedroom just as Lydia emerged from the baby's room and moved into Kenny's. He heard voices, Lydia's husky murmur and Kenny's high-pitched reply.

The discussion had nothing to do with Powell. Still he strained to hear. It soothed him. He didn't know why.

"What book are you reading?" Lydia asked.

"I can't read," Kenny replied, with enough embarrassment that Powell felt bad for him. The little tyke was only four and a half. "But I know my ABC's. Wanna hear them?"

Powell couldn't hear her response, but Kenny blasted out

the alphabet with enough enthusiasm to presume that he'd been encouraged to do so.

Lydia's reply was also enthusiastic. "That's wonderful, Kenny. You're a very smart boy."

A creak filtered down the hall, along with what sounded like the ruffle of bedclothes. "I can write my name, too. Mommy showed me how." The boy's voice quivered only a little, but it was enough to convey exquisite sadness.

There was another muffled creak, as if Lydia had seated herself on the edge of the mattress. "I know how much you miss your mommy. I miss her, too."

Powell heard a sniff, a shuffling sound. "Do you think she can see us from heaven?"

Lydia didn't answer immediately. When she did, her voice was cautious and thoughtful. "I believe that she can."

"Do you think she still loves me?"

"Yes, Kenny, I believe that she loves you very much."

"Then how come she went away?"

Another pause, shorter this time. "She didn't want to, Kenny. Neither did your daddy." Lydia's words were slow and measured. "Sometimes things happen that we don't want to happen. We lose people we love very much, and we get so angry because we didn't want them to go. But I believe that the people we love never really leave, that they are always with us here—" there was a brief pause "—and here." The bed squeaked. "Your mommy and daddy will always be in your mind and in your heart, sweetheart. Anytime you want, you can close your eyes and think about them, and remember what they looked like, and what they smelled like, and the warmth of their hugs and their kisses, and the sound of your mommy's laugh and the way she groaned at your daddy's silly jokes. As long as you remember, they'll always be a part of you."

A tingle of admiration snaked down Powell's spine. All day she'd been saying all the right things, doing all the right things, comforting an overtired baby bewildered by new surroundings and people she barely knew, then reassuring a brave little boy whose pretense of courage concealed secret fears the adults in his life couldn't possibly comprehend.

So it didn't surprise Powell that Lydia had known the right thing to say to Kenny. Everything Lydia did was right. Well, almost everything. She'd been wrong once, a long time ago. The price of that mistake had been high. For both of them.

Curled up on the sofa, Lydia peered over her book and saw exactly what she'd seen for the past two hours: Powell, reclining comfortably in that horrid old lounger, with his eyes glued to the TV screen and the wired-on remote clutched in his hand. Except for her reading lamp and flickering images from the television, the house was dark, and relatively quiet, since Powell had courteously lowered the volume when she came into the living room to read.

Or at least, she'd tried to read. But her gaze had been drawn across the room, to the man who had once meant everything to her. He still affected her. He didn't have to look in her direction, didn't have to offer that slow, lazy smile that had always melted her defenses, sent the blood boiling in her veins. All he had to do was sit there watching an old movie, and she couldn't take her eyes off him.

It was infuriating.

She angrily flipped a page she hadn't read, forced herself to stare down at the undulating mass of incomprehensible words. Where was her self-esteem? How could she allow herself to be so viscerally attracted to a man who'd used and abandoned her as if she'd been nothing more than a temporary convenience? It was appalling. She wouldn't stand for it.

"Lydia?"

She automatically stiffened. "Yes?"

Although her gaze remained on her book, she was aware that he'd shifted in the chair. He muted the television, dropped the remote so it dangled by that ridiculous twist of wire. "Do you think the kids are going to be okay?"

Slowly, she lowered the book, forced herself to look at him. "Why do you ask?"

"I don't know. They seem... different."

"Different?"

"You know, quieter. Sadder. I mean, Tami's just a baby. She was barely crawling the last time I saw her, but have you noticed that the only time she smiles is when she's playing with her brother?"

"Babies are very perceptive. They are like tiny mirrors, reflecting the tension around them. She's very confused right now, not understanding why she's been moved from one place to another, then another. It's normal that her behavior would be somewhat reserved."

He considered that. "I suppose. But Kenny's got me worried. He's always been a serious little tyke, but today..." Powell sighed, rubbed his face. "It's weird. One minute I can't take two steps without him underfoot asking if I want a pillow, or a drink of water, or if he can bring me something to eat. The next minute he's staring right through me as if I don't exist, answering questions with a couldn't-care-less shrug."

Lydia had noticed the same behavior and shared Powell's concern, which was why she'd been studying the psychology of childhood trauma in her increasingly dog-eared parenting book.

"Both children have been through a lot the past couple

of months," she said, summarizing the book's indication that both children were reacting in differing ways to the same trauma, the massive changes that had upended their young lives since the death of their parents. "Their behavior reflects that. A one-year-old is too young to understand why people she cares about keep disappearing. It's normal for a child whose emotional attachments have been broken to withhold affection."

"It is?"

"Oh, yes," she assured him with considerably more confidence than she felt. "Also, a seemingly erratic vacillation between neediness and withdrawal is common in a child Kenny's age. His solicitous behavior may be an attempt to buy your love, to be a good enough child that you won't leave him like his parents did. At the same time, he may emotionally isolate himself as a protective mechanism."

Eyes wide, Powell lowered the recliner footrest, planted his feet firmly on the floor and leaned forward. He opened his mouth, closed it, leaned an elbow on his knee. "That's just about the saddest thing I ever heard."

"Yes, it is sad."

"How can we help? What can we do?"

Moistening her lips, Lydia automatically squared her shoulders as she did during a business meeting, when poise and presentation carried more weight than substantive fact. "We need to give them love, reassurance, lots of physical affection and a rigid routine to help them overcome the fear of the unexpected."

"You make it sound simple."

"It's far from simple."

"At least you know where to start." When he looked up, admiration shone from his eyes. "Not that I'm surprised. Those kids are lucky to have you."

A fission of fear skittered down her spine. She ignored

it, as she always did when her confident facade exceeded the extent of her experience. Lydia had responded to her new role as parent figure as she had every other challenge in her life—with an outward confidence that seemed instinctive, but was in reality learned behavior gleaned from the knowledge of others.

Books were Lydia's secret weapon, along with a mind sharp enough to assimilate reams of information with computerlike speed and comprehension. Information was her salvation, her key to success in every facet of her life. Success was survival. It had always been expected of her; she'd always expected it of herself. Failure was not an option.

Powell suddenly stood, yawning. "Ready for bed?" A familiar vitality gleamed in his teasing eyes. "I promise not to grope you while you sleep. Unless you grope me first. Then all bets are off."

She fixed him with a narrowed gaze.

"Seems to me we spent considerable time agreeing that we're both adults, able to control our...let's see, what was the term? Urges? Yep, that's it. Urges." Tousling his hair with his knuckles, he tried to discipline a taunting grin and failed miserably. "Then again, if you get cold in the middle of the night and feel a need to snuggle, I'd be more than happy to oblige. Just shows you what an accommodating guy I am, and how much I'm willing to sacrifice to keep my partner-in-parenthood perky, pink and free of goose bumps."

Lydia's knuckles whitened around the paperback book she held, wondering if he'd have any trouble swallowing when she shoved it sideways into his smirking mouth.

As if reading her thoughts, Powell's grin instantly widened as he sauntered past the sofa. "Oh, by the way." Pausing, he glanced over his shoulder. "Do you still sleep in the nude?" He ducked as the book she'd been reading whizzed past his head, then he straightened with a laugh that galled her to the bone. "I'll take that as a yes."

With that, he jammed his hands in his pockets and strolled off, whistling.

Outraged and mortified, Lydia spun around and pounded a hapless throw pillow. Powell Greer was without a doubt the most arrogant, the most frustrating, the most infuriating man she'd ever laid eyes on. She'd chew salted worms before she'd give him the satisfaction of sharing a bed with him, urges or no urges. The man was incorrigibly smug, obnoxious, disgustingly sure of himself, and...and...

And he had every reason to be.

Suddenly drained, Lydia slid bonelessly back on the cushions and curled into a fetal position. It wasn't Powell that she didn't trust. It was herself.

And he knew it.

At half past midnight Powell turned off the television and covered Lydia with a blanket. She stirred slightly, a sigh escaping sleep-slackened lips. He brushed a strand of hair from her face, allowed his fingers to linger against her warm cheek, to touch the moist corner of her mouth. A shudder shook her, and he withdrew his hand. She moaned softly, sensually. Her lovely fingers flicked air, then clamped around the edge of the blanket, wrapping it tightly around her.

Powell knelt beside the sofa, gave in to an overpowering need to stroke her hair. She'd always loved having her hair caressed. Said it made her feel like warm gelatin inside. He smiled at the memory. Silken strands slid through his open fingers, fluttering to frame her sleeping face. His skin tingled at the sensation.

He'd missed her so.

"I'm sorry." The words were a whisper in his mind, a

soft thought silently circling. "I never wanted to hurt you." Only when she stirred in response did he realize he'd actually spoken.

A moment later, Lydia blinked into empty darkness, then slipped back into blessed slumber without realizing that her dream had been real.

When Lydia awakened, a gray dawn had just touched the living room windows. Pain radiated down from barbed knots in her shoulders to spasm at the base of her spine. Her neck felt like rusty rebar. She couldn't move her head.

Every movement was agony. Moaning aloud, she shifted enough to lower her legs to the floor. They were tangled in something. She blinked at the mauve blanket, would have spent more time wondering where it came from if her head hadn't felt as though it had been set on a stake beside some dreary castle moat.

Perched ramrod-straight on the edge of the sofa, she unwound the cover, grunting in pain, then awkwardly pushed herself to her feet and tottered into the hall. The only thing on earth she wanted at the moment was a long, soothing shower, as hot as her skin could bear.

But first she had to check on the children.

A quiet peek into Tami's room revealed that the baby was on her tummy with her cheek resting on her beloved blankie. She was thankfully asleep.

Scuffling sounds emanated from behind Kenny's closed door. Lydia listened a moment, then went in. "Good morning, sweetie. Did you have a good sleep?"

The startled youngster whirled around, eyes huge. He'd been frantically rearranging his bedclothes, but now stared at her with a perplexing blend of indignation and apprehension. "How come you didn't knock?" he blurted, eyes darting. "Mommy always knocks."

Taken aback, Lydia hovered in the doorway. It hadn't occurred to her that a boy so young would value his privacy with such vehemence. "I'm sorry. I didn't think you'd mind."

"I coulda been naked or something."

"Oh...well—"

"Mommy says it's rude to go into people's rooms without knocking."

"Your mommy's right," Lydia replied, feeling properly chastised. "It won't happen again."

Acknowledging the concession with an aggravated grunt, Kenny spun around to finish spreading the rumpled comforter over his bed, then speared a fierce look over his shoulder.

"I'll, ah, see you at breakfast." She took a quick step back, quietly closed the door and headed toward the master bedroom, still stinging from the youngster's rebuke. Prekindergarten modesty was one thing the child care books had failed to mention. She made a mental note of it, then found herself standing in front of another closed door, this one to the master bedroom.

She hesitated. As she'd just been reminded, courtesy dictated that she not enter a room without knocking. The knowledge that doing so would rudely awaken anyone inside was strangely satisfying. She'd just spent a torturous night on a lumpy sofa while Powell snuggled in blissful slumber. Why shouldn't she wake him up?

On the other hand, they *were* legally married and California *was* a community property state. Technically, this was her room as much as it was his. Her clothes were in there. Her toothbrush, her comb, her personal grooming supplies. A person didn't have to knock to enter her own darned bedroom.

Of course, she didn't know what she might find on the

other side of that door. As Kenny had so indignantly pointed out, a person might be naked.

She smiled, twisted the knob and walked in.

Her smile flattened. Powell was not naked. Nor was he awake. A shock of ruffled hair laced the pillow with tangled sable tufts. A mouth gentled with sleep, vulnerable lips parted slightly, quivering only a bit with each slow and easy breath. An angled jaw, still strong in repose, yet oddly deferential to the magnetic power of the man now sprawled across the bed with the covers tangled around legs clad in striped cotton pajama bottoms. But his chest was bare.

And what a magnificent chest it was.

A wistful breath slid out like a sigh. She'd forgotten how beautiful his body was, tanned and sinewy, without an ounce of visible fat. Years of physical exercise combined with a profession requiring superb conditioning had resulted in a lean, hard, muscular torso that a woman's fingers just itched to explore. Every corded bicep, every granite plane, every contour of taut, smooth skin stretching warm and elastic around blood and bone, every manly inch of him was as alluring to her as a bonfire was to a foolish moth, and just as deadly.

She knew that. Deep inside she knew that, but for a moment, for a brief, glorious moment, she allowed herself the luxury of devouring him with her gaze without considering what the next moment might bring. Appealing and tousled in sleep, he was vulnerable to her gaze, unable to recognize the desire in her eyes or to mock her for the weakness.

It *was* a weakness. He was a weakness. Not her only flaw, by any means, but the one that most disturbed her. Even now she could barely resist the compulsion to touch him, to stroke his slick chest, to lower herself into the strong arms that had once held her close even as they pushed her away.

The memory of that night six years ago jolted her back to reality. Even animals and small children learned from their mistakes.

Lydia, it seemed, did not.

Chapter Five

Powell was on his third cup of coffee when he heard the distinctive high-pitched whine of Lydia's car pulling into the driveway. He dropped the newspaper he'd been reading, pushed away from the table and headed into the entry just as Kenny blasted through the front door.

"Uncle Powell, Uncle Powell, we got hot dogs for lunch and ice cream for dessert!"

"That's great, buddy."

Beaming, Kenny dashed into the living room. A moment later, the incessant shriek of a cartoon show blasted from the television. Lydia entered the house and hurried past Powell with Tami in her arms.

He followed her into the kitchen. "Where have you been?" he asked as she slipped the baby into the high chair. "I woke up and everyone was gone. No note, no nothing, just an empty house." Lydia raised a brow, perhaps as surprised by his plaintive query as Powell himself was. He cleared his throat, bunched his own brows into a manly frown. ''The only reason I noticed was because I had to cook my own breakfast.''

''Now that's the sweet chauvinist we all know and love,'' she muttered, snapping the high chair tray into place.

''You could have told me where—'' he spun around as she swiveled past him to head out the front door ''—you were going,'' he finished lamely, focusing on little Tami, the only person left in the room. ''At least you listen to me.'' The baby regarded him silently, then slapped the plastic tray as if reminding him she was a captive audience. ''Good idea,'' Powell muttered. ''I'll tie your aunt Lyddie to a chair and talk in her face until she screams for mercy.''

Tami yawned, rubbed her eyes.

''No good, eh?''

The baby grunted.

''Yeah, you're right. Lydia doesn't get mad, she gets even. I'd probably wake up tomorrow morning with my eyebrows shaved off and my chest waxed.'' Or worse, he thought, wincing at the possibilities.

Outside, a car door slammed. Quick footsteps scuffed the concrete walk. Powell met Lydia at the front door and reached for the grocery bags she was balancing in her arms.

''Got it,'' she mumbled, muscling past him to set the bags on the counter. Without so much as a glance in his direction, she yanked out a colorful box, opened it and handed Tami something coated with pink and freckled with colorful candy sprinkles. It appeared to be a cookie, although it was unlike any Powell had ever seen. Clearly, it was a female-type cookie. No self-respecting male would ever be seen eating something so, well, pink.

Hovering in the foyer like a useless shadow, Powell glanced from the bustling woman in the kitchen to the car in the driveway with its trunk still open. He trudged out for the rest of the groceries.

When he returned, Tami had laid the cookie on the high chair tray and was crushing it into dust with a fat little fist. He set the bags on the counter. "There were calls while you were gone," he told Lydia, nodding toward a crumpled wad of messages below a wall phone with a long curly cord. "I thought your office knew you were on vacation this week."

Lydia flipped through the notes without so much as a thank-you-kindly. "There's a bond issue pending. I'm handling the contract for the deal." She snatched the phone, dialed, then proceeded to unload grocery bags and talk at the same time. "George? Lydia. What's the status...? No, I've already taken care of that.... Yes, the report is on Dressler's desk."

Powell absently retrieved a couple of cereal boxes from the nearest bag and placed them in a cupboard.

"Rumor is that the feds are fiddling with interest rates again." Without missing a beat, Lydia ducked under the phone cord, moved the cereal to a different shelf, turning each so the side of the box with nutritional information faced out. "We'll have to move quickly or investors will waiver."

Powell set a bag of apples in the refrigerator. He'd barely turned away when Lydia rushed up, the phone still clamped between her chin and shoulder, to remove the apples from the plastic bag and arrange them in a crisper drawer.

Noticing a pattern here, Powell tested his theory by stacking several soup cans in the pantry. Lydia quickly rearranged them. He placed a jug of milk in the refrigerator. Lydia moved it forward on the shelf, turning it so the handle faced out.

At this point, Tami tired of finger painting with drooled-upon cookie crumbs and started to fuss. Powell took a step toward the high chair. Lydia leaped in front of him, swept the baby into her arms and pulled a large juice jar from the cupboard. "Three-quarters of a point means the difference between a viable project and financial ruin," she said into the phone.

Balancing the baby in the crook of her arm and maintaining a chin clamp on the telephone receiver, she twisted off the cap of a small plastic baby bottle, filled it with juice and handed it to Tami, who popped the nipple in her mouth and sucked greedily. "A quarter point? Possibly. I've already run those figures." She recapped the juice jar, set it in the refrigerator, label out, then shifted Tami in her arms, rotated the telephone receiver and plucked up another crumpled message with her free hand. "I'm going to call her now, George. I'll get back to you."

Lydia strode across the kitchen like a determined tank, forcing Powell to duck under the stretched phone cord to avoid strangulation. He watched in awe as Lydia dialed, retucked the phone under her chin, grabbed a package of pork chops out of a grocery bag and pivoted back toward the freezer. "Ms. Warner, please... Marsha? Lydia. Got your message. Hmm? No, those figures have been revised...."

Lydia continued to unload groceries, balance the baby, discuss global economics and analyze the stock market without missing a beat. She didn't even blink when Tami burped in her ear and flung the empty juice bottle on the floor.

Powell's head was spinning.

Clearly he wasn't needed here. Judging by Lydia's irked frown every time she stepped around him, he wasn't wanted, either.

Jamming his hands in his pockets, he strolled into the

living room, where Kenny sat cross-legged on the carpeted floor, watching cartoons. "Hey, buddy."

At least Kenny looked happy to see him. "Can I have ice cream now?"

"That's up to Aunt Lyddie. She's kind of busy right now," Powell added when the youngster prepared to sprint toward the kitchen. "How about you and I go out and do some man stuff?"

"Man stuff?" Kenny rolled the words on his tongue as if tasting them for the first time.

"I could use your help changing the oil in my car."

The boy flicked a longing look at the TV screen. "Do we hafta do it right now?"

An unsettling image came to mind, of Lydia rushing into the garage to unbolt the crankcase cover with a pair of tweezers, then, using a hairpin and lipstick brush, rebuilding the carburetor while the oil drained.

"Yep, right now." Independent women, he decided, were hell on the ego.

"Duck down, buddy," Powell warned the youngster perched on his shoulders. "Watch your head."

Kenny, high atop Powell's shoulders, curled forward as Powell bent his knees, easing carefully through the doorway from the garage into the kitchen. Their entry startled Lydia, who knelt in front of a cupboard door, wielding a screwdriver.

Once inside, Powell straightened and splayed his feet, still holding tightly to Kenny. "Ah," he said, inhaling deeply enough to flare his manly nostrils. "I love the smell of petroleum products in the morning."

Lydia laid the screwdriver on the floor amid a peculiar scattering of odd-shaped plastic pieces, and sat back on her heels. Keeping her torso straight, she turned her entire body to look at them. "You are both filthy."

"Yes, but it's man filth," Powell replied amiably. "Grease, oil, engine dirt, the stuff dreams are made of."

"Your dreams, my nightmares." Her nose wrinkled adorably. "Don't touch a thing until you've washed up."

Chuckling, Powell squatted down, allowing Kenny to scramble off his shoulders. Flushed with excitement, the grinning youngster danced from foot to foot, sharing his experience with a torrent of exuberance. "Aunt Lyddie, Aunt Lyddie, Uncle Powell took all the old oil outta his car and put new oil inside, and I helped!"

She issued a weak smile, but her gaze was riveted on the child's grease-stained hands. Powell's gaze was riveted on her. Pale cheeks, purplish smudges beneath her eyes, hair mussed and tucked haphazardly behind her ears—she was clearly weary, clearly stressed. Clearly beautiful. Just the sight of her warmed him. Aroused him.

He shifted, spoke to Kenny. "Go scrub up in the bathroom, buddy. Use lots of soap."

"Okay."

As the boy sprinted away, Lydia called after him, "Make sure the dirt is gone before you use the towels." A muffled grunt was the only indication he'd heard her. She sagged a bit, flinched and squared her shoulders, wiping a forearm over her forehead.

Powell wanted to hug her. Instead he went to the sink, flipped on the water. "Where's Tami?"

"Taking a nap. She was...cranky."

"She always is," he said, snatching a paper towel from a roll mounted under a high cupboard. "Maybe it's that ear infection Rose told us about."

"She doesn't have a fever." Lydia gave a weary sigh, a touch of frustration in her voice. "She doesn't care for the medicine, either. It's been difficult to convince her to take it.''

''Aren't you supposed to rub her throat while she swallows?''

Lydia regarded him as if trying to decide whether he was serious. ''She's not a dog, Powell.''

Since he had indeed been serious, he glanced away to prevent her from noting his embarrassment. ''Just trying to lighten things up.''

Oddly enough, she accepted that. ''I'm sorry. I guess I've been a little cranky myself lately.''

Offering an empathetic nod, Powell tried to open the sink cupboard using the paper towel to protect the knob from his greasy hands. The cupboard opened an inch, then jammed. He frowned, yanked harder, rattling the thin door enough to get Lydia's attention.

''Here, let me show you.'' She leaned over, slowly and with a peculiar stiffness, to slip her index finger into the opening. Something clicked, and the door yawned open. ''Childproof latches,'' she explained, gesturing toward the screws and plastic parts scattered beside her. ''I'm installing them on all the lower cupboards.''

''Oh. Good idea.'' Wishing he'd thought of it, Powell retrieved a can of kitchen cleanser, kneed the door shut. He lathered his hands with gritty cleanser, snaking occasional glances over his shoulder. Lydia was marking the location of another plastic piece inside a neighboring cupboard. ''I could do that for you.''

For a moment, her eyes lit up in something that seemed very much like gratitude. She glanced away. ''Thank you, I can manage.''

Of course she could manage, Powell thought, and wondered why he was so disappointed. There was nothing on earth that Lydia couldn't do, and do well. Her independence was one of the things that had initially drawn him to her. She wasn't clingy or needy. She was her own person, able to handle anything life dished out. He liked that about her.

So why did he suddenly feel aimless and isolated?

The question hung in his mind unanswered as Kenny dashed in to display his shiny pink hands. "All clean," he announced. "Can I have ice cream now?"

Lydia's smile was genuine. And ravishing. "As soon as your sister wakes up from her nap, okay?"

Her pronouncement was met with a pained sigh, a disappointed slump of small shoulders. "She's gonna sleep a long time."

"Not nearly long enough." At the sight of Kenny's fractured frown, Lydia actually smiled, then turned her rigid torso to reach for him, slip an arm around his little body and pull him over for a hug. The gesture was plainly unexpected by the child, who stiffened in surprise and stepped away. To her credit, Lydia's smile never wavered. "Hey, guess what we're going to do tomorrow?"

Kenny tilted his head. "I dunno."

"Well…" Shifting painfully, Lydia pivoted from a kneeling position to a sitting one, then stretched her legs out with an almost audible sigh of relief. "First, we're going to visit a very special place, with lots of children for you to play with."

The boy's eyes widened. "Really?"

"Uh-huh. It's called Happy Home Day Care, and there are lots of toys to play with, and a whole big playground in the backyard, with swings and slides and all kinds of wonderful things."

Kenny grinned. "Cool."

"And then we're going to spend the rest of the day at the aquarium." That was news to Powell, who tried to question Lydia with a look. She stubbornly avoided his gaze. "Won't that be wonderful, sweetie?"

Kenny shrugged. "I guess so. What's a 'quarium?"

"It's a marvelous place where we can see all kinds of different fish, like sharks and stingrays, and even saltwater puffers that blow themselves up like prickly balloons. When I was a little girl, the puffers were my favorite."

"Wow," Kenny said, plainly awed by the image. "Will we get to see goldfish, too?"

"Goldfish? Well, possibly. I know there's a freshwater exhibit there, too."

"Way cool! Goldfishes are my very best favorite!" Kenny leaped up, clapping, then hopped happily away, chanting, "Goldfishes are old fishes, goldfishes are old fishes...."

When television sounds emanated from the living room, Powell rounded on Lydia, who was efficiently fastening a plastic latch to the inside of the cupboard frame. "Okay, I understand the bit about the day care visit. We agreed the kids should see the place and meet some of their new playmates in advance. But what's all this about aquariums?"

She speared him with a glance. "We took this week off to spend time with the children. The aquarium is a good place to do that. The kids will enjoy it, and they'll learn something as well."

"Didn't it occur to you to check with me first?"

"No."

"Why on earth not? I might have had plans or something."

She twisted one screw into place, reached for another. "Do you?"

"Do I what?"

"Have plans."

"Well, no. But that's not the point. You should have asked."

"Asked?" She flicked him a look. "As in begged for permission?"

Exhaling all at once, Powell sagged sideways to brace one hip against the sink counter. "That's not what I meant."

"I didn't think so."

There was more warning in her voice than acquiescence, although Powell noted a peculiar softening around her mouth and a strange sadness in her eyes. When she twisted her taut torso to reach for another screw, she flinched slightly.

"Is something wrong with your back?"

"Hmm?" She turned her upper body to look at him. "Oh, no. My neck is a little stiff, that's all."

The image of Lydia curled awkwardly on the sofa flitted through his mind. Guilt pricked him. But not very hard. He moved to kneel behind her. "Where does it hurt?" he murmured, wrapping his palms gently over the top of each shoulder. Her knotted muscles responded to his touch with a quiver. "Here?" He flexed his fingers, pressing firmly, gently. She moaned, a quiet guttural sound vibrating low in her chest. He rolled his thumbs against the taut muscles at the base of her neck. She gasped, nearly purred in relief. "Feel good?"

"Um-hmm."

Leaning forward until the scent of her hair made him dizzy, he whispered against her ear, "Roll your head with my hands…that's it, slowly, slowly…. Left, front, right, back…" He repeated the mantra, whispering each command in a voice raw with surging emotions. Silken hair brushed his knuckles with every roll of her head, a whisper of scent, a tickle of softness on his skin. Beneath his hands, her flesh trembled, melted, warming his palms until his own blood heated in response. "Left, front, right, back..."

Sweet jasmine, a hint of baby powder, a whiff of strawberry—a dizzying blend of fragrance wafted around him, through him. "Left, front, right, back..."

She moaned, a kittenish sigh of pleasure that shot straight into his veins with molten force. His groin tightened; his belly burned. "Left..."

He wanted to hold her.

"Front..."

Wanted to taste her.

"Right..."

Wanted to sweep her into his arms.

"Back..."

Wanted to bury himself inside her.

She uttered a tiny cry of pleasure and went limp under his hands. "I'd forgotten how good you are," she whispered. "I give up. You win."

His hands went perfectly still. "I win?"

"Of course." Eyes closed, face relaxed in serene repose, she allowed a soft breath to slide from between sensually slackened lips. "You've got me all warm and tingling. It would be a shame to let all that effort go to waste."

Powell froze. "Do you mean it?"

"Yes." It was a sigh. "If your offer is still good."

"My offer?"

"Umm." Lydia rolled her head, massaged the back of her neck, levered herself to her feet, nearly knocking Powell backward. "And while you finish installing the cabinet latches, I'm going to soak in a hot tub. No sense letting everything stiffen back up on me."

Seated awkwardly on the floor, Powell stared up in disbelief. "No, certainly no sense in that."

She flashed a vixen smile, then strolled away, rolling her

hips like a runway model doing a victory lap, leaving a throaty chuckle and Powell's deflated ego in her wake. Not only had she been aware of his arousal, she'd taunted him with it to make certain he understood that she was in control here. There wasn't a doubt in his mind that he'd just been played like a randy fiddle.

This, Powell decided, was war.

"I'm gonna name him Sidney," Kenny announced the moment he walked in the front door. "He's gonna be my best friend in the whole wide world."

Lydia lifted Tami from the stroller, cast a pained glance at the spotted orange-and-black creature placidly circling the round bowl clutched in the child's arms. A goldfish wouldn't have been her first choice for a best friend, although she grudgingly admitted that Kenny seemed pleased enough. "A pet is a big responsibility."

"I know," the child said solemnly, gazing into the water-filled bowl with something akin to adoration. "I'm gonna take real good care of him."

Powell strolled inside the house carrying a diaper bag, a cooler filled with now-empty juice cans, and Tami's newest toy, a stuffed dolphin purchased in lieu of yet another finny creature that would doubtless add to Lydia's misery. A bag of fish food, bowl-cleaning paraphernalia and a "How to Care for Your Goldfish" booklet dangled from a mesh bag hanging on his wrist.

Shifting Tami in the crook of one arm, Lydia unzipped the baby's jacket, skewered Powell with a frumpy stare. "I hope you're pleased with yourself."

"Look on the bright side. I could have bought him a Labrador retriever." Ignoring Lydia's irked frown, he flashed a grin at Kenny, who'd set his precious goldfish bowl on the kitchen counter, lowered a finger into the water and was diligently attempting to pet his finny friend. Powell chuckled. "Have you trained him how to heel yet?"

Kenny looked up and blinked. "Are fishes smart enough to learn that?"

"Sure they are. Look how much time they spend in schools." Beaming at his own joke, Powell angled a smug glance at Lydia, who rolled her eyes and groaned.

"Fissy!" Tami blurted, pointing a fat finger at the gold-fish bowl.

"Yes, that's a fishy," Lydia murmured, struggling to extract the child's flailing arm from the padded sleeve. "Hold still, sweetie, so I can get your jacket off—"

"Fissy, fissy!"

"It's *my* fish." Kenny hugged the bowl against his tummy as if it were a basketball. "It's going to live in *my* room, and you can't even look at it." Water sloshed from the bowl as the boy dashed into the hallway.

"*Fissy!*" Tami shrieked, arching her back and kicking her feet into Lydia's midsection with enough force to double her over.

Gasping, Lydia spun around, tripped over the stroller and sank to her knees. The wriggling baby twisted out of her grasp, toddled toward the hall screaming wildly. Lydia sat back on her heels, panting, with an empty baby jacket clutched in her fist.

Powell stared down at her with only a slight flinch as the wailing toddler fiercely pounded on her brother's bed-room door. "Would you like me to hang that up for you?"

She gave him a look that could freeze meat. "If it wouldn't be too much trouble."

Fighting a smirk, he unloaded the cooler, stuffed toy and fish supplies on the counter, then hung up the baby jacket in the hall closet. By the time he'd finished putting the folded stroller away, Lydia was on her feet, dusting herself off.

He bit his lower lip, tried to look patriarchal. "So..." *Thump. Pound. Rattle.* "Fiss-ssy!"

"Is there anything else I can do for you?" Powell asked politely, as if it hadn't occurred to him that he might want to investigate the small war erupting just down the hall.

Wild shrieks joined a deafening series of thumps, as if the baby had thrown herself on the floor and was kicking the closed door with her feet.

Lydia felt as if her head might explode. "No, thanks," she hissed. "You've done quite enough."

To Lydia's mind, a goldfish had caused this noisy discontent. Powell had purchased the goldfish. Therefore, Powell was clearly responsible for the current squabble, her blinding headache, the lousy weather and probably the decline of the Asian stock market.

He responded to her accusatory stare with an unconcerned shrug. "We went to an aquarium. There were lots of fish there. Kenny liked the fish, so I bought him one. What's the big deal?"

"That—" she jerked a thumb toward the hallway, where Tami was screeching and Kenny was yelling and the walls were vibrating with sounds of battle "—is the big deal."

Spinning on her heel, she marched into the hallway, where Tami was flat on her back kicking her fat legs, swinging her little arms and screaming at the top of her lungs. Lydia sucked in a breath, certain she had to do something to stop the baby's temper tantrum, but not sure exactly what that something was.

She knelt down and tried soothing the child. "Shh, Tami, honey, it's okay, I'm sure your brother will let you see the fishy."

"No, I won't," warned a muffled voice on the other side of the door. "Sidney is *my* fish."

"Kenny, you have to share your things."

"Uh-uh. Mommy says I don't have to, 'cause Tami always breaks stuff."

"She's not going to break your fish," Lydia said with considerably more conviction than she felt. Visions of a goldfish flopping on the carpet came to mind. "Maybe you could just let her look at it sometimes when you're there to make sure she doesn't hurt it."

"No!"

"Kenny—"

"She can't ever look at him, ever, ever, ever!"

By this time Tami was screaming so loudly that her face was red as a boiled beet.

"Hush, sweetie, hush." Lydia tried to scoop the flailing baby into her arms. It was like trying to hug an angry octopus.

Suddenly Tami stiffened into silence, her wide-eyed stare riveted on the far end of the hall. Lydia followed the child's gaze and saw the stuffed dolphin leaping in the air at the end of a hairy, masculine arm.

A series of interesting clicks and squeaks seemed to emanate from the toy, which paused in midair. "Tami, Tami," the stuffed toy called out in a voice that sounded suspiciously like a grown man struggling in falsetto. "I'm lonesome. Come play with me."

Tami quivered. Her head spun around, tear-stained eyes huge with wonder. "Fissy?"

"Yes, sweetie," Lydia assured her. "That's Tami's fishy. Do you want to go play with it?"

The baby hesitated, eyeing the dancing dolphin with a somber frown. The dolphin squealed and whistled. Tami smiled, actually smiled. Lydia was stunned. The dolphin called her name again. Tami jammed her chubby fists against her mouth and giggled. The sound of baby laughter warmed Lydia to the marrow.

The mesmerized toddler watched the dancing toy for another moment before waddling over to snatch it away with a happy squeal. Powell stepped forward, scooped the now-thrilled baby into his arms. "I'll put Tami and her 'fissy' in the playpen to get acquainted," he told Lydia.

She could have kissed him.

Then he ruined the mellow mood with a gloating grin and a comment deliberately designed to aggravate. "You see, parenting isn't so difficult for those who know how."

He exited the hallway, chuckling, and strolled back a couple of minutes later without the baby, but still gloating. "She's happy as a clam. I guess buying her the dolphin was a good idea. It was my idea, by the way, but who's keeping track?"

Lydia was fuming. "Don't you *ever* do that again."

"Do what?" he asked innocently. "Calm a crying child? I thought that was my job."

"It's *our* job, and I was doing just fine until you interfered." She hadn't been doing fine at all, but the words rushed out on a torrent of embarrassed anger.

He chuckled. "Yeah, I could see that."

Furious now, Lydia felt a burning sensation in her cheeks, which were probably the color of ripe apples. "I was talking about Kenny's fish. He's too young to care for a pet, any pet. Who do you think is going to get stuck taking care of it, cleaning the bowl, making certain it's properly fed? How dare you make a decision like that without asking?"

"Asking?" Powell's smile flattened like a steamrolled onion. "As in begging for permission?"

With her own words slapped in her face, Lydia wobbled

back a step, feeling supremely stupid for having overreacted, for behaving like a drill sergeant on steroids, for wanting to throw her arms around Powell, for wanting to confess that she didn't know what she was doing and was scared out of her mind.

But most of all she felt stupid because Kenny had opened his bedroom door a crack and was peeking out with huge, frightened eyes. "I'll take care of Sidney, honest, Aunt Lyddie. Please don't be mad at Uncle Powell, please don't..."

"Oh, honey." Kneeling, Lydia opened her arms, and Kenny ran into them, sobbing. She hugged him fiercely. "Of course you'll take good care of Sidney. You're such a big boy. You even went into the playground at day care this morning. I was so proud of you."

The youngster hiccuped, wiped his teary eyes. "Really?"

"Absolutely," Lydia assured him, although their first day care visit had been less than a roaring success. Tami had clung to Lydia's leg the entire time, and Kenny had ventured into the playground only because Powell had gone with him. "You were very brave, and you made so many new friends." Actually, he'd spoken to only one child, a little boy who'd asked Kenny to play ball with him. Kenny had said no. All in all, the visit had not gone well, but Lydia wisely chose to accentuate the positive in an attempt to bolster the boy's confidence.

Slightly mollified, Kenny now sniffed, his wary glance skipping from Lydia to Powell, who also looked chagrined to have been caught arguing in front of the children. Powell squatted down to the child's level. "So, did you have a good time today?"

Kenny shrugged. "It was sorta fun."

Powell teased him with a smile. "Only sorta?"

Another shrug. "It wasn't real fun, 'cause you guys were all mad at each other."

Somehow Lydia kept the moan stifled in her throat. She and Powell exchanged a look. They'd been sniping at each other all day, Powell teasing and Lydia reacting, each trying to gain the upper hand without so much as a thought as to how their verbal jousting was affecting the children. At the time, neither had paid much attention to Kenny's worried looks or long periods of silence.

A shaft of pure misery sliced through her. "Kenny sweetheart, Uncle Powell and I aren't angry with each other."

The boy's brows rose a notch. "How come you were yelling?"

She forced a smile, tried to think of a reasonable response. There wasn't one.

Powell cleared his throat. "Do you like your sister, Kenny?"

"Huh? Sure, I guess."

"But you yell at her sometimes, don't you?"

"Uh-huh."

"Do you think it might hurt her feelings?"

He shrugged again, but this one was coupled with a glimmer of understanding in the boy's bright blue eyes. "She makes me real mad."

"Yeah, I know, but you still like her, don't you?" Powell waited for the child's affirming nod, then continued. "Aunt Lyddie and I like each other, too, but sometimes we do things that hurt each other's feelings. We don't mean to, and it's not right, but sometimes grown-ups do dumb things, too."

"They do?" Kenny's eyes widened as if the thought had never occurred to him.

"Yeah, they do." Smiling, Powell ruffled the boy's hair.

"Why don't you go warm up the television? I'll be there in a couple of minutes, and we'll see if we can find a good ball game to watch."

"Okay."

Powell stood, waited until the boy had scampered out of the hallway. He skimmed a glance at Lydia, then lowered his gaze as if embarrassed to meet her eyes. "We blew it big time."

Folding her arms, Lydia leaned against the wall for support. "Yes, we did. I'm..." she paused to moisten her lips "...sorry for being so, well..."

"Bitchy?" The amused grin died on his face. He muttered a curse, roughly rubbed his chin. "I'm sorry, Lyddie. That was uncalled for."

"Yes, it was." Actually, she agreed with him. She was not proud of her prickly behavior, but was so tangled up inside with emotion every time she looked at him, she couldn't seem to help herself. Her defensive shield bristled every time he looked at her.

Because inside, she was melting. And she didn't want him to know it.

Now, however, Powell seemed completely sincere with his apology. She kept waiting for the zinger, the hidden taunt. It never came. "I'm hopeless," he told her, seeming genuinely piqued with himself. "Absolutely hopeless. I know this is all my fault, Lyddie. I stay up nights thinking of ways to tick you off. I don't know why. You're just so damned adorable when you get mad...."

"Adorable?"

A rush of color stained his face. He coughed, turned away. "Maybe I should have said predictable."

Oddly deflated by the correction, she hiked her chin as if his opinion didn't matter to her. "I suppose I am. Insults make me predictably cranky."

"You're right." He shifted, jammed a fist on his hip. "We've both brought old baggage with us, stuff from a long time ago. It's affecting the kids."

A lump wedged in her throat. "Yes, it is."

"I guess that's one more thing we're going to have to control." His smile was a little sly, a little sad. "Along with those pesky urges."

"No insults, no sex," she murmured, with an exaggerated sigh. "What a drag."

Chapter Six

Happy Home Day Care was in chaos.

Shrieks, sobs and distressed howls reverberated through the playroom, rattling walls and adult nerves until the beleaguered owner of the facility, a portly, poodle-faced woman with a normally hospitable smile, wrung her hands in dismay. "Perhaps," she said in a voice rising only slightly above the din, "we should reevaluate Kenny and Tami Lynn's suitability for day care at the current time."

Lydia, kneeling on the cartoon-carpeted floor in a vain attempt to quell Tami's terrified screams, looked up in horror. "But this is the finest facility in the city. I've done extensive research. The programs you offer for emotionally fragile children are the most comprehensive available."

Wringing her hands, the woman flinched as yet another of the day care's small clients, frightened by the hysteria, broke into tears. "I'm sorry, Mrs. Greer, I know how difficult this is for you, but clearly the children aren't—" she cringed as Tami arched her baby back, screeching like a trapped animal ''—er, suitably adjusted at this point.''

As Lydia stood, preparing to plead her case, Tami flung herself over and grabbed her aunt's ankles. Hiccuping, shaking violently, the wailing baby sobbed so hard she started to choke. Lydia scooped her up, frightened as the child's face darkened to ominous crimson. Lydia spun around, threw a desperate look at Powell, who was still trying to convince a sniveling Kenny that he really would enjoy the day care experience if he'd just give it a try. Kenny wasn't having any of that.

Neither was Tami. The baby locked her fat arms around Lydia's neck, shaking with wretched sobs. ''Oh, sweetie,'' Lydia murmured, hugging the child fiercely. ''It's all right, precious, it's all right.''

It wasn't all right at all. Lydia's detailed and meticulous schedule of introduction and familiarization with the day care facility had been prepared specifically to avoid the very abandonment terrors that both children now displayed. During the first two visits the children had accepted the new environment with cautious curiosity. Today's visit was to include a one-hour get-acquainted session, during which Lydia and Powell would actually leave the facility.

As soon as they'd offered a cheery goodbye, Kenny had bolted to his feet, shrieking, and whipped his arms around Powell's knees. It had taken Tami a few minutes longer to figure out what was happening, but when she'd toddled out of the playroom and seen Powell and Lydia trying to dislodge her screaming brother long enough to get out the front door, she'd let out a bloodcurdling shriek, flung herself forward and beat her little head on the carpet until Lydia hurried over to comfort her.

Comfort, however, had not been enough for Tami Lynn. She'd continued to screech until every child in the center was terrified. Many were howling; some simply stood by watching with frantic eyes, hugging favorite toys, or each other, until they also burst into frightened tears.

To his credit, Powell was doing his best to calm Kenny. Squatting down, he wiped the boy's wet face, spoke in a slow, soothing voice. "Hey there, buddy, we're not going to be gone long. Why, before you know it story time will be over, your aunt Lyddie and I will be back and we'll all head over to the ice cream place for the biggest chocolate swirl cone they can make. How does that sound?"

Trembling all over, Kenny clutched at Powell's shirt. "I'll be good, Uncle Powell, I promise. I won't tease Tami no more, and I won't drink all the juice without asking, and I won't hide cookies in the sofa, and I won't turn the channel when you're watching a ball game, only please don't go away. I don't want you to go away."

"I'm not going away, sport." Powell frowned, heaved a sigh. "Well, maybe for just a few minutes so you can get acquainted with your new friends—"

A fresh round of ragged sobs shook Kenny to his sneakers. "I don't wanna stay here! I don't want you to go away, I don't, I don't!" The child flung himself against Powell's chest, crying his little eyes out. Powell stood, hoisting the frightened boy in his arms, and cast a resigned glance at Lydia. "This isn't going to work."

Lydia felt as if she'd swallowed a brick. "I know."

As several teachers swarmed to calm the rest of the children, the day care owner held out a helpless hand. "Perhaps we could try again next week—"

"No," Lydia said, shaking her head. A week wouldn't be nearly enough time to overcome Tami's and Kenny's terror of being left alone. They'd been in day care on the fateful afternoon of their parents' accident, and clearly associated being left with strangers with the loss of the people they loved.

The warm baby body quivered in Lydia's arms and shuddered from the force of her sobs. Blond ringlets lay plastered against the child's scalp, moistened by perspiration and tears that had run behind her ears as she'd lain on her back, shrieking and kicking.

A dull ache revolved inside Lydia's chest, a protective response so fiercely intense it was frightening.

Lydia had warped into mommy-mode.

It was a strange and totally unexpected sensation, one so powerful that she knew instantly her life would never be the same. At that moment, there was nothing on earth she wouldn't do to nurture this precious child, to keep her safe and happy.

She kissed Tami's damp little cheek, whispered soft assurance. "It's okay, sweetheart, I'm not going to leave you. I'll never leave you."

Sniffing, Tami turned a wet, pink face toward Lydia as if gauging the sincerity of that promise. The baby popped a thumb in her mouth, suckling madly. She shivered twice, issued a contented sigh and buried her face in the warm crook of Lydia's throat. Lydia's heart felt as if it had been squeezed dry.

Beside her, Powell held Kenny in his arms and studied Lydia as if he didn't know what to make of her. Not that she blamed him. It had been Lydia who'd insisted the children be instantly enrolled in day care. Powell had been reluctant, to say the least. Under the circumstances, however, he'd been forced to agree that since they both held full-time jobs, there didn't appear to be any viable alternative.

There still wasn't, although judging by his surprised and hopeful expression, Powell clearly wondered if she'd come up with some magical solution to the problem. She hadn't. All she knew for certain was that forcing children into a situation that terrified them was wrong, dead wrong, and she was not going to allow it.

Without responding to the silent question in Powell's eyes, Lydia focused on the day care owner, managed a thin smile. "You've been very kind, truly you have, but we'll have to give the children some time to adjust before we try again. I hope you understand."

"Of course." The woman nodded empathetically. "What will you do in the meantime?"

"Whatever is best," Lydia replied without hesitation. "For the children."

In the bedroom that had been converted into an office, Lydia hung up the phone, heaved a sigh and wondered what had possessed her to flush a burgeoning career down the toilet. The answer was clear. There hadn't been another option.

Even Lydia's mother had agreed, as soon as the shock dissipated and her daughter's marriage of convenience had been thoroughly explained. Lydia had expected her parents to be disappointed in her decision to marry for the sake of her best friend's children. Instead, they'd been wonderfully supportive. Particularly Mama, who'd always wanted Lydia to marry Powell, and seemed less concerned by the circumstances than relieved that her daughter had finally become Mrs. Greer.

It always amazed Lydia that the perfectly proper Farnsworths were so taken with a man from a family so far from their own social loop. But they clearly adored Powell, and had been plainly disappointed when the relationship had dissolved six years earlier.

Even more surprising, they steadfastly supported Lydia's

decision to sideline her own career for the children's sake. It was the right choice, of course. They knew it. Lydia knew it.

That didn't make her feel any better.

Leaning back in the swivel chair, she rubbed her eyelids with fingertips so icy they made her shiver. She was scared, scared to the bone. Everything she'd strived for, everything she'd meticulously created to express her vision of herself, was in jeopardy. She felt lost, out of control.

Trembling inside, she went to the living room. It was empty, but the backyard pulsed with laughter. She peeked through the sliding glass door and saw that Powell was tossing a fat beach ball for the kids. He was wearing the faded whale cap that had been her gift to him so many years ago. A smile touched her lips, and she allowed it. The sight she beheld was heartwarming. Lydia's heart needed to be warmed.

Outside, Kenny laughed and scampered after the ball, then tossed it to his sister, who blinked as the soft plastic sphere bounced off her tummy. She glared at the impudent toy, huffed over to retrieve it, but every time she toddled within range, her tiny foot kicked it away. Lydia chuckled aloud at the baby's befuddled frown. It felt good to laugh, to smile, to forget for a few sweet moments that she was married to a man who didn't want her, that she was responsible for children who deserved so much better than a woman trapped in a lie of her own making.

Even worse, she felt incompetent to effectively handle either the man or the children.

Despite her determination, despite having read every child care and parenting book she could get her hands on, Lydia still didn't trust herself to be a proper mother. The more she learned about these precious, perplexing creatures called children, the more she realized how arrogant she'd been to believe she could give them all that they needed.

All that they deserved.

The ball bounced against the glass, startling her. Taking a deep breath, Lydia opened the door, gave the ball a gentle kick back toward the grassy yard. Kenny dashed after it.

By the time Lydia lowered herself into a woven web patio chair, Powell had loped over to join her. Fine beads of perspiration glowed on his brow, moistened his upper lip. His hair was attractively ruffled, with a tousled strand flopped across his forehead and stuck to his damp skin. Slightly out of breath, he dropped into a folding chair. It creaked beneath his weight. "Are you all right?"

Focusing on the scampering youngsters, she clasped her hands primly in her lap. "Of course. Why wouldn't I be?"

He shrugged, wiped a rugged forearm over his moist face. "This morning's fiasco at day care kind of throws a monkey wrench into your plans. I figured you'd be upset."

She was very upset. "Not really."

"Oh. Well, that's good." He studied her for a moment, then flicked an absent gaze toward the children. "I guess we've still got a problem to solve."

"It's already solved."

He hiked a brow. "I hope you don't expect me to stuff the kids in a backpack and take them out to the job site with me."

"I don't expect anything of you," she replied with more frost than she'd intended. "I've already made other arrangements."

Frowning, he leaned forward, propped his elbows on his knees. "Did you find a sitter or something?"

"A sitter won't solve the problem, Powell. The children are terrified of being left with strangers."

"I just figured they might be more comfortable in their own home."

"I'm sure that's true."

"So you found someone to come here and watch them while we're at work?"

"In a manner of speaking."

"Who?"

She cleared her throat, avoided his gaze. "Me."

The patio chair creaked. From the corner of her eye she saw his incredulous expression and was wounded by it.

"That's not even funny," he declared.

"I didn't intend it to be, Powell." A steadying breath, a slow exhale and she was prepared to face him. "Fortunately, much of my job can be accomplished via modem hookup through the computer. I'll have to give up certain accounts that require extensive client contact, of course, but for the most part I should be able to handle portfolios with e-mail, fax and telephone communications. I've already made the arrangements."

He was silent a long moment. "What does your boss think about this?"

"He's not thrilled," she admitted, "but is willing to see how things go."

"And if things don't go well?"

She skewered him with a look. "I can handle this, Powell."

The concern in his eyes instantly drained away, replaced by a blank stare. "Yeah, sure. You're superwoman. You can handle anything."

"I'm glad you've noticed."

A nonchalant shrug indicated that he'd noticed, but it didn't matter to him. Nothing really mattered much to Powell. He cruised through life, taking neither himself nor others seriously, shrugging off obstacles with a carefree "so what?'' attitude that made Lydia crazy. He had no desire for power or control, preferring to be a neutral observer rather than an active participant in his own life.

To Lydia, life was serious business. Ambition was the key to success; success was the key to acceptance; acceptance was the key to everything. And the underlying tool for every facet of life was control, or at least the appearance of control.

Despite presenting a confident face to the world, Lydia was not the eternal rock Powell perceived her to be. Inside she'd always had nagging doubts, secret fears. Those doubts and fears pushed her, propelled her at breakneck speed to be the brightest and the best. She'd never failed to focus her ambitions; she'd never failed to achieve her goals.

But there had never been so much at stake before. The future of two children rested squarely on Lydia's wavering shoulders. And she was terrified.

It was after midnight before Lydia finally turned off the computer and dragged her aching body toward the master bedroom. She tiptoed in the darkness, as she had all week, to keep from waking Powell. Quietly making her way to the bathroom, she slipped into the fat, fleecy pajamas she now wore in concession to the lack of privacy and chilly nights. Powell preferred cool nights, and turned the thermostat down to frost level.

Normally she wouldn't have minded, except stretching out on the sofa with only a thin blanket between herself and cold air was hardly conducive to a restful sleep. Her aching neck creaked at the thought of spending another night twisted like a human cruller on that sofa-from-hell. She'd repeatedly proposed that they share the misery, switching from bed to sofa on alternate nights.

Powell, of course, had refused. He'd just plastered that maddening grin on his face, assured her he was more than willing to share the bed, but flatly refused to fold himself onto a sofa the size of a Scout cot simply to humor her absurd and ridiculously belated sense of modesty.

At the leering reminder that he'd already seen and tasted her feminine wares, she'd blushed like a virgin, which had amused him even more. Lydia hated the man, flat-out hated him.

The intense emotion circled her mind, kicked at the inside of her skull with a stunning rebuke. She didn't hate Powell Greer at all. Oh, she wanted to hate him. He'd broken her heart, strolled out of her life as if she'd been nothing more to him than a casual fling.

He'd been so much more to Lydia. She'd loved him. Deeply. Sweetly. Irrevocably.

If she was honest with herself, she would grudgingly admit that on some level she still did love him. It wasn't the same, of course. It would never be the same. According to common wisdom, a woman's first love always held a special place in her heart. Powell had been her first love. In truth, he'd been her only love, but she'd be damned if she'd give him the satisfaction of knowing that.

He'd left her, abandoned her, deserted her with less concern than one bestowed upon a loyal pet. And he'd lied to her, lied to her about something so precious, so intensely personal that she'd never forgiven him for it.

If she was brutally honest with herself, she'd admit that truth hadn't been her finest virtue back then, either. Lies of omission, perhaps. Little things, like making a deposit on a New York City apartment without consulting him. At the time it had seemed reasonable. Powell had been studying mechanical engineering, a profession he could pursue anywhere, but a career on Wall Street had been Lydia's dream.

Powell had known that, so she'd presumed his silence when she discussed living there had been tacit agreement.

Clearly, it hadn't. When he'd learned that she'd already planned the move, he'd been furious and had accused her of trying to control his entire life. Lydia hadn't seen it that way at the time. In retrospect, she charitably agreed she should have been more cognizant of his feelings. New York had lost its luster without Powell. She'd made a foolish mistake.

Lydia had never gone because when Powell admitted he'd lied about having been in love with her, he'd deliberately torn her heart out. It had shattered her then. It shattered her now.

Shaking off old memories, Lydia concentrated on her tedious bedtime routine. She meticulously washed her face, applied a soothing cream guaranteed to reduce the appearance of fine lines, brushed her teeth for a full two minutes, then sterilized the brush with steaming hot water before wiping down the sink and counter and polishing both with a towel. Once finished, she carefully placed the towel in the hamper, along with the damp linens dumped on the floor after Powell's last shower. Lydia also took pains to wipe splattered shaving cream off the mirror and scrape a hardened blob of toothpaste from the faucet handle.

Powell's slovenliness had always irked her, but it didn't seem to bother her as much as it used to. She wondered why. His scent lingered in the air, a hint of the minty soap he favored mingled with the tangy smell of other grooming products that clung to his body to create a fragrance uniquely his own.

She inhaled deeply, enjoying the guilty pleasure. She told herself that the lingering scent of him didn't affect her, didn't warm her belly and make her dizzy with memories of how that same special essence had once clung to her own damp skin.

She told herself she didn't care that Powell was just outside the door, so vulnerable in slumber that she could reach out without disturbing him to touch his ruffled hair, stroke his stubbled cheek. She told herself she had no desire to do so, that she was over him forever. She told herself a lot of things.

Too bad none of them were true.

Exhaling slowly, Lydia cast a quick glance around the tidy bathroom, then opened the door. A stream of light sprayed from the bathroom to illuminate the massive king-size bed. Decorator pillows were still carefully arranged against the headboard. The elegant comforter was smooth and undisturbed. The bed was empty.

Surprised and curious, Lydia went to the living room and found Powell asleep in his grungy recliner beneath a familiar blanket. The television was off; the room was dark.

A wave of gratitude brought a smile to her lips. Bless his heart, she thought. Despite all his protestations to the contrary, he was clearly offering her the use of that huge, soft bed. Lydia could have kissed him.

Excited beyond belief, she returned to the master bedroom, fluffed up the crisply cased pillows and slipped beneath the downy comforter with a contented sigh. "Heaven," she purred to herself. "Pure heaven."

Then she nestled into the luxurious softness and drifted into a sound, satisfying sleep.

A harsh grunt awakened Powell. He snorted, blinked at the darkness and realized the sound had come from him.

Disoriented, he sat up, kicked at the tangled blanket he'd tossed on to ward off the chill and stared at the blank television, which had an automatic timer to turn the set off every night at eleven. Annoyed that he'd fallen asleep before the end of the movie he'd been watching, he lowered the chair's footrest, swept the blanket into a heap on the floor and rubbed his tired eyes. His neck ached. His back throbbed. The fact that the sofa was empty didn't register in his fuzzy mind as he padded toward the bedroom, yawning.

He pulled his sweatshirt off over his head, dropped it by the dresser. A snap, a zip and his jeans puddled on the floor. He stepped out of them, removed his briefs and wandered naked to the bed. Only when he'd reached under his pillow for his wadded pajama bottoms did he notice the human-shaped lump on the other side.

It took a moment for the grin to reach his face. When it did, he tossed the pajamas behind him and climbed into bed. A moment later Lydia moaned, flipped over and burrowed right into his arms.

Heaven was such a warm place. Soft. Blissful.

Sighing, Lydia stretched buttery muscles that for the first time in days didn't shriek in protest. Something stroked her hair, a gentle caress that sent delicious shivers down her spine. A melting heat radiated through her shoulders. Something was touching her, a delicate flex of flesh against flesh. Loving, sensual. She uttered a moan of approval, rolled her head on the fluffy pillow until her face pressed something hard, hot and slightly hairy.

She frowned, tried to force one eyelid open. It stubbornly refused. Something brushed her forehead, a flutter of moist velvet. Like a kiss. Heaven had kisses, too. How delightful. How perfect.

How strange.

The recalcitrant eyelid opened with a snap. Something large and warm and lightly furred loomed in front of her face. Her nose seemed to be pressed against the peculiar object, which radiated an odd heat. It also appeared to be moving, a slight but rhythmic rise and fall as if it was alive and breathing.

It took a moment for Lydia to realize that it was most assuredly alive, and it was indeed breathing.

She reared up with a gasp, tore her startled gaze from what was clearly a human chest to blink up into Powell's amused eyes. "Good morning," he said amiably. "Sleep well?"

"What are you doing here?"

"I live here."

"I mean, what are you doing *here?*"

He shrugged in that maddening way of his. "I'm lying in my own bed holding a beautiful woman in my arms."

For a moment Lydia was struck with an absurd desire to look for this woman, but lucidity won out and she realized he was referring to her. She was definitely in his arms. One strong hand was splayed possessively against her shoulder blades, the other was softly caressing her hair. It felt so wonderful she swallowed a stab of disappointment that she hadn't feigned sleep awhile longer so she could enjoy the delicious sensation.

But she was awake now and mustered appropriate indignation. "Get out of my bed this instant."

An annoying grin tweaked the corner of his mouth, and his eyes gleamed with good humor. "Half of this bed is mine. This half, as a matter of fact. You're certainly welcome to return to your own side anytime you want."

A quick glance confirmed that he was indeed squished up against the edge of the mattress, and she was squished up against him. Face flaming, she reared up on her knees and scrambled crablike to the cold side of the bed. "How dare you violate our agreement!"

He stretched, rolled lazily toward the center of the mattress without extending beyond it, then propped his elbow on the pillow and his head on his fist. "What agreement was that?"

"It was my night to use the bed."

"Was it?" He pursed his lips, hiked a brow. "I don't recall agreeing to that."

"Well, not in so many words, but you were asleep in the living room, so I naturally presumed..." Her voice trailed away. "You deliberately tricked me."

"I tricked you?" His laugh made her flinch with embarrassment. "Then why is it that you were the one who spent the entire night climbing all over me?"

If Lydia could have made one wish, it would have been for the mattress to split apart and swallow her whole. "I can't be held accountable for what I do in my sleep."

He cocked his head, widened his eyes. "I wish I'd known about that rule last night, when I was being so good at keeping my hands to myself. Despite being seriously tempted, I might add. You are quite a wild woman in your sleep. Even begged me to kiss you."

"I did not!"

"Oh, but you did." He sat up, pivoted around until he, too, was kneeling. Kneeling and naked. Very naked. Very, very naked. Lydia nearly went into shock, but Powell simply continued to chat, as if his manhood weren't issuing a happy salute barely an inch from her chastely pajama clad body. "Of course, I was too much of a gentleman to take advantage of a sleeping lady." His eyes darkened; his voice lowered into a husky rasp. "But you're awake now."

A tremor vibrated from her shoulders to her knees. Her traitorous gaze jerked downward. Aroused flesh, glistening and gorgeous, beckoned her. "You wouldn't dare."

"I would," he whispered, leaning so close his breath

brushed her cheek. "I would, I could and I will. Unless you tell me not to."

Molten heat built deep inside her, a radiating warmth that quivered from belly to thighs. She caught her breath, tried to speak, was stunned when all that emerged from her lips was a sensual sigh.

He moved a wayward strand of hair from her cheek with his lips. She felt the softness of his mouth against her skin, the gentle puff of his moist breath. "Say it, Lyddie. Say you don't want me as much as I want you. Say it."

She couldn't. Lydia wanted him, all right, wanted him more than she wanted her next breath.

And Powell knew it.

Chapter Seven

Her eyes betrayed her. His eyes told her so.

Powell's fingers flexed at the brink of her shoulders, holding her, caressing her, melting her with insistent warmth. A tiny rattle vibrated her chest. The breath caught in her throat.

They knelt in the center of the huge, soft bed, her fleece-clad thighs brushing his bare ones, her nipples hard and straining against her pajama top, which was mere inches from his gleaming, naked chest. Her gaze didn't waver from his eyes, didn't angle a glance downward to gauge the extent of his arousal. It wasn't necessary. She felt his desire pulsating at her belly, quivering against the loose fabric of her sleepwear. He wanted her. She wanted him. It had always been that way.

Her fingertips rested against his collarbone, not to push him away but to balance herself for the passion to come. It arrived quickly, with a sharp breath, a ragged groan. He pulled her close, brought his mouth to hers in a kiss so sweet, so incredibly powerful that it brought tears to her eyes.

Blood pulsed through her veins; her heart thrummed in a drumroll. She was drowning in sensation, enveloped by the heat of his body, the scent of his need. Images spun through her mind, memories of passion and promise, of happy days and erotic nights. Memories of a sweeter time, when Lydia had believed that the heart never lied, that love was forever.

Their passion breathed a special perfume—of slick skin, moist breath, the musk of desire that clung to every pore of the body, every crevice of the mind. The sounds of long-ago lovemaking echoed through her thoughts, haunted her dreams. She still remembered those ragged whispers from the past, when he'd throbbed deep inside her.

"I love you," he'd said softly. "Only you."

Then he'd murmured her name, over and over and over again in a voice trembling with wonder.

If happiness had been fatal, Lydia would have expired on the spot. In that long-ago time of youth and innocence their future seemed spread out like a sumptuous feast. It had been a time of rapture, of ecstasy, two soul mates as much in love as it was possible to be. At least that's what Lydia had believed.

But it had been a lie.

Two days later, Powell had dropped out of her life, dusted off his passport and headed to Central America. She hadn't seen him again until last month, when they'd met in Clementine's office.

Now she was in his arms again, tasting him, wanting him, preparing the stage for more pain, more disappointment.

More lies.

Lydia jerked back with a ragged gasp, turned away from Powell's startled expression. Breathing hard, she stiffened her arms, managed a single word. "Don't."

For an instant, Powell seemed frozen in place. Then his arms dropped away, freeing her to collapse into a boneless puddle. "All right."

It took a moment before Lydia gathered the strength to move. Panting, trembling, she pivoted to the edge of the bed, sat there with her back to him. "This was not part of our agreement."

There was a thoughtful silence. "No," he said finally. "It wasn't."

"I don't want it to happen again."

"It won't." The bed jiggled, creaked. Footsteps across the room were followed by the rustle of clothing, a metallic zip. A moment later, the bedroom door rattled. A puff of air rushed in from the hallway. "I'm sorry," he said.

Then the door clicked shut. He was gone. Again.

In the hallway, Powell sagged against the wall, feeling like the world's biggest rat. It hadn't been her dismissal that troubled him; he'd expected that. But the pain in her eyes had sliced through him like a sharpened blade.

Hurting Lydia was the last thing on earth Powell wanted to do now; it had been the last thing on earth he'd wanted to do six years earlier. When he'd left for the Peace Corps, he'd known she'd be angry with him, just as he knew she was still angry with him. It simply hadn't occurred to Powell either then or now that a woman of Lydia's unbendable inner strength would allow him or anyone else to wound her emotionally. That she'd trusted him with that kind of power stunned him. It was a sobering responsibility.

In fact, Powell now realized that he faced a truckload of the same responsibilities he'd spent a lifetime struggling to avoid. The responsibility of emotional entanglements, of children, of family. Of a wife. That all of these were temporary responsibilities did little to lessen his uneasiness.

In a very real sense, Powell was in danger of becoming a clone of his own unhappy father and the overworked, emotionally burdened Dan Houseman, all rolled into one. It scared the spit out of him.

This wasn't what he wanted. It had never been what he wanted. Responsibility. The end of freedom, entrapment of the soul.

Unlike Lydia, Powell had never sought to control his environment, or those who inhabited it. If a situation discomfited him, he removed himself from its sphere. If one place held him too tightly, he wriggled free to seek another. If a woman brushed too close to his heart, he ruthlessly reined in his emotions and walked away—walked away from the entrapment, walked away from the crushing responsibility.

Walked away from the lies.

I love you.

The words haunted him.

But not as much as the lie that followed.

Six years ago, Powell had left without realizing that he'd left a piece of himself behind. Lydia had kept that fragment all these years. Powell had told himself that he'd returned only to reclaim the missing part of his heart. It hadn't occurred to him that she would end up capturing even more of it.

Pinching the bridge of his nose, Powell spun on his heel and strode down the hall. He planned to keep on going, to march out to his car and drive somewhere, anywhere, until this ache in his chest eased.

A frantic rustling beyond Kenny's door stopped him. Powell leaned closer, heard a childish whisper, tight, strained, tinged with panic. "We gotta hide everything. If someone finds it, we'll say you got real excited and splashed a whole bunch of water out of the bowl, okay?"

Powell's hand hovered over the knob for only a moment before he made the decision and entered the startled boy's room.

Whirling, Kenny clutched the armload of sheets, tangling his bare feet as he stumbled forward. "Go away!" he blurted, his eyes wide with alarm. "You're not supposed to come into people's rooms without knocking. It's not nice."

Powell took in the sight calmly, noting a sizable blotch of dampness on the exposed mattress.

Kenny's head swiveled to follow his gaze. "Sidney did it! He was swimming real fast and splashed water all over my bed."

Nodding quietly, Powell deliberately angled a glance from the water-stained mattress to the dresser nearly five feet away, on which the bowl had been placed. He eyed the orange-and-black creature swimming placid laps around its miniature world. "That must have been quite a splash."

"Uh-huh, a real big one." Gulping, Kenny's eyes darted to his closet door, already propped open to receive the soiled linens.

"I wonder why the top of the dresser didn't get wet."

"I cleaned it up already."

"Ah. You did a fine job. Not a single water spot."

"Yeah, I rubbed real hard."

"What did you use?"

"Huh?"

"To wipe the water off the dresser."

"Umm, uh..." Kenny's gaze dipped to the linens wadded in his arms.

"Oh, the sheets," Powell said. "Of course, they were already wet, so it didn't matter."

Kenny's small shoulders rounded in relief. "Yeah."

Rubbing his chin, Powell moved toward the mattress, studied the dried rings around the fresh dampness and realized that this hadn't been an isolated accident. Clearly, the boy had been too embarrassed to admit his problem or seek help in dealing with it. Powell could relate to that. He sat at the foot of the stripped bed, motioned for Kenny to join him.

After a moment's hesitation, the child dropped the wad of sheets and inched over, eyes downcast and head drooping. Powell tossed a chummy arm around the boy's shoulders. "Did I ever tell you what happened to me at Scout camp?"

Kenny looked up without raising his head. "Uh-uh."

"Well, I was older than you, but I'd never spent the night away from home before. Everything was so different. There were dozens of kids, all hollering, and running and jumping and teasing each other. They were all excited. Heck, so was I, but I was kind of scared, too."

"Scared?" Engrossed, Kenny scrambled up to sit on the foot of the bed beside Powell. "How come?"

"Because everything was so new to me, so different. We had to eat outside, sitting on rocks while bugs flew into our food. There were eight kids in each cabin, and we had to hike a quarter of a mile to use the outhouse."

"What's a outhouse?"

"It's like a little closet in the middle of the woods that people use when they have to, er, go to the bathroom."

"Oh."

"Well anyway, this outhouse was kind of a scary place. It didn't smell very good, and there wasn't any light in it, so at night it was black as pitch inside. You couldn't see your hand in front of your face.''

"Wow," Kenny said, his eyes huge. "I wouldn't like that.''

Powell laughed. "I didn't like it, either. There were spiders hanging in the corners, and someone told me that snakes went in there at night to keep warm.''

"Snakes?" The boy vibrated in shock, his voice little more than a strained squeak.

"Yep, snakes." Powell squeezed Kenny's shoulders, lowered his voice to a conspiratorial whisper. "Don't tell your aunt Lyddie, but I don't much care for spiders, and I'm scared to death of snakes.''

"I saw a snake once. Daddy found it in the backyard.'' Kenny shuddered at the memory. "Mommy said a really bad word and made Daddy put it over the fence.''

Powell didn't have to fake an empathetic nod. He wasn't kidding about his fear of snakes. "Then you can understand why I didn't want to make that long, dark trip to the outhouse in the middle of the night." He waited for Kenny's confirming nod. "Unfortunately, I'd had about three cans of soda before I went to bed, and with all the excitement…'' He paused for effect, added a melodramatic sigh. "I wet the bed.''

Kenny's eyes nearly popped out of his head. "You didn't!''

"Yes, I did, and in front of all my buddies. I just about died of embarrassment. And that wasn't the worst part.''

The boy's horrified pallor indicated that he couldn't think of anything on earth that could possibly be worse.

"I was so stressed out over wetting the bed that first night that I ended up wetting the danged bed every single night of camp. The rest of the kids ended up calling me…er, well, let's just say they chose a nickname for me that I'd prefer not to repeat." Grinning, Powell angled a look at Kenny, whose little mouth dangled open like a gate with a broken hinge. "I couldn't wait to get home."

"Yeah," Kenny murmured when he finally regained control of his drooping jaw. "Did you...I mean, when you got home...?"

The unfinished question dangled in the air. Powell smiled. "I was fine when I got home. Later I figured out that the tension of being away from home combined with the nervousness of wanting so much to be accepted by new friends had caused the problem."

"You think?"

"Absolutely. After I grew up I discovered that bed-wetting is one of those things that happens to almost everyone at one point or another, usually when they're stressed, or going through a dramatic change in their life." He squeezed Kenny's shoulders. "It's no big deal, buddy. It happens all the time."

A quiver worked its way across the small chin. "How do you make it go away?"

Caution alarms went off in Powell's mind. He inhaled slowly, exhaled all at once. It was an impossible question. Honesty was the only answer. "I don't know." At the child's crestfallen expression, he quickly added, "Sometimes it just stops as fast as it starts. Sometimes it takes longer, but there are things that can be done to help."

"Like what?"

"Well, take my case, for instance. If it hadn't gone away on its own, I would have told my parents."

Kenny nearly choked. He wriggled out from under Powell's arm and leaped from the bed, staring in disbelief. "Get outta here!"

"I would have told my parents," Powell repeated calmly, "so they could have taken me to the doctor to make sure there was nothing physically wrong. Sometimes an infection can cause this kind of problem, and the proper medicine can fix things right up.''

Frowning fiercely, Kenny folded his arms across his chest. ''I don't like medicine.''

''Even if it makes you feel better?''

The frown wavered. ''I don't wanna go to the doctor.''

Leaning forward, Powell rested his elbows on his knees. ''Is there something you'd like to tell me, buddy?''

Kenny blinked twice. Tears leaked from his eyes. He gulped, darted a glance toward his fish, then back toward the damp spot in the mattress. ''Sidney didn't splash my bed.''

Gathering the miserable child in his arms, Powell pulled him onto his lap, wiped the boy's damp cheek with the pad of his thumb. ''I know.''

A shuddering breath. ''Please don't tell Aunt Lyddie.''

''Are you afraid she'll be mad at you?''

''No. Aunt Lyddie's real nice. She wouldn't get mad. Only, well…'' He gulped again. ''She's a girl.''

''Ah, gotcha,'' Powell said with a manly nod of commiseration. ''In that case, this will be just between us guys.''

''No lie?''

''Cross my heart.''

''But what about that?'' Kenny nodded toward the rumpled heap of sheets on the floor.

''We'll just have to wash them.''

''Do you know how?''

''Hey, you're talking to the king of the Fifth Street Wash-and-Dry.'' He gently elbowed the boy's ribs. ''All we have to do is wait until your aunt Lyddie is out of the house for a couple hours, and presto-chango, clean dry bedsheets.''

"What if she doesn't go anywhere?"

Powell considered that. "Hmm. In that case, we'll have to be a bit more devious. If you were to keep your aunt Lyddie busy in the living room, I could sneak the sheets out to my car. Then I'll drive off to do some errands and hunt down the nearest laundromat. Sound like a plan?"

At first Kenny nodded with enthusiasm, then he sent Powell a concerned frown. "What if it, y'know, keeps happening?"

He was ready for that question. "There are some things we can do to help."

"Like what?"

"First we can protect the mattress with a rubber sheet, just in case." At the child's embarrassed flush, he hurried on. "But it might not happen again, especially if you don't drink water or soda after dinnertime. And I can wake you up before I go to bed so you can, er, use the facilities."

Kenny swallowed hard, issued an agreeable nod. "About the doctor? I guess it's okay. I mean, if it doesn't go away and stuff."

Smiling, Powell ruffled the boy's hair. "We're going to beat this, buddy. We make a great team."

Kenny beamed.

The door was open only a crack, barely enough for Lydia to see the man and boy seated at the foot of the bed. But she could hear them. She heard the emotion in Kenny's voice, the calm candor in Powell's. She heard the whispered conspiracy, understood the impact of secrecy on a young child's self-esteem.

A lump wedged in her throat. Tears threatened. She tiptoed away before her presence was betrayed by the thudding of a heart so tender it literally ached. She'd never seen this side of Powell before, never believed him capable of such empathy. It touched her almost as deeply as had little Kenny's humiliation and fear. She wished Kenny had felt comfortable coming to her with his problem, but understood why he hadn't. He'd needed a father. He'd needed Powell, and Powell had been there for him. Powell had been wonderful. He'd said all the right things, done all the right things, wiped away a frightened child's tears with such tender compassion that Lydia had nearly wept.

The shield she'd so carefully erected around her wounded heart cracked into dust. She was doomed.

The bedroom door creaked open. Powell's head poked out first. He looked right, then left, then down at the smaller head peering out below him. "The coast is clear."

Powell tiptoed across the hall, plastered his back against the wall. Kenny mimicked his uncle's movements precisely. They both sidled down the hallway, halted abruptly at the opening into the entry. Powell peered around the doorjamb. Kenny peered around Powell.

Neither of them heard the master bedroom door open behind them. "Looking for someone?"

At the sound of Lydia's voice, they both gave a guilty leap and spun to face her. Powell cleared his throat, managed a grin. "We were just trying to be extra quiet so we wouldn't disturb you."

Kenny's wide-eyed gaze rolled from Powell to Lydia. He emulated his uncle's charm-filled grin.

"Yeah, real quiet."

"And we were going to, er, surprise you by fixing Sunday breakfast."

"Yeah, breakfast!" Kenny's chirpy acquiescence faded into a frown. "We were?"

"Yeah," Powell replied through clenched teeth. "We were."

Kenny's eyes widened. "Uh-huh, right."

Lydia flicked them a cool look, but her eyes held a peculiar gleam that Powell couldn't quite identify. "How thoughtful. I'm sorry I'll have to miss it."

Only then did Powell notice the car keys in her hand and the woven straw bag slung over her shoulder. "Going somewhere?"

"Tomorrow will be a busy day. You'll be going back to work, and I'll need some things—items to help me organize myself around here. Since Tami has just awakened, I'm sure she'll enjoy the breakfast you two have planned. You can handle that, right?"

Powell was stunned that she thought he could handle anything. "Uh, sure."

"Good." She stepped around them into the foyer, glanced over her shoulder. "As a matter of fact, I'd appreciate anything you two could do to help out. Washing a few dishes, picking up the living room—" a glimmer of amusement disappeared beneath the dark sunglasses she slipped on "—doing a couple of loads of laundry."

She knew, Powell realized. He forced a nonchalant expression as a jubilant Kenny elbowed his thigh. "Sure, we can do that."

"Thanks, I'd appreciate it." She paused at the front door, bouncing her car keys in her palm. "Umm, don't bother washing any of my things."

"Wouldn't dream of it," Powell assured her.

With a relieved smile, Lydia left.

As the front door clicked shut behind her, Powell and Kenny slapped a high five, scooped up the soiled linens and headed into the laundry room.

By the time Lydia returned, it was nearly noon. The house smelled of detergent and warm cotton. Delighted aughter emanated from the living room, where Powell and Kenny raced miniature cars using Tami's fat tummy as a peed bump. The normally somber baby was giggling nadly, with happy drool glistening on her chin.

So engrossed were they in the game that they didn't hear Lydia enter, which allowed her to enjoy the joyful sight for a few moments before quietly unloading her purchases on the kitchen counter. Two cookbooks, a time-management text, a magnetic corkboard for the refrigerator, all of which he left in the kitchen while she toted a box of manilla files, several plastic file holders and a bag of paper clips, marking pens, Post-It notes and other office sundries into her workroom. She returned to the car for the final item, a four-foot-by-three-foot erasable marker board on which she planned to map out every minute of every day. Organization was the key to success, Lydia had learned.

And success, after all, was the key to everything.

They stared at each other warily, glumly. Powell shifted his stance, cast a longing look at the cushy king-size bed. Lydia, having just completed her nighttime ritual, had emerged from the master bath wearing fresh pajamas and a determined frown.

They circled each other, Lydia with her arms crossed, Powell with his hands jammed in his jeans pockets, like two people playing musical chairs. Both kept one eye on the prized bed and the other on the competition.

"I have to work tomorrow," Powell said. "I need a decent night's sleep."

"I have two jobs ahead of me," Lydia countered. "I need sleep twice as much as you do."

"You'll be here all day. You can take a nap."

"I'll be working all day, taking care of the kids with one hand and faxing conference reports with the other."

"I have to get up at six to be at work by seven."

"I have to get up at five-thirty to get closing figures for the Asian stock markets."

They circled the room again like hungry wolves eyeing a deer carcass.

"We could flip for it," Powell said.

"No."

"Why not?"

"There's a fifty percent chance of losing."

"There's a fifty percent chance of winning."

"I don't like the odds."

Powell heaved a sigh, pulled his hands from his pockets and jammed them on his hips. "Well, I'm not sleeping on the sofa."

"Neither am I." She studied him, studied the bed. It really was huge. Soft. Comfortable. And that squishy down comforter was to die for. "Okay, these are the rules."

Powell tilted his head hopefully.

"One, pajamas are required, both top and bottom."

He frowned, but nodded.

"Two, no encroaching on the center line."

"Okay."

"Three, somnambulistic groping is not allowed. No excuses."

He hiked a brow. "That goes for you, too, right?"

She didn't dignify that with a response. "And four, last one up makes the bed."

"Aww—"

"Take it or leave it."

"I'll take it."

A deal was struck, and the deed was done.

This wasn't the first compromise the intimacy of their living arrangements had required. It wouldn't be the last. It was, however, the most significant. Lydia hoped she wouldn't regret it.

Chapter Eight

Outside, a gray dawn cast a sleeping pall at the edge of a moonless sky. Inside, the monitor blinked, the computer whirred, the printer mewed with muffled squeaks and clatters. An overhead light glared. A swivel chair squeaked. From across the hall came the soothing thrum of the master bedroom shower.

Lydia worked smoothly, with practiced efficiency. Confidence born of experience propelled her fingers across the keyboard, while her mind collated the information like a speeding mainframe. Bond points. Market share. Interest analysis. Mentally graphing financial flux, she whirled the mouse over its prim blue pad as gracefully as a skater glided on polished ice. A click here, a highlight there. Figures dragged, dropped. Columns became updated, graphically displayed.

Click *print*.

With a comforting hum, gleaming documents spit forth one by one, colorful charts awaiting a final destination.

Click *fax*.

Processing, processing, processing.

Weekly financial updates buzzed into a dozen waiting modems.

Click *send*.

Queued reports bounced through cyberspace, settled into electronic mailboxes from Atlanta to San Francisco.

With a satisfied grunt, Lydia circled the mouse, clicked to another waiting report and started the update cycle all over again, her ears attuned to the shower sounds in the adjacent room.

A moment later, the sounds ceased. Lydia glanced at the clock, scribbled a note of the time, went back to work.

Ten minutes later, footsteps vibrated into the hallway. A cupboard rattled in the kitchen. She dutifully wrote down the time.

At six-thirty, she heard the scrape of a kitchen chair pushing away from the table. More footsteps sounded, dull at first, then muffled by carpeting in the hall. As Lydia marked the time, she felt Powell's presence in the open doorway.

"I'm leaving."

She laid down the pencil, swiveled her chair far enough to see him. Somehow she managed not to suck in a betraying breath. Freshly shaven, with his hair still gleaming from a damp comb, he wore slim jeans and an aviator-style jacket that made his shoulders look like mountains. It should be illegal to look that good before the sun was up, particularly since Lydia had spent a sleepless night trying to ignore not only the sensual specimen of a man in beside her, but the insistent call of her own libido as well.

Powell had apparently suffered no ill effects of sharing

a bed. He'd fallen asleep the moment his head hit the pillow. Lydia wished she could say the same.

A strained swallow, a self-conscious tug at the collar of her ratty chenille robe and she angled another glance in his direction. "You'll be off at four, right?"

He shifted a booted foot, shrugged a suede-clad shoulder. "Give or take."

Licking her lips, she managed a tight nod, scribbled "four o'clock" on her time list. It was a twenty-minute drive from the telephone company maintenance yard where Powell's crew met each morning and returned each afternoon. She charitably allowed ten minutes for locker-room banter, and rush-hour traffic, then decided he should be home by 4:30. She jotted that down. "I packed a lunch for you. It's in the refrigerator."

"You didn't have to do that." She made a point not to look at him, although from the corner of her eye she caught the surprised tilt of his head. "I usually just grab a burger with the guys."

"You should eat healthier food."

"I like hamburgers."

"So do I, but not every day." She laid down the pencil, tucked her slippered feet beneath the chair and focused her attention on the monitor. "Take the lunch. Your arteries will thank me."

Silence stretched a long moment before he cleared his throat. "Are you going to be all right?"

That startled her. "Why wouldn't I be?"

"Well, you'll be here alone with the kids."

She pivoted all the way around, saw her own secret fear reflected in his eyes. "Are you implying that I'm incapable of caring for two small children?"

His eyes narrowed. "Hell, no. You're not incapable of anything."

Instantly regretting her snippy tone, Lydia lifted an apologetic hand. "Powell, I—"

But the doorway was empty, and angry footsteps already echoed on the entry tile. The front door was opened noisily, as if yanked in anger, although it wasn't shut immediately. After a split second of silence, she heard Powell move back toward the kitchen. The refrigerator opened with a distinctive whoosh, after which the heavy footfalls returned to the entry. Only then did she hear the front door close.

Outside, a car engine hummed to life, idled briefly, then shifted in tone and disappeared. Lydia forced her attention back to the blinking monitor.

Twenty minutes later, the sound of a cranky baby filtered down the hall. Lydia made a note of the time.

"Hey, buddy! How's married life treating you?" The grinning pole-puller elbowed Powell in the ribs. "Anything worn out yet?"

The rest of the crew guffawed, added a few more ribald comments to the fray. Pasting on a manly grin, Powell retrieved his work belt and hard hat from the locker. "Bite me, boys."

Guffaws rose up, along with a few high-pitched whoops. Powell feigned amused indifference. The good-natured ribbing from his workmates was neither unexpected nor particularly welcome. It was, however, a necessary part of working with a bawdy crew capable of displaying adolescent taunts and feats of heroism with equal ease.

He snatched the lunch Lydia had packed from the long skinny bench running between the rows of lockers, only to have a co-worker, Joe Batista, yank the bag from his hand.

"Woohoo," Batista chortled, holding the bulging brown bag over his head. "Wifey made his lunchie. Isn't that just the cutest thing?" Batista batted his eyes, sending the rest of the crew into convulsive laughter. ''Look, look, it's even got his name on the bag!''

Powell groaned. He hadn't noticed that.

But the crew had noticed and roared with delight.

''Hey, Powell, where's your Barney lunch pail?''

''Just like summer camp.''

''Next thing y'know she'll be a'labeling his underwear.''

With the tips of his ears burning like a hot match, Powell snatched his lunch bag and glared at Batista. ''Aren't you supposed to be scheduling out work orders?''

The squat man flung up a pair of hairy forearms in mock horror. ''Touchy, touchy.''

Sam Perenkski, the foreman, sauntered over to slap Powell on the shoulder. ''Now, boys, can't you see the poor guy's plumb tuckered? Probably worn himself to a frazzle pleasuring that pretty bride of his.'' Sam winked at the group, turned a semiserious face to Powell. ''Just remember where you are. I know it's a big adjustment after a week of sweet loving, but if someone hollers your name out on the job site, don't automatically reach for your zipper. That ain't what we got in mind.''

''I don't know,'' Powell drawled, affably mimicking his foreman. ''Some of these guys look pretty desperate.''

Sam shrugged. '''Course they're desperate. They're married.''

The wry comment raised another round of guffaws as the crew sauntered out to the truck yard. Powell hesitated, pretending to adjust his tools until he was alone in the locker room. Heaving a sigh, he shut his locker with a satisfying slam, snatched up the humiliating, personalized lunch bag and shuddered at the sight of his name penned in a loopy, feminine scroll. Lydia, he decided, was taking this temporary-wife role much too seriously.

* * *

"That kind of financing isn't the safest way to go," Lydia told the manager of a small, financially strapped municipality in the northern foothills. "I know the interest rates are attractive compared to issuing redevelopment bonds, but when a project has no concurrent revenue stream…" she paused to ladle bubbling oatmeal into two small bowls "…there are significant risks to the bondholders."

Clinching the telephone receiver between her chin and shoulder, Lydia placed one bowl on the kitchen table, the other on the high chair tray. "Kenny, breakfast!"

"Excuse me?" The startled reply crackled through the line.

"Hmm? Oh, sorry, Mr. Morris, I'll be right with you." She laid the phone on the counter, hurried toward the living room, where cartoons blared from the television. "Kenny? Kenny!"

A twist of wire stretched from the ugly recliner to the television remote control clutched by the small, pajama-clad figure seated cross-legged on the floor. The screen clicked from one cartoon show to another to another.

"Kenny!"

The boy's head tilted, but did not turn. "Uh-huh."

"Your breakfast is ready."

An animated creature wearing a Viking helmet screeched from the television. "Uh-huh," Kenny mumbled.

"Turn off the TV and come into the kitchen."

Click, flip. Kenny thumbed the remote, changing channels until a trio of masked turtles exploded on-screen to wreak havoc on a helpless gaggle of sharp-nosed villains. Kenny stared at them with huge, glazed eyes. "Uh-huh."

A telephone rang down the hall. Her fax line. Lydia tensed, hoping the figures she'd requested from Standard & Poors were coming through. "Hurry up, Kenny," she called on her way down the hall. "Breakfast is getting cold."

"Uh-huh."

Frustrated, she headed to the office, caught each warm sheet as it emerged. "Oh, no," she murmured, studying the figures. Muni bond ratings had dropped from A— to double B, which meant the cost of financing just leaped at least two points, a catastrophe for several of her current clients. More sheets spit from the fax; more disaster loomed as she scanned them. She spun, snatched up her cordless office phone and dialed quickly.

A frustrated yelp emanated from the other end of the line.

"Mr. Morris? Oh, I'm sorry." She'd forgotten that the finance officer was still holding on the line, and had just shot a piercing fax wail directly into the poor man's ear. "Now that I have you back on the line, I must repeat my caution about securing private bond futures with public funds—"

A horrific crash from the kitchen was followed by a bloodcurdling shriek. Papers fluttered from Lydia's hands. She dropped the phone, was out of the office before they hit the floor.

She skidded into the kitchen, gasped in dismay. Oatmeal was everywhere, on the floor, globbed on the cupboard doors, stuck to the walls. And in her highchair, Tami was red faced and screaming, pounding her own sticky scalp and looking for all the world as if she'd been dunked head-first in her own porridge.

"Oh, sweetie, what happened?" Snatching a handful of paper towels, Lydia picked her way across the slippery floor, stepping around sharp shards of the broken bowl. Her heart sank. She knew better than to give a glass bowl to a baby. What on earth had she been thinking? Her heart sank another notch as she spied the spoon still lying on the counter where she'd left it, which meant the poor child had been forced to eat oatmeal with her fingers. Lydia felt horrible.

"There, there," she crooned to the furious toddler, whose hands, face, hair and pajamas were thoroughly coated with sticky oatmeal. Tami shrieked in reply, pounded the messy high chair tray with one hand while Lydia wiped off the other. "I know, sweetheart, it's all my fault. I'm so sorry, I…" She reached for another towel, spotted the kitchen extension phone lying on the counter, just where she'd left it before going to check on Kenny. "Oh my God. Mr. Morris."

She leaped over the oatmeal on the floor, snatched up the receiver. "I'm terribly sorry. Could I possibly call you back in a few… Mr. Morris?" The line was dead.

Lydia heaved a sigh, hung up the phone and reached for a mop. She glanced at the clock. It was barely 8:00 a.m.

She made a note of it.

Powell wiped a sweaty forearm over his brow, found a fairly flat rock to serve as a lunch table. The day was cool, brisk, still damp from the ground fog that rose from the forest at this elevation. The crew had been repairing phone lines damaged by a windstorm that had swept down the canyon last night. Usually Powell enjoyed working in the rural foothills, enjoyed the breathtaking Sierra views from pastureland dotted with placid cattle. Today he'd been distracted, out of sync with the rest of the crew.

He kept thinking about Lydia and the kids. It was stupid, he knew, but he just couldn't help himself. At the most inconvenient times an image would flash into his mind, a mental picture of Kenny scurrying across the backyard to catch a thrown ball, or of Tami's scrunched-up face when a beetle crawled over her tiny bare foot.

Or of Lydia's beauty, serene in slumber, her sweet scent permeating the air, her hair spread like spun gold across the pillow. Through a spray of moonlight he'd watched her, aching to stroke her soft skin, caress the silken mass of tousled hair. He hadn't, of course. Not that he'd feared waking her, because Lydia slept like the dead. No, Powell had feared only that if he succumbed to his desire, gave in to the burning need to feel her warmth, her softness, he wouldn't have been able to stop.

Those pesky urges, Lydia had called them. He'd assured her he could control them. He'd lied.

"So Papa Bear said, 'Who's been eating my porridge?'" Sitting cross-legged on the office floor, Lydia fed a sheet into the fax machine. It sucked the paper in with a satisfied hum. "And Mama Bear said, 'Who's been eating *my* porridge?'"

A tawny-haired blur dashed past the open door with a flapping bath towel wrapped around his shoulders. "I'm Super*man!*"

Tami sat on the floor beside Lydia, eyeing the humming fax with great interest. "Bub-bub," she said.

"You just had a bubble bath, sweetie. Now it's story time."

A swish, a scamper of little-boy feet. "Super*ma-a-an!*"

Lydia retrieved the faxed document, filed it, then placed another in the holder and dialed. When the fax connected, she returned her attention to the solemn child, who clutched a fat pink marker pen and fingered pieces of graph tape and cut construction paper strewn across the floor. "Then Baby Bear came in and squeaked, 'Someone's been eating my porridge, too, and ate it all up!'" Lydia pulled over a large sheet of uncut construction paper on which the child had been scribbling. "Can you draw a picture of Baby Bear?"

"Bub-bub!" Tami insisted, her tiny brows crashing into a baby frown.

"Sweetie, you just had a bubble bath to get all the oatmeal out of your hair. Now it's story time. See?" Lydia found herself pointing to the appointed time posted on the large organizational chart she'd been preparing.

Unimpressed, the toddler flung the pink marking pen across the room. It bounced off the same wall that vibrated with the sound of stomping, little-boy feet.

Swish, stomp. "Super*ma-a-an!*"

Huffing a breath, Lydia retrieved the pen, groaned at the pink marker stain on the wall, then returned to feed another chart into the fax. Daunted but determined, she carried on. It was story time, darn it, and one way or another, a story would be told. "Then Papa Bear went into the bedroom and said, 'Who's been sleeping in my bed?'" The fax hummed, Lydia's head throbbed. "And Mama Bear—"

"Super—" *Swish...*

The phone shrieked like a siren.

...Stomp. "*Maa-an!*"

"Bub-bub, bub-bub, bub-bub!" Tami screeched.

"Later, sweetie, later." Lydia snatched up the telephone just as the fax alarm signaled a paper jam. "Oh, good grief."

A startled voice replied. "A simple hello would do."

"Hmm?" Clamping the receiver against her shoulder, Lydia scrambled to her knees and struggled to extract the twisted document. "Oh, good morning, George."

"Good morning. Listen, Lydia, I just got a call from Ben Morris and he—"

"Super*ma-a-an!*" *Swish, stomp, thud.* A yelp of pain thundered from the hallway.

Lydia leaped to her feet. "I can't talk now, George. I'll call you at nap time."

"Nap time?"

"Bye." A flick of her thumb disconnected the cordless phone. She tossed it in the general direction of the desk as she dashed into the hall, to find Kenny hopping on one foot with his towel-turned-cape flapping madly as he clutched his bruised knee and howled at the top of his lungs. "Oh, honey, did you hurt yourself? Let me see."

As Lydia knelt to examine the injury, the tearful child reared back. "Don't touch it, it hurts, it hurts!"

"I know, sweetie," she soothed, gently rolling up the leg of his corduroy pants. "I'll be very careful." A tiny red welt puffed his little kneecap. "Ooh, that looks sore. You are such a brave boy."

Kenny sniffed, wiped his wet face. "It hurts real bad."

"I'll bet it does." As she gave him a hug, little Tami toddled out of the office with the marking pen clutched in her hand and pink ink smeared from the top of her forehead to the tummy of her new white T-shirt.

"Bub-bub," the baby announced with a satisfied smirk.

Lydia gasped, groaned, sat back on her heels. She might have been a fine investment analyst, but as a parent she was a total bust. She buried her face in her hands, whispered into her palms. "Oh, Susan, you made it look so easy."

Then Lydia huffed, heaved a sigh and went to prepare Tami's second bubble bath of the day. It was barely noon.

She made a note of it.

Using his work vest as a napkin, Batista wiped mustard off his fingers. He shifted his rump on the flat rock, smacked his fleshy lips and peered over Powell's shoulder. "What in hell is that?"

Powell stared at the peculiar item he'd retrieved from his

personalized lunch bag. It appeared to be some kind of edible pouch stuffed with salad greens. "I have no idea."

The foreman sauntered around the rear of the tech truck, tossed down his hard hat and squatted to observe the strange entrée. "That there's a pita sandwich. Seen 'em at that yuppie soup shop over at the mall."

"There's no meat in it," Powell said. "What kind of sandwich doesn't have meat in it?"

Batista shrugged. Sam, the foreman, scratched his scraggly chin. "You didn't marry yourself one of them vegetarians, did you? Not that there's anything wrong with it for women, but a man, well, a man needs meat, y'know?"

Powell did indeed know. He tucked the peculiar lettuce-filled pouch back into the lunch bag, held out his hand. Sam dug into his pocket, dropped the truck keys in Powell's palm, then called out to his work crew. "Greer's going for burgers!"

Instantly conversation around the site stopped as unhappy men exchanged cash with grinning co-workers who'd won the bet on whether the groom would or would not eat the lunch his new bride had packed.

Lydia tucked the screwdriver in her back pocket and stood back to admire her handiwork, the newly purchased conference board on which a daily time chart had been carefully sculpted with graph tape and markers. "Organization," she told the wide-eyed boy standing beside her, "is the key to success."

Kenny regarded the massive board with obvious skepticism. "It is?"

"Indeed. And success, my precious little man, is the key to everything." Scooping the child into her arms, she planted a noisy kiss on his cheek and was rewarded with a heartwarming giggle. "All you have to do is look at this chart. These are the days of the week, and the times are listed down the sides. You'll always know exactly what we're going to be doing and when we're going to be doing it.''

The boy's grin faded. "But I don't know how to read."

"Which is why I've drawn these little pictures for you." She lowered him to the floor and pointed to a sketch of a box within a box, topped by a V-shaped antenna. "This represents the television, here, here and here, which means you can watch TV from 7:00 a.m. until 8:30 a.m., from 3:00 p.m. until 3:30 p.m. and from 6:00 p.m. until 7:00 p.m. Seven is bath time. See the little bathtub I drew?"

The child squinted at the tiny icon. "How am I s'posed to know when it's seven o'clock? I can't tell time, either."

"Ah, that's why I made this." Thrilled by her own perceptiveness, Lydia retrieved a clock cut out of thick construction paper, the movable hands tacked to the center with a round paper fastener. "We'll set the clock for the time your program comes on, then you can compare that to the clock in the kitchen, and before you know it, you'll be telling time like a pro! Isn't that terrific?"

"Umm, I guess so."

Humming happily, Lydia taped the paper clock beside the family's organizational chart and set the hands for six o'clock. "There. Now as soon as the kitchen clock has the big hand on the twelve and the small hand on the six, you can go turn on the television."

"I wanna watch television now."

"It's four o'clock now. That's playtime."

"I don't wanna play."

"Of course you do, sweetie. Playtime is very important for building young minds."

"I wanna watch TV."

"Uncle Powell will be home in thirty minutes, then he'll

spend a whole hour of quality, role-model time with you before dinner, which is at precisely 5:30.''

Kenny brightened considerably at the thought of spending precious time with his uncle. ''Really?''

''Really.'' Lydia ruffled his hair, felt a peculiar tingling in her heart. Such an adorable boy, with those huge, curious eyes and tweaky, stubbed nose. She was overcome with another sudden urge to hug him, and gave in to it. ''Now, you go play with your toys while I put a chicken in the oven, okay?''

''Okay.'' Kenny stepped out of her embrace, angled a glance at the paper clock on the wall. ''Can you make it show when Uncle Powell will be home?''

''You bet I can.'' After she rotated the paper hands into place, Kenny studied the crayoned clock face intently before scurrying off to play. Things were looking up already, Lydia thought with a sudden burst of optimism. Organization was the key.

Will you be all right?

The question Powell had asked early this morning still irked her. It implied a lack of confidence in her ability to handle both her business responsibilities and the more important task of caring for two children. The fact that Lydia's own confidence had wavered more than once throughout the day was beside the point. Powell should have trusted her, should have realized that she was an intelligent, capable woman able to do whatever was necessary to achieve the goals she'd set for herself. He hadn't trusted her, hadn't seen that.

But he would. As soon as he walked in the door tonight, he'd realize that she had everything under control. He'd be pleased. He might even be proud. Lydia would, of course, gloat graciously.

Smiling to herself, she went to the kitchen, laid out her

newly purchased cookbooks and began preparations for a delicious and nutritionally balanced evening meal.

The locker room buzzed with raucous laughter punctuated by the metallic clang of locker doors and language too raw for mixed company. Powell tossed his loaded tool belt on the locker floor, set his hard hat on the upper shelf and had just shimmied out of his canvas work vest when Batista slapped him on the back.

"Let's go, Greer. Half the keg will be gone before we get there."

"Go where?"

A hearty laugh vibrated Batista's stubbled jowls. "The Iron Duck, m'boy, where else would this motley crew throw a wake for our dearly departed bachelor?"

Powell's jaw drooped. The groom party, a tradition the crew had carried on for all the years he'd worked there. Of course, Powell's status as bridegroom was as fake as the marriage, but the guys didn't know that. "Cripes, Joe, I don't think I can make it tonight—"

A beefy arm flopped around his shoulders. "You gotta make it, it's your party." Although Batista continued to grin, his eyes narrowed just a touch. "Unless you're already so damned henpecked that the little woman won't let you out of her sight. Now, that couldn't be it, could it, buddy?"

Powell stiffened, felt the muscles in front of his ears twitch. "Of course not."

A mischievous gleam danced in the big man's eyes. "So, how 'bout we get us a beer?"

"Sounds great," Powell muttered, slamming his locker door. "Let's do it."

At five-thirty, Kenny studied the paper clock with a crestfallen expression. "The little hand is all the way down here,'' he said, pointing. ''How come Uncle Powell didn't come home when the little hand was up here?''

Lydia wiped baby food off Tami's sticky face before hoisting the toddler from the high chair. She tried to answer Kenny's question with a smile, but ended up responding through clamped teeth. ''I don't know, sweetie. We'll have to ask him when he finally deigns to join us.''

''Oh.'' He followed Lydia to Tami's room, stood patiently while she dressed the baby in pajamas. ''I'm hungry.''

''I know, honey.''

''Isn't it dinnertime yet?''

''Yes, as a matter of fact, it's past dinnertime.'' It was a strain to keep an even voice. ''But we have to wait for Uncle Powell.''

''Oh.''

Lydia tugged a flannel sleep shirt over Tami's head, muttering to herself. She'd been trying to reach Powell for almost an hour. His crew had returned from the field on time. Powell had clocked out on time. The truck yard was only a twenty-minute drive from the house. So where the devil was he?

''Aunt Lyddie?''

''Yes, sweetie?''

''Can I have a samwich? I'm real hungry.''

''Let's wait a few more minutes. I'm sure Uncle Powell will be here soon.''

The boy considered that. ''Can I turn on the TV?''

''It's not television time yet.''

''Then can I take my bath?''

''It's not bath time, either.''

He jammed his little fists on his hips in a comical imitation of his uncle's favorite gesture of frustration. "Well, what time *is* it?"

Lydia heaved a long-suffering sigh. "It's dinnertime." Balancing Tami on her hip, she reached out for Kenny's hand. "Uncle Powell is on his own, sweetie. Let's get you something to eat."

By six o'clock, Kenny was happily fed and in front of the television set, Tami was playing with blocks in her bedroom and the roasted chicken, sans one drumstick that had been served to Kenny, was back in the oven waiting for Uncle Powell's esteemed appearance.

By six-thirty, Lydia was pacing the kitchen, babbling to herself and mad enough to spit staples.

By seven o'clock, Tami had been tucked into her crib for the night, Kenny was running a hot bath and Lydia was in the living room, dialing Powell's car phone number for the fifteenth time in as many minutes.

Anger had evolved into terror. Maybe something awful had happened. Maybe he'd had an accident. Maybe he was in a hospital somewhere, bleeding and unconscious. Maybe the police were at his old apartment, the address on his driver's license, vainly searching for next of kin.

Maybe—

A shrill siren nearly deafened her. Dropping the telephone, Lydia recognized the sound of the fire alarm at the same time she smelled smoke. "Oh my God," she muttered, realizing that she'd returned the chicken to the oven without lowering the temperature. Sprinting to the kitchen, she turned off the oven and waved at the billowing smoke with a flimsy dish towel.

The fire alarm continued to shriek.

Kenny's frightened voice echoed from the hall bathroom. "Aunt Lyddie!"

"It's all right," she called back, between fits of coughing. "Just a little smoke, nothing to worry about." She flung open the kitchen window, leaped onto the counter and ripped at the alarm until it dangled by a cord from the ceiling, but continued to screech.

"But Aunt Lyddie—"

A final yank, and the disk-shaped alarm came off in her hands. Except for Kenny's frightened wails, the smoke-filled house was blessedly silent. Jumping down from the counter, Lydia dropped the dead fire alarm and went to calm the frightened boy, only to run smack-dab into a knee-high mound of bubbles oozing out of the hall.

A tiny voice called out, "Aunt Lyddie, Aunt Lyddie, the bubbles are eating me up."

She gaped at the heaving surge, wondering why on earth she was even surprised. Steadying herself against the wall, she cast her eyes upward. "This is your doing, isn't it, Susan? Look, I'm sorry about giving you a home permanent that turned your head into a haystack. I honestly thought the directions said thirty minutes instead of ten. Please, can't we just call it even?"

Lydia could have sworn she heard soft laughter ooze out of the bubbles.

Powell sat at a corner booth nursing the same beer that had been thrust into his hands two hours earlier. Around him men laughed, drank, played pool and generally had a raucous good time. Usually Powell would be right in the middle of the fun. He loved a get-together with his buddies. For some reason, he couldn't get into the spirit of this one. He kept glancing at his watch, wondering when he'd be able to leave without causing eyebrows to raise. It wasn't that he felt guilty. Even if he had, he wouldn't admit it. Guilt was his father's cross to bear, not Powell's. Powell did what he wanted to do, plain and simple. If he wanted to drink with his buddies, he'd drink with his buddies.

He just didn't feel like it at the moment. Of course, leaving too soon would open him up to hoots and howls and accusations of being henpecked that he didn't feel like dealing with, either. So he sat there, bored, watching his friends have fun, and wondering why he couldn't get into the spirit of a party thrown in his honor.

By seven, he was tired, he was hungry and the flat beer in his glass tasted like diesel fuel. He wanted out. Now. Fortunately, most of his crewmates had downed too much brew to note his departure, and he was able to slip out without much of a stir.

A strange sense of relief washed over him as he pulled in front of the small tract home he shared with Lyddie and the kids. He didn't examine that relief too closely, nor did he scrutinize the anxiety he felt as he hurried up the walk. He hoped the children weren't asleep yet. For some reason, he really wanted to see them, maybe even help tuck them in.

The smell of smoke hit him the moment he opened the front door.

Frowning, he stepped inside, shrugged out of his jacket. "Lyddie?" There was no answer. The house was quiet, too quiet. Not even the comforting sound of the television greeted him.

He followed the smoky scent to the kitchen and saw a charred lump of something that might once have been edible on top of the stove. A twist of frayed wires dangled from a hole in the ceiling. The disemboweled smoke alarm lay on the counter.

Tossing his jacket over a kitchen chair, Powell headed toward the hallway and jerked to a stop, gaping, as Lyddie emerged from the bathroom looking like a half-drowned rat. Her clothes were wet, her bedraggled hair looked as if it had been caught in a rain shower, and a peculiar clutch of bubbles dripped from her scalp.

Grasping a wet dustpan, which also dripped bubbles, she spoke through clenched teeth.

"How nice of you to drop by."

"What happened?"

"Nothing important, just a small demonstration of what happens when a four-year-old dumps an entire bottle of bubble bath in the tub." She brushed past him, clearly furious, and disappeared into the kitchen.

Powell followed, perplexed by her anger. "Kids do stuff like that all the time."

"Yes." She flung the dustpan into the broom closet, spun around and speared him with a look. "I know."

It dawned on him that she might be perturbed by something other than a few bubbles. His gaze fell on the blackened lump on the stovetop. Wisely, he said nothing. As it turned out, he didn't have to.

Lydia followed his gaze. "That," she snapped, "is what happens to a chicken left in the oven for an extra two hours. And that—" she jerked a thumb toward the dead smoke alarm on the counter "—is what happens to loud, obnoxious, inconsiderate things that stretch my patience to the breaking point." The final words were uttered at a decibel level slightly below that of a jet plane on takeoff.

Powell had the distinct impression that she was referring to something more personal than a malfunctioning smoke alarm. "So you had a bad day, hmm?"

Her eyes widened, then shuttered into angry slits. "A bad day? Whatever gave you that idea?" She stomped past him, leaving a scent of sweet soap and baby powder in her wake.

The smell of her aroused him instantly. Angered by his

lack of control, he spun on his boot, followed her toward the living room. "What are you mad at me for? I didn't burn the damned chicken."

"You might as well have. It's your fault."

"*My* fault? How in hell do you figure that? I wasn't even here."

"That's the point, isn't it?" She stopped short, slammed the palm of her hand on a large board filled with peculiar numbers and drawings that was hanging on the dividing wall between the kitchen and living area. "Dinner was scheduled for five-thirty and *you weren't here.*"

"So what? There's no collar around my neck.... Hey, wait a minute." Powell did a double take, stared at the board. "What the devil is that?"

"It's our time schedule, and it says quite clearly that dinner is served precisely at—"

"Schedule? *Schedule?*" To his horror, Powell realized that the huge marker board had every daily activity mapped out in fifteen-minute increments. "You've scheduled my shower? When I get dressed? How long I'm allowed for breakfast, and when I can *read the damned newspaper?*"

Lydia's cheeks grew pink. "The indicated times are preliminary estimates. I'm willing to make some adjustments."

"Oh, well, *that's* a relief." Furious, Powell marched into the kitchen, snatched his jacket off the chair. He had one arm in it when Lydia appeared in the doorway.

"Powell, for once will you please try to see things from my perspective?"

"Your perspective is pretty damned clear. You've made a chart of it."

"Now don't get on your high horse with me, buster, I'm the one who has to cram two full-time jobs into one day." She turned sideways as he marched through the kitchen door, then squared off in front of him with her hands on her hips. "Time schedules allow me to accomplish twice as much in half the time. It works for me in the office, and it will work here, too, if given half a chance. All I'm asking for is a little cooperation."

"You don't want cooperation, honey, you want control. And it flat tears you up that I won't give it to you."

With that, Powell ended the argument as he'd always done. He walked out.

Lydia stood as though rooted, staring at the front door. She heard Powell's car start up and drive away. Still she couldn't move, was locked into place by the anger in his face, the fury in a voice still ringing in her ears.

You don't want cooperation...you want control.

Her legs trembled; her mouth went dry. Memories spun through her mind, memories of other arguments, other slamming doors. Through it all, she'd huffed silently, secure in the righteousness of her position and hurt because Powell hadn't understood her.

A voice from the past circled in her mind like a hungry vulture. "You've got my entire life mapped out," Powell had said six years ago. "Didn't it ever occur to you that I might not want to move to another state, that I might not appreciate being told where I'm going to live, what I'm going to eat, how I'm going to make a living? Did it ever occur to you that I might want control over my own damned life?"

It hadn't occurred to her, not then, not now.

For the first time, Lydia realized that Powell was right. She had wanted control, had been terrified of losing it. That's why she'd lost Powell six years ago.

It's why she'd just lost him again.

Chapter Nine

Lydia was in her office when Powell returned. She heard the front door open, felt her heart leap into her throat. He'd been gone nearly two hours, two of the longest hours of her life. Part of her had thought she'd never see him again; part of her had known better.

He'd never leave his precious chair.

Their confrontation earlier that evening had been yet another in-your-face reminder of the issues that had separated them in the first place. They hadn't dealt with the issues then. They would have to deal with them now. The children were counting on them.

Swiveling away from her computer, she held her breath, listening to the sound of his footsteps echoing on the tiled entry. Heavy, booted footsteps, a substantive sound, masculine, determined, brisk, without hesitation. The footsteps stopped. She swallowed hard, forced herself to remain rooted in her chair.

What could she say to him? He'd been right about her. She *had* tried to control him, had tried to control everything and everyone around her. That she hadn't recognized the flaw was no excuse. She recognized it now.

Still, Lydia wasn't certain she could change, not when she panicked at the thought of losing command over her environment, losing ownership of her own soul.

A successful person takes charge of life, her father had told her. *Victory is not bestowed by circumstance. It is seized by those with the courage of conquest in their souls.*

Odd, Lydia thought. She'd heard those words a hundred times in her youth, yet she'd never analyzed them, never realized that her father had equated success with victory, and victory with conquest.

Conquest.

The defeat of others.

The footsteps began again, startling her. They were slower this time, more deliberate. Two steps, three, then the sound was muffled by carpet. Her heart raced. He was in the hallway.

Breathing hard, Lydia spun around to face her computer monitor, clutched the electronic mouse as if it were a lifeline. He was in the doorway. She knew it. She felt it.

Behind her, he cleared his throat. "Are you about ready for a break?"

Her fingers convulsed around the mouse. She allowed her shoulders to straighten, forced herself to glance at him slowly, as if his appearance was a surprise. She wanted to speak to him, she really did, but a frustrating swell of warm moisture gathered in her eyes and she was struck mute. The very sight of him standing there, tousled and sheepish, the collar of his bomber jacket rumpled and askew, begged her to leap up and fling her arms around him. It was a dangerous compulsion, one she dared not indulge.

He shifted, knuckled the back of his skull. "You still like broccoli beef, right?"

"Broccoli beef?"

A nervous shrug vibrated the supple leather of his jacket. He shifted his stance, gazed back down the hall as if not trusting himself to look at her. "There's a neat little Chinese place over by the mall."

It took a moment for her to comprehend what he was saying. When she did, she was stunned. "You brought Chinese food?"

He angled a glance at her, his lips twitching with the hint of a smile. "I was hungry. Under the circumstances, I figured you might be hungry, too. Unless you got desperate enough to gnaw the charcoal off that burnt bird."

The amusement he struggled to suppress suddenly sprang free with extraordinary results. Laugh lines crinkled at the corners of his eyes, deepened the rugged grooves bracketing a firm, sculptured, deliciously tantalizing mouth. A chuckle rose up from deep inside, a mellow, manly vibration that sent shivers of appreciation down her spine.

As was his habit when he had the upper hand in a given situation, or was trying to gain it, he cocked his head, flashed a devastating grin. "Well, are you?"

Lydia used her tongue to pry her dry lips off her teeth. "Am I what?"

"Hungry?"

"Starved," she whispered.

He issued a satisfied nod, shifted his stance, then jammed his hands in his pocket. "It's getting cold," he mumbled before disappearing down the hall.

She stood, steadied herself on the desk, thankful her wobbly knees hadn't buckled. She found him in the kitchen ladling steaming noodles and vegetables onto dinner plates.

"I hope pork chow mein is okay." He scooped out a

final spoonful, then closed the white carton and opened another, sending her a mischievous glance. "I thought you might be kind of soured on the idea of chicken."

She smiled in return, recalling that she'd flung both the blackened fowl and the ruined baking pan in the trash with a satisfied shudder. "If I never see another chicken, it will be too soon."

"I'd rather have steak, anyway."

"Seven days a week?"

"Eight if I could." He licked sauce from his fingers, reached for a towel. "Of course, pizza's good, too."

"Ah, yes, we can't live without pizza."

"Well, we could, but what's the point?" He carried the plates to the table, swung a lean leg over a chair back and seated himself, only to bounce up a moment later and pull a second chair out for her. The gesture was unlike him. Lydia couldn't recall the last time he'd pulled out a chair or opened a door for her. He'd once said that women's liberation had eliminated a man's responsibility to perform such niceties, adding that he had no use for a female too puny to open her own danged door.

Lydia still recalled how his eyes had sparkled when he'd made the provocative statement, as if he'd been baiting her to quarrel with his logic. She hadn't. In fact, she'd agreed with him. Women, she'd replied with prodigious gravity, were capable of performing any function a man could perform, and many others beyond the grasp of the male gender altogether. Like having babies, for example.

Powell had laughed, hugged her and amiably agreed that women were indeed the stronger sex. That's why they could open their own doors.

The conversation came back to her now as clearly as if it had occurred only moments ago. Lydia had always appreciated Powell's willingness to treat her as an equal. It was more than a willingness, actually. It was a natural instinct on his part. He'd never patronized her, never shrugged off anything she wanted to do as being beyond her capabilities, had always been supportive and encouraging. He'd reminded her of her father in that regard.

Her father never pulled out chairs, either.

Now, as Lydia sat in the proffered chair and smiled her thanks, she was oddly touched by the gesture. "Such chivalry. Clearly you've put all those years since the college cafeteria to good use."

"I've learned a couple of manners." He reseated himself, began to enjoy his meal.

Lydia picked at hers, then laid down the fork. "Powell?" He grunted, stabbed at an egg roll. "About what happened earlier..." Moisture evaporated inside her mouth. Her tongue scraped dry lips; her throat constricted as if squeezed by a giant hand. "You were right. I'm sorry."

He chewed a moment, reached for a paper napkin from the holder in the center of the table. "No, you were right."

"I was?"

"Yeah." Seeming to stall for time, he dabbed at his mouth, wiped his fingers and finally laid the crumpled napkin beside his plate. "You're the one who's here all day taking care of the kids, the house, a goldfish and a business. If you think a stupid—er, an organizational time chart will help you do that, the least I can do is go along."

Relief was too benign a word to describe the joyous warmth flooding through her. The Powell she remembered would never have admitted he was wrong about anything, never backed down from a position on which he'd taken a stand. This glimmer that his trademark stubbornness might be softening was more than a surprise. It was a shock, albeit a delightful one. "Do you really mean that?"

Resting his forearms against the table edge, he spoke

without looking at her. "Yes, I guess I do." He frowned, leaned back, regarded her thoughtfully. "You didn't ask for this any more than I did. We're here and we both have to make the best of it for as long as we have to."

She felt as if she'd swallowed a brick. *For as long as we have to.* True as they were, the words were an unsettling reminder that nothing about their relationship was real, that she was married to a man who didn't want her, caring for children she'd barely known a few weeks earlier, and struggling to maintain a tenuous grip on a career she'd spent years cultivating.

Logically she understood that Powell had every reason to be unhappy with the situation. Lydia should be unhappy with it, too. Oddly enough, she wasn't unhappy. She'd just never realized that before. Oh, she was frustrated by a lack of time, a lack of perfection in matters with which she lacked experience, but she wasn't unhappy with the situation itself.

Unhappiness crept in when she allowed herself to consider what would happen later, when this phase of the guardianship proceedings had been completed.

This was temporary. She knew it. She'd always known it. She understood exactly what was supposed to happen after the legalities had been settled. Powell would move out; Lydia would take over. They'd already agreed to that, but she hadn't allowed herself to consider how she'd actually cope with the inevitable separation. She didn't want to consider it now.

Fear bubbled into her throat. "Powell, I—"

He held up his palm. "I know what you're going to say."

"You do?"

"I know you don't need my help, Lyddie, and you don' need me getting in your way, either."

That wasn't at all what she was thinking, but something in his eyes kept her silent. He pursed his lips, raked his fingers through his hair. "Look, I've been selfish. I admit it. This whole thing has ticked me off, screwed up my life in ways I didn't even want to think about. I've been mad at the world, mad at Dan and Susan for getting themselves killed, mad at Clementine for dragging me into this, mad at you for going along with it. Mostly, I've just been mad at myself."

"At yourself? Why?"

"Because I don't know what I'm doing here. I'm useless, Lyddie. I don't know squat about raising kids. If it wasn't for you..." His eyes shifted, he licked his lips, focusing his gaze on his dinner plate.

She laid an encouraging hand on his forearm. "Go on. Please."

After a moment's consideration, Powell took a breath, pivoted to face her. "You aren't going to like it."

She managed to keep a steady gaze. "Like it or not, we're in this together. Keeping secrets from each other isn't going to help."

"All right." Drumming his fingertips on the table, he avoided her gaze, seemed to be struggling to find the right words. "If it wasn't for you, I would have turned Clementine down flat. It wouldn't have mattered that Dan was my best friend, it wouldn't have mattered that the kids would have ended up in foster care, I would have said no."

Apparently her shock was evident. "I don't believe that."

"Believe it. I am not a nice person, Lydia. But then, you already know that."

It took a moment for her to gather her thoughts. "That's simply not true. I've seen you with those children. You care about them. You care deeply. And I know how much Dan's friendship meant to you. I can't believe you would have turned your back on that."

"I would have, not because I didn't care about Dan's children, but because I cared too much. You know me, Lyddie, you know that sooner or later I would have let them down."

"Why do you say that?"

"Because it's true. I've never been a person who can be counted on for the long haul. There's something inside me that flares up like an itch that can't be scratched. I feel claustrophobic, like I've been folded into a box and there's nothing I won't do to get out."

His candor sliced her to the quick. All that he'd said about himself was true. Deep down, she'd always known that. Hearing the words from his own lips, spoken with such calm acceptance, hit her like a body blow. She swallowed, took a sip of ice water from the glass beside her plate, then twirled the glass between her palms. "So you accepted Clementine's proposal because of me?"

"Yes."

"Why?"

He flinched slightly. "Because I knew you wouldn't expect anything of me."

"I see." She carefully set the glass aside, wiped the moist table ring with her napkin.

"I'm not proud of myself, Lyddie, but I am what I am." He lifted her hand, cupped it between palms roughened by hard labor, gentled by a caring heart. "I know you don't want my help, or need it, but I can promise that if you ever do, I'll be here for you. All you have to do is ask."

A soothing warmth spread from the comfort of his touch to the center of her soul. Her breathing slowed; her pulse calmed. She did need Powell's help, needed it desperately. But she also knew that if she took him up on his magnanimous offer of assistance, the gleam of raw panic would return to his eyes. He'd feel trapped again, locked in a prison of responsibility that he'd do anything to escape.

What Powell said and what he meant were two different things. Lydia had learned that the hard way, years ago. He'd said a lot of things back then. He hadn't meant any of them. Despite the soft words and gentle touch, Powell was now and always had been a man who answered only to the whisper of his own heart and the haunting song of freedom.

As always, Lydia was on her own.

"Okay, buddy, the Navy SEALs are gathered at the beachhead, preparing to attack the giant sea monster that's been destroying the San Francisco fishing fleet." Propped up on an elbow, Powell stretched out on Kenny's bedroom floor, positioning his legs around the wicker toy box that had been pushed beside the dresser to serve as a step so the boy could reach the goldfish bowl, which now sat on the floor surrounded by tiny toy soldiers. Sidney swam laps in his diminutive glass world, fanning his fins and focusing buggy fish eyes on the activity beyond the bowl, where Powell drove a jeep the size of a small matchbox through the front line of tiny plastic soldiers. "Here comes the admiral, buddy. Everyone salutes."

Scooting forward on his knees, Kenny marched a slightly larger action figure dressed in a wet suit toward the jeep Powell was racing around the fishbowl. "The monster is in the bay," the boy squeaked. "We're gonna toast him, Admiral, sir."

"Good man." Powell emitted a sound like screeching tires, jerked the tiny vehicle to a stop, then grabbed a small plastic figure to play the part of the admiral. "Carry on, Ensign."

"Yes, sir." Kenny's smart salute was interrupted by a delighted squeal from the doorway.

"Fissy!" Wearing nothing but a T-shirt and a thrilled grin, Tami clapped her pudgy hands, shrieking wildly. "Fissy, fissy, fissy!"

As she toddled forward, her brother leaped up to block her way. "You're not supposed to be in here. This is my room, and we're in the middle of a war." Thwarted, the baby tried to push past her much larger sibling, grunting, pointing and babbling. Kenny's frustration reached the boiling point, but instead of turning to Powell for adult assistance, he screeched for Lydia. "Aunt Lyddie! Tami won't leave us alone! Aunt Lyddie!"

Frowning, Powell sat up. "There's no reason to bother your aunt Lyddie, pal. I think you and I can take care of this."

Before he could get to his feet, Lydia swept in from the hallway with an oven mitt in one hand and a tea towel draped over her shoulder. "There you are." She tucked the mitt in the back pocket of her jeans, gathered the half-nude baby in her arms, planted a kiss on the fat little neck. "You were supposed to call me when you were done on the potty."

"Fissy," Tami insisted, pointing and grunting and wriggling to get down.

Shifting the agitated baby on her hip, Lydia swept her eyes around the war room with obvious disapproval. She flicked Powell a disgruntled look, then turned her attention to the shuffling youngster with a scuba-diving action figure clutched in his fist. "Kenny, I've told you a dozen times not to put your fish on the floor."

"But he has to be there 'cause he's a sea monster and the navy has to keep him from eating up the whole city."

"If you knock over his bowl, all the navy will end up

with is a year's supply of orange sushi. I've told you, sweetie, that Sidney can't live out of his bowl, which is why you can't take him out and pet him.''

Tami let loose a frustrated shriek, arched her back and bucked wildly. "Fiss-sy!"

Struggling to maintain her grip on the squirming baby, Lydia angled a withering stare softened by a sparkle of genuine humor. "Honestly, Powell, you're as bad as Kenny. Can't the two of you play something quieter and more educational?''

"Battlefield strategy is very educational. It teaches how to think on your feet, outwit the enemy." Powell stood, followed her gaze to the breast pocket of his shirt, out of which a miniature soldier in full battle gear peeked. He removed the plastic figure, held it behind his back. "Think of it as ROTC for preschoolers."

Her laugh slid down his spine like a warm bath. "In that case I stand corrected. In the event of a giant goldfish attack, I'm sure that you and Kenny will be at the top of the Pentagon's call list. I mean, how many boys can brag about having completed military training before entering kindergarten?''

She was beautiful when she laughed. Even the weary smudges shadowing her eyes like tired bruises couldn't disguise the sparkle in her smile every time she looked at the children. That smile warmed when she turned it on Powell, but there was always a trace of wariness in it, as if she expected a criticism or complaint.

He blamed himself for that, and had spent the week since the burnt chicken incident evaluating his every word and deed with political precision. Despite his promise to stay out of her way, Powell couldn't help but worry about her. She worked too hard. Everything had to be perfect, from the shine on the kitchen floor to the gravy on their evening meal. Then, after the children were asleep and the supper dishes had been washed, dried and neatly stacked by size, shape and utilitarian purpose, Lydia would slip into her office and work until well after midnight.

No wonder she was exhausted. Only with the children did stress lines bracketing her mouth loosen into a smile. As Powell watched her calm her agitated charge by blowing affectionate bubbles on the baby's fat little neck, he realized how much he enjoyed just gazing at her. Lydia was at her best at moments like this, unguarded and outgoing, when her natural tenderness spilled from behind the prickly shield she'd erected around her emotions. She was like that with the children, warm and wonderful, glowing with love.

Lydia swished Tami in her arms until the baby's irked grunts dissipated into tickled giggles, then she turned to Kenny. "Put Sidney's bowl back on the dresser, sweetie, and wash up. Dinner will be on the table in five minutes."

Powell stepped forward. "Can I help you with anything?"

The question seemed to startle her. Caution crept back into her eyes. "No, thanks. Everything's under control."

Although not unexpected, the rebuff hurt. It was a reminder that he was neither wanted nor needed in any capacity other than that of male role model, as specified in their original agreement. Which was fine with him, of course. At least, that's what he kept telling himself, although he'd long since stopped listening. As much as he cherished his freedom to come and go as he pleased, he didn't like feeling useless. He didn't like the feeling in his gut when the children looked through him as if he didn't exist, and called out for Lydia when they were hurt, or scared, or hungry.

Most of all, he didn't like the way Lydia's eyes changed from lustrous to circumspect when turned in his direction.

Once her eyes had glowed for him, had shimmered and smoldered, had turned his heart to butter with the merest glance. There had been no wariness in her gaze then, no shuttered secrets, no cynicism or distrust. She'd poured her soul into those lovely eyes, allowed him unfettered access to her heart and her mind.

He hadn't appreciated her openness then, had even felt threatened by it. The effect she'd had on him had been powerful, frightening. She'd made him feel things he hadn't wanted to feel, see things he hadn't wanted to see. She'd made him think about his future, their future, a boring, predictable string of events leading to the same boring, predictable life from which Powell had yearned to escape throughout his own boring, predictable childhood.

The life he'd envisioned with such dread, the daily drudgery of job and family, had been very much like the one in which he was now ensconced. Strangely, it wasn't as dreary and oppressive as he'd imagined, probably because none of it was real.

Except the children. They were real. And the peculiar ache in Powell's gut every time Lydia walked into the room, that was real, too, just as real as the mistrust in her eyes every time she looked at him.

That mistrust wounded him more deeply than he cared to admit. Whatever feelings she'd once had for him had died long ago. Powell had made certain of that.

The eleven o'clock news had just ended. Powell yawned, stretched, flicked his thumb on the remote. The TV screen snapped into darkness. He stood, rolling his head, massaging the base of his neck as he turned off the living room lights and made his way into the hall. A thin beam of light sprayed from Lydia's office door. She was still working.

Powell went to Kenny's room, gathered the sleepy

youngster in his arms and carried him to the bathroom, then settled him back into bed, a nightly ritual that had apparently been effective, since the bed-wetting had not recurred.

''G'night,'' he mumbled as Powell tucked the covers around the small body.

Powell allowed himself the luxury of stroking the boy's soft hair. ''Good night, buddy. Sweet dreams.''

With a languid sigh, a contented groan, Kenny nuzzled into the covers and drifted quickly back to sleep.

Returning to the hall, Powell continued his bedtime routine by quietly peeking into Lydia's office. Sometimes she was hard at work, so engrossed in the blinking computer screen that she never heard the door creak open, never knew that he was checking up on her. On other occasions he found her slumped over her keyboard, sound asleep. She was asleep now, her head tilted forward, her chin resting on her collarbone, one hand cocked beside the keyboard and the other dangling beside the arm of the chair.

Moving quietly, Powell fingered the keyboard, executing the system shutdown. After turning off the computer, he wrapped one arm around the small of her back, slipped the other beneath her limp knees and lifted her gently.

She stirred, as she always did, moaning softly and burying her face in the curve of his throat. One of her hands rested against his collarbone, the other was trapped between her rib cage and his chest. Her breath slipped out in a sigh, condensing against his skin like warm fog. Her warm body, so supple in slumber, molded against him with a sweetness that made him shudder.

He bent his head, brushed his lips across her forehead, sipped the moist corner of her mouth. She was so beautiful, lying there in his arms. It felt so perfect to him, so right.

He savored the moment awhile longer. Then, as he'd done so many times over the past two weeks, he pressed his cheek to her silky hair, shrugged off the light switch with his shoulder and carried her to bed.

The tiny sound seeped into her consciousness, distant at first, then closer, with more insistence. "Ba-ba-ba-ba, ma-mamama, lee-lee, lee-lee." Sweet baby sounds, a contented child singing softly to herself.

From the warm darkness of her mind, Lydia stirred, groaned, then bolted upright, blinking. A dim gray light sprayed through the lacy sheers. The sound of a television wafted into her mind. Horrified, she swiveled toward the clock. It confirmed her fears. It was past eight. Eight! She should have been up three hours ago.

Vaguely aware that she was fully clothed, Lydia leaped from bed, rushed down the hall and found poor little Tami standing in her crib, eyes bright and fat cheeks pink from sleep, rocking back and forth to the rhythm of her own baby song. The toddler squeaked happily as Lydia entered the room, flinging out her arms, grunting to be picked up.

"Oh, sweetie, good morning." Lifting the chortling child from the crib, Lyddie hugged her fiercely and kissed her warm face. "You are such a good little girl, and I am such a bad mommy. I'll bet you're starving, aren't you, precious? Let's go check on your brother, then we'll get some nice fresh diapers and have a big bowl of yummy oatmeal. How does that sound?"

Tami reached up and patted Lydia's nose. "Oo-meel."

"I'll take that as a yes," she murmured, and hurried into the living room, vastly relieved to find Kenny engrossed in watching a children's program on television. "Why didn't you wake me up, honey?"

Kenny glanced over his shoulder. "Uncle Powell said you were real tired."

"You were up before Uncle Powell went to work?"

"Uh-huh. He came in and told me I should take good care of you today, on account of you working so hard and all."

Lydia couldn't argue about that. She had been working hard. So hard, in fact, that half the time she couldn't even remember climbing into bed at night, but had apparently done so in such a zombielike state that she hadn't even bothered to undress. That had happened frequently over the past couple of weeks, but this was the first time she'd overslept.

The disarray of her carefully orchestrated schedule was unnerving, to say the least. Lydia hadn't even been awake five minutes and she was already hours behind. The daily analysis reports should have been faxed to the office twenty minutes ago, and she hadn't even downloaded the Asian market figures. Considering the fact that George had been less than pleased with her performance on the Morris account, she couldn't afford to alienate him further by missing her daily deadlines.

"Listen, sweetie, I'm going to get Tami dressed and fix breakfast, then I'll have to work for a little while—"

"I already did."

"Pardon me?"

"I fixed my own breakfast." Grinning proudly, he hopped up, adjusting the stretched elastic band of his pajamas. "I fixed yours, too."

"You did?"

"Yeah! Come look!"

Stunned, Lydia followed the scampering child into the kitchen and saw a massive bowl of cornflakes on the table. Or at least she presumed it had once been cornflakes, although at the moment it more accurately resembled a large mound of milk-soaked mush. A grateful mist warmed her eyes. "That was so sweet of you."

Kenny beamed. ''Uncle Powell said you'd like it.''

''Did he, now?'' An image pulsed through her mind, a flicker of strong arms and warm lips. When she tried to clarify the memory, it evaporated like so much steam. ''I...I didn't pack his lunch for him.''

''That's okay. Uncle Powell said he was sick of rabbit food wrapped in cardboard.''

''He said what?''

Kenny's grin faded. ''Maybe I wasn't s'posed to tell you that part.''

Before she could digest that tidbit of information, the phone rang. She suspected it was George, and knew he wouldn't be happy by the delay in supplying his precious financial reports. Lydia had a choice to make. Either pick up the phone and let Tami crawl around hungry and in wet diapers for the next twenty minutes, or let the call go on the answering machine and risk losing her job.

By the time the machine answered, Lydia was already in the bedroom, changing Tami's damp pajamas and tickling her fat tummy. Between the happiness of a child or a boss, there really was no contest. It didn't occur to Lydia how much her priorities had shifted to make that choice.

The day had started poorly, gone downhill from there. Lydia had sneaked away during playtime to prepare the morning reports, although she'd been interrupted so often that by the time she'd gotten them faxed to the office, the figures were probably obsolete.

She'd returned George's call shortly before noon and found him less than amiable about the delay. In fact, he'd been coldly furious.

And there had been more, much more.

By the time she hung up the phone, the ramifications of her earlier choice had come home to roost. The results weren't pretty. Five years of ambitious effort were teetering in the balance. Lydia hadn't exactly been fired, but she'd come close enough to be disheartened. After having been demoted to part-time research and analysis work, she'd had her major accounts shifted to an up-and-coming investment banker who could show up at power lunches without searching for a baby-sitter and wearing sour milk on his lapel. Even worse, she'd been put on a six-month probation, after which her job performance would be reassessed.

Reassessed. In business jargon, that meant she'd either have to resolve her parenting problems and return to work full-time or her position would be filled by someone else, someone whose life wasn't in utter pandemonium.

Someone who wasn't a failure.

The word pounded her brain. *Failure, failure, failure.* Failure in her career, failure in her relationships, failure with the children. Failure with Powell.

Of all the failures, all the hurts and disappointments, the last one sliced the deepest. Years ago she'd chosen ambition and career over love. It had been a bitter mistake, one she'd been determined not to make again. Now she'd chosen her love for the children over her career.

Still the quandary remained. The children needed her time and attention, but they also needed food and clothes, all the necessities that money could buy. Powell wouldn't be around forever. As soon as the guardianship papers were filed, Powell would pack up and move on with his life. He'd made that clear.

Sooner or later, Lydia would be on her own. How would she manage? The answer was that she simply didn't know how she'd manage. That scared her to death.

"Icky." Red-eyed and furious, Tami vainly wiped at the smeared mud on her shirt while Lydia wheeled the stroller into the entry hall. The baby hiccuped, whacked at her filthy shirt, kicked her feet in the stroller and began to wail again, as she'd been doing for the entire three-block walk from the park.

"Hush, hush, sweetie, we're home now. We'll get you all cleaned up."

"Icky!" Tami shrieked.

Parking the stroller in the foyer, Lydia extracted the frustrated baby, trying to calm her before she flew into yet another rage. "The doggie was just trying to give you a kiss. He didn't mean to push you in the puddle." The dog in question, a hyperfriendly terrier belonging to a little boy with whom Kenny had struck up a friendship at the local playground, had bounded through the park with unabashed glee, paw-printing one child after another with its personalized canine signature. Tami, less than pleased by the attention, had promptly thrown a temper tantrum that had every parent in the park shaking an empathetic head.

Lydia had been mortified.

All in all, it was not shaping up as a particularly good day. The only saving grace Lydia saw at the moment was that nothing worse could possibly happen.

Kenny stomped inside, slamming the door behind him. "I wanna go back to the park."

"Tomorrow, Kenny." Lydia hoisted Tami on one hip and headed toward the bathroom for another futile lesson in potty training.

Kenny followed, grumbling madly. "But I was having fun. It's not fair."

"Well, I doubt Tami thinks it's fair that she is all wet and muddy because your friend's little dog knocked her down." Working quickly, Lydia stripped off the baby's muddy shoes, socks, pants and diaper, and sat her on the little potty chair that her parenting book specified as the most appropriate training tool for a child this age. She'd just started to pull the filthy T-shirt off over her head when Kenny suddenly kicked the door.

Lydia straightened and spun around. "Kenny!"

The boy looked properly chagrined. Tears spurted into his eyes. "What's *adopted* mean?" he asked suddenly.

Lydia's heart dropped like a rock. "Why do you ask?"

"Joey is adopted."

"Joey?"

"My friend from the park. He says he's special 'cause his parents wanted him forever and ever, and that's why they adopted him."

"I see." Absently handing Tami a small toy, Lydia slipped an arm around the boy's shoulders and ushered him toward his room. "*Adoption* is a legal term. It means that people who want to be parents of a child who has no parents will adopt that child, and become his legal mommy and daddy."

The boy frowned. "Are you and Uncle Powell going to adopt Tami and me?"

"Well, not exactly. Uncle Powell and I are your guardians. But that's just a legal term, too. We're—" She opened his bedroom door and groaned. "Oh, Kenny, what have I told you about putting the fishbowl on the floor?" A shriek from the bathroom spun her around. "I'm coming, Tami! Kenny, please put your fish back on the dresser. I'll be right back, and we'll talk about adoption some more, okay?"

Before Kenny could respond, the walls vibrated with a horrific thud, followed by another angry shriek. The phone rang as Lydia sprinted to the bathroom to release the furious, mud-smeared baby from her potty-chair prison. Tami toddled off. Lydia ducked into her office to answer the phone. The answering machine light blinked frantically.

Lydia ignored it. She'd check messages later—perhaps after a few stiff drinks.

"Clementine, thank heavens." Lydia sagged against her desk. "I was hoping it was you. Listen, we have to talk—"

"Tami, no-o!"

Lydia went rigid. "Kenny, what's wrong?"

"No, no, no!"

"Fissy, fissy!"

"Ohmigosh. I'll call you back." Dropping the phone, Lydia leaped forward in time to see the bare-bottomed baby scuttle out of Kenny's room hugging the fishbowl to her mud-smeared tummy. Kenny shot out, shrieking at the top of his lungs, and chased her into the living room.

Lydia sprinted after them.

"Gimme my fish!" Kenny hollered, grabbing his sister's arm.

"Fissy!" Tami screamed, and flung the fishbowl on the floor in a fit of pique. Water gushed onto the carpeting as the bowl rolled like a ball before righting itself, but not before an orange blur washed out on a wave and disappeared beneath the sofa.

"Oh, no! *Sidney!*" Horrified, Kenny flattened himself on the floor, stretching his arm under the sofa, while his frustrated sister flung herself backward onto the floor and went into a full-fledged temper tantrum.

Lydia cleared the kicking, screaming baby like a worldclass hurdler and dropped to her knees beside the sobbing boy, whose arm was clearly not long enough for the job at hand. Peering into the darkness, Lydia saw the gasping goldfish flopping just out of reach. "It's all right. We'll get him." A quick dash to the broom closet and Lydia was armed for fish retrieval.

The entire house was in chaos. Kenny was sobbing wildly while his dirty, bare-bottomed sister screamed at the top of her lungs and a gasping goldfish prepared to flip his final flop.

Using the broom to sweep the fish forward, Lydia stretched her free arm under the sofa until her shoulder felt as if it had been dislocated and her face was squished against the upholstered frame. Something slimy swished against her palm. She grabbed it, rolled over and sat up, cradling the quivering fish in her palm. "Got it," Lydia shouted over the baby's furious wails. "Bring the bowl, Kenny, quick."

Lydia leaped to her feet and froze.

A woman wearing a business suit and a horrified expression, clutching her briefcase like a shield, stood in the doorway. Her puzzled gaze went from Lydia, who held a half-dead fish, to Kenny, who grasped a half-filled fishbowl, to the muddy, half-naked one-year-old prostrate on the floor, red faced and shrieking.

The woman sucked in a breath, blinked at Lydia. "I knocked, but…ah, well—" she raised her voice to be heard over Tami's indignant wails "—I heard all the screaming and thought someone might be injured."

Momentarily startled by finding a strange woman in her living room, Lydia had to be prodded by Kenny to release Sidney into the bowl he held up. Once returned to his own environment, the dazed fish righted himself and began to swim familiar circles around his tiny world. Kenny dashed into the kitchen, presumably to refill the bowl.

Lydia returned her attention to the visitor, who was staring at the howling baby with something akin to pity in her eyes. At this stage of a tantrum there was little anyone could do but let it run its course. Foolishly smoothing her own mud-splotched shirt, Lydia spoke to the stranger with as much dignity as she could muster under the circumstances. "As you can see, things are a little hectic at the moment. Whatever you're offering, we don't need it."

"Excuse me?" The woman hiked a brow. "I'm sorry, I presumed I was expected. I left a message."

"I...that is, we just returned home. I haven't had a chance to check messages."

"In that case, allow me to introduce myself." The woman retrieved a business card from the pocket of her stylish blazer, presented it with a frosty smile.

Lydia nearly fainted. Only moments ago, she'd believed this day couldn't possibly get any worse. She'd been wrong.

"Martha Renault," the woman said coolly. "Department of Social Services." Her eyes flickered around the cluttered living room, settling on the screaming toddler. "And I must respectfully disagree, Mrs. Greer. It appears you do need what I have to offer." Her wintry smile froze Lydia to the bone. "Whether or not it's available, well, that's what I'm here to determine."

With that chilling reminder, Lydia felt her world collapse.

Chapter Ten

The first thing Powell noticed when he arrived home that evening was the absence of aroma, enticing or otherwise, which would normally be wafting from the kitchen. The second thing he noticed was the sound of the television blaring during an hour of the day Lydia had stridently deemed as quiet playtime.

A peek into the kitchen revealed no sign of recent activity. Lunch dishes were piled in the sink. Spilled milk was dried on the table. A few colored pebbles similar to those lining the base of Sidney's fishbowl were scattered in peculiar locations across the floor, from the entry tile to the carpeted landing of the living area.

Upon entering the kitchen, Powell noticed more such pebbles on the counter and in the sink. He moved past the breakfast nook, exited into the dining area of the elongated living room, where Kenny was engrossed in watching cartoons while his sister napped on the floor beside him with her ratty blanket tangled around her corduroy-clad legs. "Hey, buddy. Where's Aunt Lyddie?"

Powell posed the question twice more before the mesmerized boy glanced over his shoulder with cartoon-glazed eyes. "Huh?"

"Aunt Lyddie," Powell repeated slowly. "Where is she?"

"I dunno."

"Are you supposed to be watching television now?"

Kenny gave a limp shrug. "Aunt Lyddie didn't say it was time to turn it off."

Frowning, Powell pivoted toward the hall and went to the master bedroom. Lydia wasn't there, nor was she in the bathroom, the office or either of the children's rooms. A frisson of fear slid down his spine. This wasn't like her. With her time charts, chore maps and rigorous routines, Lydia was as predictable as the tide. Something definitely wasn't right.

Heading toward the garage, Powell passed the laundry room, jerked to a stop and back-stepped to the open doorway. "Lydia?"

She didn't respond, but that wasn't surprising, since she was sitting cross-legged on the floor with her face in a bag. The brown paper expanded and contracted, crinkling with every breath.

Powell stepped inside, squatted down. "Are you all right?"

She yanked the bag away with a gasp, stared up with huge, frightened eyes hollowed out of a face the color of bleached concrete. Pale lips moved. Tears leaked onto her lashes. She took a ragged breath, then another.

Unable to speak, she dived back into the bag, which crinkled in and out, in and out until Powell finally took hold of her wrists and pried the wrinkled sack from her hands. He tossed it aside, touched her cheek with his knuckles. Her skin was moist and cold. "You're ill. I'll call the doctor."

"N-no." She clutched his forearm to keep him from rising. "Not sick, just stupid. Stupid, stupid, stupid…" Gasping for breath, she reached for the wad of brown paper.

"Shh, you don't need that. Breathe slow and easy, slow and easy." Grasping her icy hands in his palms, he coached each breath until her skin grew pink and her eyes cleared. "There, that's better."

She licked her lips, leaned back against the washing machine with a pitiful moan. "I've ruined everything."

"I don't understand."

Covering her eyes with her hand, Lydia curled forward again. In a halting voice, she relayed all that had happened that day, from the muddy dogs in the park and her demotion at work to the disastrous interview with the social services investigator. Apparently Powell couldn't keep the disbelief from his eyes, because she peeked through her fingers, uttered a helpless cry and began to rock to and fro like a miserable child. "I told you I ruined everything. What if they decide I'm not capable of caring for Kenny and Tami? What if they take them away and put them in foster care? What if—"

"Hey, that's not going to happen."

"How do you know?" Her head reared up. Tears streamed down her cheeks. "How do you know that woman isn't filling out paperwork right this very minute to make our kids wards of the state?"

The term "our kids" did not escape Powell's notice, but he wisely chose not to comment on it. Instead, he wiped at her tears with the side of his thumb, tried to keep his gaze from wandering to her rumpled clothing, which appeared to have been used for belly-surfing on a muddy lawn.

"Look, you're just tired, that's all. You've been working too hard, not getting enough sleep—"

"What has sleep got to do with anything?" She flung up her hands in disgust. "Aren't you listening to me? It's ruined, everything is ruined."

"Nothing is ruined. You told this social services person what happened in the park with the dog—" his gaze skittered to her smeary green, paw-printed ensemble "—and the mud. I'm sure she understood."

"I should have kept the children away from the dog. What if it had bitten them?"

"It didn't bite them. It got them dirty. Dirt," he pointed out logically, "is not fatal."

With a pitiful sniff, Lydia wiped the back of her hand across her face, heaved a long-suffering sigh. "You don't understand. When that woman walked into the house, everything was in shambles. The fish was flopping under the couch, Kenny was in hysterics and his shirt was all torn, Tami was beating her head on the floor, half-naked and shrieking at the top of her lungs, and both of the kids looked like filthy, homeless urchins, and—"

"Look, does this woman have children?"

Lydia blinked up at him. "Yes, three."

"Aha. So after the initial chaos, you two obviously spent some time talking." He waited for her affirmative nod. "And clearly she felt comfortable enough with you to tell you something about herself."

A small frown puckered between her brows. "We talked while I cleaned Tami up and put her down for a nap. I fixed her some tea. She told me a story about her kids and a pet gerbil that escaped into the walls through an opening around a water pipe. It didn't have a happy ending." Lydia heaved a sigh, scratched at a green stain on the hem of her white shirt. "There was a cat next door...." She shrugged, let the words trail away. "Anyway, she said that she understood children and chaos go together."

"So you see, things worked out."

Lydia's eyes were filled with misery. "Tami is too young to potty train."

"Excuse me?"

"That's what Martha said."

"Martha? You're on a first name basis with this person, and you're worried about whether or not she likes you?"

"Liking me has nothing to do with whether or not she thinks I can take proper care of two small children. I don't even know when it's appropriate to potty train—"

"Wait a minute. How did personal hygiene instruction get into the conversation?"

"I had to explain why Tami was running around with a bare bottom, didn't I?"

Powell charitably allowed that had probably been a good idea.

"Anyway, I told her that my books said one was a good age to start, but she just gave me this funny look and said that books aren't the answer to everything…" Lydia rubbed her eyes again. "What am I going to do?"

Powell was having difficulty believing this was truly the crisis Lydia considered it to be, but would have sewn his own lips together with a pole hook and 220-volt cable before he'd have dismissed her concerns. She was clearly upset by the incident. Powell was upset that she was upset.

"We," he said finally.

"Hmm?"

"This is a joint effort, remember?"

She stared at him as if he'd grown antlers. "It isn't your problem."

For some reason, that stung. "Then why am I here? Frankly, I've got better things to do with my life than hang around like a seasonal decoration to be dragged out whenever company arrives.''

"Isn't that all you agreed to be?"

The question rocked him. He sat back on his heels, hard. Denial stuck on his tongue. Deep down, he knew she was right. He'd agreed to this only because he'd known that little would be expected of him, that there would be only minimal interference in his life. When it came to emotional involvement, to the acceptance of actual responsibility, he'd drawn a line in the sand, sending signals that he didn't want to be a real part of Lydia's life, or the children's. To his surprise, he realized that wasn't entirely true. He did want to be a part of their lives. On his terms, of course.

Words moved slowly to his lips, hesitated there as if fearing the consequence of escape. "I know what I agreed to. That was then. This is now. Now I believe the children need more from me than I've been willing to give. I think you need more from me, too."

A small flash in her eyes could have been anger. Or fear. "I don't need anything from you, Powell."

He stiffened, felt foolishly betrayed. "Of course you don't need me. You don't need anyone. You never have. You're perfect. You can do it all by yourself, be the perfect parent, the perfect cook, the perfect housekeeper, the perfect employee. That's why the kitchen is empty, the house is a mess, the children are vegged out in front of the television, while you, now one step away from the unemployment line, are hiding in the laundry room hyperventilating into a damned paper bag. A *perfect* paper bag. Oh, hell, what's the use?"

Powell straightened fiercely, feeling anger in his gut— fury not at Lydia, but at himself. Emotions carefully suppressed for years bubbled deep inside with a vengeance that frightened him. He was haunted by her tears, touched to the core by her vulnerability. The first time he'd laid eyes on Lydia, he'd admired her strength, her focus, her tenacious independence. She'd told him a dozen times that she didn't need him. In the past, Powell had reveled in those words. They'd been like an aphrodisiac to him.

Now he despised them, and he despised himself for fearing the need he saw in her eyes. Because for the first time in his life, he relished that need, cherished it.

But he simply didn't know how to fulfill it.

He stood with his back to her, shoulders bent, one fist jammed on his hip, the other pressed to his temple as if he could eliminate unwanted thoughts by physical force.

Behind him fabric rustled. There was a dull metallic thump, as if Lydia had levered herself upright against the washing machine. When she moved closer, the fragrance of fresh meadow grass from her clothes mingled with the lingering scent of laundry detergent. A whiff of herbal shampoo joined the collage, along with a faintly familiar astringent he recognized from a bottle of skin freshener on her side of the bathroom sink.

"Powell." Her voice was soft, tremulous, almost a whisper.

If he turned, he'd be doomed. He felt it; he knew it. In the end, he couldn't help it.

The pain in her eyes carved a hunk out of his heart. "I know I've let you down," she whispered. "I've let the kids down. But please, please don't leave them. They're so alone, so frightened. You and I, we're all they have. They need both of us, Powell. They need you." The final words escaped with a whiff of breath. "And I need you, too."

His arms opened without conscious thought. She slid into them with a sigh, a quiver of warm flesh melting into his embrace, awakening a protective ferocity of heart that shook him to the marrow. At that moment, there was nothing he wouldn't have done to protect her, to calm her, to keep her safe. He would fight dragons for this woman. He would even fight the terror of his own soul for her.

Her hair smelled so sweet splayed across his shoulder. He rubbed his cheek against its silken softness, felt the moist heat of her tears soak into his shirt. "I'm sorry," she whispered against his collarbone. "I wanted to do it all, but I can't. I don't know how."

"It's okay." He brushed his lips across her brow, felt the responding tremor of her breath. "We'll work it out together."

"How?" Her voice trembled. She scraped her lower lip with her teeth to quell a quiver. "If I force the children into day care before they're ready, they could be emotionally scarred for life. But if I don't, I'll lose my job, I won't be able to support them and the state will take them away. I've never been so confused before, I've never felt so hopeless—"

His lips covered hers quickly, swallowing her fears in the heat of his kiss. Pressing his hand to her cheek, he held her tightly to him, drinking deeply of an essence so sweet his knees nearly buckled.

Hers did. His arm looped her waist, holding her upright while his free hand caressed the curve of her throat, and gentle strands of golden hair tangled in his fingers.

A weak moan vibrated from deep inside her. Or perhaps from deep inside him. He couldn't tell. They were joined, body and soul, until he couldn't feel where he ended and she began.

Her fingers twisted the open collar of his shirt, pulling him closer. Her lips parted, inviting him in. He accepted, tasting her moist sweetness until he was dizzied by it, his mind spinning, his body weakening in some places, strengthening with sexual yearning in others.

He wanted her. Desperately.

That's why he let her go.

The kiss ended as suddenly as it had begun. Lydia clung weakly to him, gazing up with startled eyes, her breath coming in tiny gasps. He pressed her face to his shoulder, laid his cheek against her hair. "I know how much your career means to you," he said. "Keep your job. I'll quit mine."

A shudder moved through her. "You don't mean that."

"I mean it."

She twisted to look up at him. "No, it's not fair. I can work part-time for a few months, even take a leave of absence if I have to. You'd have to give up everything."

"It's only a job. I can find another."

"It's a job you happen to love."

He couldn't dispute that. "Not as much as you love yours."

Guilt clouded her eyes, and he knew she was remembering the argument they'd had years earlier. He'd discovered the rental agreement by accident, had stumbled over the signed lease while searching for something else. The confrontation had not been pretty. Powell had been furious. Lydia had been shocked by his reaction.

After all, it made sense to her. Everything was charted, delineated, a spreadsheet representing their lives. Only Powell hadn't been consulted.

He hadn't been consulted, and he didn't want the life that Lydia seemed hell-bent on pursuing. He hadn't wanted to move to New York, had shuddered at the thought of climbing a corporate ladder. He'd liked working with his hands, being outdoors. He'd liked his freedom.

He still did.

Lydia knew that about him. She'd always known that,

which was why the generosity of his offer now stunned her into silence.

She stepped away, just enough to allow a breath of air between their overheated bodies. The power of Powell's kiss still burned on her lips and in her heart. Her pulse still raced like hot steam through her veins. She needed a moment to gather her thoughts, to consider the magnitude of what Powell had been willing to renounce for her sake, and for the sake of the children.

She moistened her lips, avoided his gaze. "Let me make certain I understand this. You've just offered to quit your job and stay home with the children?"

"Sure, why not?" A gleam of amusement fought its way through the sexual heat in his eyes. "Unless you don't think I can impress the state social workers in the same way you can."

A warm flush crawled up her throat, but she couldn't suppress an embarrassed smile. "Touché."

"I can take care of kids."

"I know," she said, although she didn't know at all. "But I really want to do it."

If he was surprised by that, so was Lydia. The words had slipped out unbidden, but they were nonetheless true. "I want to be with them. I want to see them wake up in the morning, watch them feed the ducks in the park. I want to read stories before naptime and be there when it's time to have afternoon juice and cookies. I love them, Powell. I don't want to be away from them, not for eight hours, not even for one hour."

He regarded her for a moment. "If that's what you want, then that's what I want. Take that leave of absence."

"But the money—"

"I'll support the family. I mean, I don't make as much as you—" his gaze skittered "—but I can keep us in Pampers and milk for a few months.'' His Adam's apple bobbed. A glint of panic hovered in his eye for only a moment, then was gone. ''Not that I'm ready to settle down for life or anything—''

''Of course not.''

''But hey, a few months as breadwinner won't kill me, right?''

''Right.'' She flinched at the breathless sound of her voice, so needy. ''We'll be partners. A team.''

''A team,'' he repeated, seeming to savor each word like an unfamiliar taste. ''Yeah, sure, why not?''

Before Lydia could reply, a cranky sound filtered from the living room. Lydia swallowed disappointment, rubbed the back of her neck. ''Tami's awake.'' She glanced at her watch and moaned. ''Look at the time. The kids must be starving.''

Powell shifted, shrugged. ''Umm, I could eat, too.''

''Oh, of course you could. I'm so sorry. I'll just tend to Tami, then I'll fix something—''

''I'll take care of Tami.''

''No, I'll do it—'' She caught herself, took a breath and stepped back. ''Okay, great. That would be a big help. You take care of Tami, and I'll see to supper.''

It wasn't a huge step. It was, in fact, a very small one, but it heralded a minuscule release of control, and a willingness to share responsibility to which she'd always clung as if it were a lifeline.

The smile Powell flashed in her direction was a clear indication that he, too, understood the effort it took for her to relinquish even that tiny facet of domestic sovereignty. ''After the day you've had, you deserve a break from kitchen duty. If you want to toss on some mud-free clothes, I'll get the kids ready and we'll go out for dinner.''

''Who's buying?''

"Always the financial analyst, aren't you?"

"I am what I am."

"I'll buy. You're unemployed, remember?"

"Technically I'm a part-time research consultant on a limited budget." She forced a smile. It made her cheeks ache. "But I can still spring for a hamburger and fries."

"Suit yourself." Another loud wail from the living room caught Powell's attention. He paused in the doorway as Lydia called his name.

She moistened her lips. "About what just happened, you know, between us…"

A wary shadow shuttered his gaze. "You mean the kiss."

"Yes, the kiss."

"I apologize for that. It won't happen again." With that, he left.

Lydia touched her lips, remembering. "Yes," she whispered to the empty doorway, "it will."

Balancing the frowning one-year-old in the crook of his arm, Powell tossed a bottle and two jars of toddler spaghetti into the diaper bag, then headed to the living room, where Kenny still sat glassy-eyed in front of the television. "Where's your sister's jacket?"

"I dunno." Only the boy's lips moved. His hypnotized gaze remained glued to an animated explosion of superheroes karate-chopping across the screen.

"Well then, where's your jacket?"

"I dunno."

"Find it. It's cold outside." Powell yanked the remote control up by the braided wire on which it hung from the ratty lounger, performed an awkward one-handed flip that landed the instrument in the palm of his hand, then thumbed the blaring TV into blessed silence.

"Hey!" Kenny pivoted on his bottom to glare upward. "I was watching that."

"We're going out for dinner. Get your jacket on."

"Where's Aunt Lyddie?"

"She's changing clothes. Hurry up, now. She'll be ready any minute—"

"Ban-kee." Tami, having spotted the tattered hunk of flannel pooled on the floor, suddenly lurched forward with a grunt, stretching out her fat arms and nearly propelling herself out of Powell's grasp.

Shuffling the diaper bag dangling over his shoulder, he dropped the tethered remote to tighten his grip on the wriggling baby. "You don't need your blanket," he said reasonably. "We're going out for dinner."

He realized his mistake the moment her tiny blond eyebrows crashed into a ferocious frown.

"Ban-kee!" she shrieked, arching backward with a furious lurch and kicking frantically. *"Ban-kee!"*

"Hey, wait—oof." One sneakered baby foot jammed into his midsection. The other hit perilously close to a sensitive part of his anatomy. Within three seconds, Tami's face was red as a boiled beet, and she was completely immersed in a shrieking, kicking, arching, flailing, full-blown temper tantrum.

Kenny wisely left the room while Powell futilely tried to calm the angry child. Failing, he carried the howling toddler to her crib and ran for help.

The master bedroom door was closed, a signal that one should knock before entering. Flustered and slightly panic-stricken, Powell simply blasted into the room. "Tami's having a fit. What do I do…?"

The question died on his lips. He closed the door to muffle the baby's angry screams and moved quietly into the room. Muddy garments were heaped on the floor. Clean clothing was laid out beside Lydia, who sprawled across the bed wearing nothing but a pair of lacy panties and matching bra that left little to the imagination.

She was also sound asleep.

Something cracked deep inside him. She looked so peaceful, so lovely. Because he couldn't help himself, he brushed the hair from her face, allowed his fingertip to linger at the edge of her soft mouth.

How many times had he seen her like this? Dozens, perhaps hundreds, yet he never tired of it. Never tired of her. Over the years, he'd dreamed of waking with her in his arms. In the weeks they'd been sharing this marital ruse, he would sometimes lie beside her just watching her sleep. He'd wanted desperately to reach out for her, to pull her into his embrace and feel her healing warmth seep into his wounded soul.

But he hadn't dared to touch her. If he had, he'd never let her go. He remembered the last time they'd been together, made love together. He remembered the words that had slipped out unbidden. *I love you,* he'd said.

I love you.

Later he'd denied it, pretended it was just one of those things men said to the women they bedded. He'd seen the hurt in her eyes, the shattered stare. That's when he'd realized that she'd found a niche in his heart and moved right in.

Powell hadn't wanted her living inside him, hadn't wanted anyone living there, not then, not now, not ever. It had taken all of his strength to leave her, a strength that was nothing more than the manifestation of his cowardice.

I love you, he'd whispered then.

"I meant it," he whispered now. "I always meant it."

Then he covered her with a blanket, turned off the light and went into the kitchen to order a pizza.

Chapter Eleven

Beside a winding lane in the heart of California's pictur-esque Nevada City, a fiery maple rested a crimson branch along a snow-white picket fence. Kenny studied the foliage with childish curiosity. "How come the leaves don't stay green?"

Lydia glanced up, but it was Powell who answered.

"Because it's fall, buddy, time for the leaves to fall off so the tree can rest all winter. Up here in the foothills, where it gets cold enough to snow, the leaves turn even brighter colors than they do down in the valley."

To Lydia's delight, Powell shifted the baby carrier on his back, causing Tami to grab his ears and giggle. "Sharp little fingernails," he muttered, twisting out of her pinching baby grasp. He angled a glance at Lydia, who simply chuckled and retrieved another fallen leaf for the autumn scrapbook she and Kenny were creating. "I don't know if this kiddie backpack was such a great idea. She thinks my ears are handles.''

Amused by Powell's struggle with the baby carrier, or rather with the baby inside the carrier, Lydia simply batted her lashes and flashed an evil smile. ''Daddy ears *are* handles. That's why old men have droopy lobes.''

She handed the scarlet leaf to Kenny, who examined it carefully before tucking it into his bag. ''That's a maple leaf. See that huge tree across the street?''

Kenny followed her gaze. ''The big yellow one?''

''Yes. That's an oak. What say we go get some of those for our book?''

Bright-eyed with enthusiasm, Kenny gave a vigorous nod and would have scampered across the road without looking had Lydia not snagged his hand. ''Uh-uh, remember what we've discussed about streets?''

''Oh, yeah. Look both ways—'' he carefully complied with exaggerated motions ''—and always hold on to a grown-up.'' Grinning, he squeezed her fingers.

Lydia squeezed back and felt as if her heart might actually explode. It seemed impossible to believe that she'd once survived without these beautiful children in her life. She couldn't fathom how. They were so much a part of her now, as was the man who was digging through the diaper bag to comply with Tami's request for ''joose.''

The baby emitted a joyful squeak when he produced a small bottle, snatched it with grabby little hands, popped the nipple into her mouth and sucked greedily.

From across the street, Lydia watched, smiling. In the weeks since that first disastrous visit from social services, her life had clicked into perspective. Time once slated for business pursuits was now lavished on the children, who thrived on the attention. They'd adapted so well that Lydia had been able to return to the day care facility for twice-weekly visits. She never ventured beyond their sight, of course, and kept their stays brief. Still, the children seemed less and less cautious now, and even seemed to enjoy themselves.

At home, Powell had been true to his word, and had taken on the role of father-figure with a vigor that was startling. Lydia had to admit that sharing parental responsibilities had been a relief. Beyond that, it had allowed her to view Powell through new eyes. She admired his resilience, was amused by his wry humor and utterly charmed by his befuddled struggle to understand those curious creatures called children.

Lydia had always admired Powell's easygoing nature, but now, whenever she watched him comfort a sobbing toddler, tend a scratched hand or nurse a wounded little ego, she saw a man who was not only comfortable in his own skin, but had gifted insight into the needs of others.

He'd changed, she realized, not only from the callous college youth with whom she'd once been enthralled. He'd continued to evolve since their lives had become inextricably entwined, and she found herself depending on him more frequently, and at a level beyond what she would have suspected.

Lydia even found herself trusting Powell, albeit not emotionally. It hadn't been easy to separate her feelings for him as a parenting partner from her feelings for him as a man. The last thing on earth she needed was to fall in love with him all over again. She'd promised herself she wouldn't.

It had been a promise increasingly difficult to keep. Every night had become a trial by fire, with Lydia retiring early each evening in the vain hope that she'd be asleep before Powell came to bed.

Sometimes it worked. More often she'd find herself lying beside him listening to the steady rhythm of his breath basking in the radiant heat from a body she'd once known so very well. Darkness amplified the sweet memories until she wanted him so much her teeth ached.

The past haunted her, reminding her of the intimacy they'd once shared. Those had been wonderful days, rich with passion and with promise. But the passion had died, and promises had been broken.

Powell had only pretended to love her then, and she held no illusions about him loving her now. He only stayed for the children. Lydia told herself that was enough.

Across the street, he still fussed with baby things, adjusted the happy toddler strapped to his back. Lydia called out to him, "You're getting pretty good at this daddy stuff."

"Yeah?" Seeming pleased by the compliment, Powell straightened, shifted the diaper bag over his shoulder and crossed the narrow lane to the large yellow oak tree where Kenny was bagging a stash of brightly colored leaves.

As Powell stepped over the slanted curb, Tami, still brandishing her juice bottle, swung around and whacked him in the back of the head. He ducked, muttering, and frowned at Lydia's thinly veiled chuckle. "I suppose you're going to say this is why old men have bald spots?"

"It's one explanation."

"Tell me again why we couldn't just use the stroller?"

"Because we're on a nature walk. Some of the most breathtaking fall colors are along Deer Creek, accessible only by hiking path. It's pretty, but not particularly stroller friendly."

Powell pivoted his head sideways as Tami flipped the juice bottle again. He flinched as it caught him above the left ear. "Last week it was a picnic in the rain. This week it's leaf-picking nature walks. I never realized how adventurous you are."

"There's a lot you don't know about me."

"Yes." His eyes warmed, sending a shiver of heat down her spine. "But I'm learning."

Lydia swallowed hard, averted her gaze. *For the children,* she reminded herself. *Only for the children.*

"Where's Deer Creek?"

"Hmm?" She blinked, realized that Powell was speaking to her. "Oh, it's right over there." She pointed to a strip of shrubs and trees running through the quaint old country town. "They have duck races in the summer."

"Duck races?" Eyes wide with wonder, Kenny rose from a squat, stuffing a handful of vibrant saffron leaves into his collection sack. "Real live ducks?"

"Well, not exactly." Taking his hand, Lydia guided her little troop toward the bridge crossing the creek. "They're little plastic ducks like the one you play with in the bathtub." They paused at the rail, gazing down at rushing, crystal-clear water that sluiced from snow-fed mountains to carve a lush, forested waterway through the center of town. "Each duck has a number on it. They're all put into the creek beyond that white gazebo." She pointed to the octagon structure not far from the water's edge, across the creek from a restaurant with a balcony extending to the edge of the ravine.

Powell leaned against the rail while Kenny shaded his eyes, gazing at the rippling water. "So what happens to all the ducks?"

"Ah, well, they float downstream over the rapids, and the winners line up in a chute right below the bridge."

The youngster hopped up on a curb to lean over the railing. "I don't see a chute."

"Careful." Lydia quickly took hold of his arm, urged him off the curb. "It's only set up for the summer races, when the creek is calm and the water is only a few inches deep. During the winter rains, the creek is more like a roaring river than a lazy little stream. The water can rise all the way to the bridge.''

Powell propped an elbow on the railing. "How did you learn so much about duck races and raging rivers?"

"My folks drove through the area on the way to their Tahoe cabin," Lydia said. "I saw the duck races when I was about fourteen, and loved them. There are pictures in the restaurant of the creek at flood stage. It's fairly awesome."

"I can imagine," Powell mumbled, eyeing the twenty-five-foot drop from the bridgehead to the water below. The creek was substantial even now, due in part to an unseasonably wet autumn, followed by a warm spell that had melted the early snowpack and sent it careening into rivers and streams. "It's hard to believe this ravine could ever be full."

"Trust me, it can." A tug on her shirt hem caught her attention. Inquisitive blue eyes stared up at her. She tousled the boy's thick hair. "What is it, honey?"

"What happens to the ducks that win?"

"The people who have adopted them get prizes."

Kenny's eyes snapped wide-open. "People get to adopt the ducks?"

"Yes, indeed."

Clearly thrilled, the boy jumped up and down, clapping madly. "I wanna adopt a duck. Can we, huh, can we?"

"Of course we can, sweetheart, but we'll have to wait until next summer."

"Can we adopt a whole bunch of ducks?"

"A whole bunch? Well, I don't know—"

"Oh, please? I'll keep them all in my room, and they won't be any trouble, honest."

Smiling indulgently, Lydia slipped an arm around the

boy's quivering shoulders and gave him a squeeze. "We won't be able to take the ducks home, Kenny."

The news obviously crushed him. "How come?"

"Because the duck races are a charity event. People pay to adopt one duck for one race. Someone else adopts the same duck for the next race. That way, the charity earns more money. At the end of the day, all the ducks are packed up until next year's duck races."

A light flickered in the boy's eyes, then dimmed into darkness. His lip trembled; his gaze dulled. "So people just play with them for a little while, then give them back?"

"Yes, I guess so."

"It's not fair."

Lydia felt rather than saw Powell stiffen. She swallowed a surge of alarm, knelt down to the boy's level. "Why isn't it fair, Kenny?"

He gave a limp shrug, and blinked back a tear. "'Cause it means people are just guarding the ducks. Nobody wants to keep them."

That night Kenny wet his bed again, the first such accident in weeks. While Powell escorted the whimpering boy into the bathroom for fresh pajamas and man talk, Lydia discreetly changed the bedclothes.

"How is he?" she asked when Powell returned to the living room.

He shrugged, sat in his lounge chair, oblivious to the ominous creak it gave beneath his weight. "He's asleep. I'm not sure he was ever completely awake. If we're lucky he might not remember this episode."

"He'll remember." Heaving a sigh, Lydia set aside the magazine she'd been absently perusing. "Clementine left message on the machine while we were out this afternoon

She said the guardianship papers will probably be finalized by the end of next week.''

"That's good, isn't it?"

"Yes." After the first disastrous meeting with social services, two subsequent surprise visits had gone very well, and according to Clementine, the investigators had issued glowing reports on the children's home life. Lydia had been massively relieved. Powell had just smirked and said something to the effect that he'd told her so.

He was smirking again. "See there? All your worrying was for nothing."

"I suppose so." Lydia was still worried, but not for the reason Powell implied. "Powell, I've been thinking."

"Always dangerous," he muttered, reeling up the remote and flipping on the television. "Try to control it."

"I'm serious."

Something in her voice apparently got through to him. He stared at her for a moment, then turned the television off. "What's wrong?"

"I'm not sure." She chewed her lip a moment, avoided his withering gaze. "Don't look at me like that. It's Kenny. I'm worried about him."

Powell sat forward. "The bed-wetting thing? Look, he's just a kid. It's no big deal—"

"I think it is, Powell, because it only happens when he's deeply stressed about something."

"We had a big day, that's all. Too much soda, too much excitement. He was overtired and fell asleep without attending to his nightly routine. By tomorrow he'll be fine."

"I hope so."

"He will be." The statement was punctuated with almost enough fervor to sound desperate.

"Powell?"

"Hmm?"

"What Kenny was saying this afternoon, about guarding the ducks instead of adopting them—" When he stiffened slightly, she rushed on. "It's not the first time he's said something like that. The other day Tami called me Mama for the first time. Kenny scolded her."

That got Powell's attention, although he clearly tried to conceal his concern with a haphazard shrug. "He's old enough to remember his mother. He might not like hearing someone else called by that special name."

"I thought that was it, too, until later, when I heard him telling her that we were only 'guarding' them until a new mom and dad came along." The expression on Powell's face was telling. "You've heard him say the same thing, haven't you?"

He nodded reluctantly, and fidgeted with a loose thread on his sweatshirt. "That may be my fault. The first day we brought them here, he asked me about that. I tried to explain that we were their guardians. Maybe I messed it up."

"I don't think so, Powell. I think Kenny understood only too well, and now that he has this little friend Joey, who loves to talk about how special he is because he was adopted, Kenny seems to be obsessed that we're going to give him away."

"That's silly."

"Is it?"

"Sure it is. I'll set him straight."

"How?"

"Well—" he worried the shirt thread a moment longer "—I'll just explain that guardians are every bit as permanent as parents, that we'll both always be here for him."

A weary heaviness settled in her chest. "You can't tell him that, Powell."

"Why not?"

"Because it isn't true."

Their eyes met. For a moment, she saw bewilderment in his gaze, then the clouds lifted into clarity as he remembered the terms of their agreement. "After the guardianship papers are finalized, Clementine will initiate divorce proceedings. You'll be moving out. I'm terribly concerned about how Kenny will deal with that. He's crazy about you."

Powell pinched the bridge of his nose. "Yeah. I know." There was no reason to add that he was crazy about Kenny, too. They both knew it. "I don't suppose there's any big rush. I mean, unless you've made plans or something."

"Plans?"

"For after we're, you know, not together anymore."

A sharp breath burned the back of her throat. "No," she whispered. "No plans."

He rolled his head, rubbed the back of his neck, avoided looking at her. "So I don't have to be out of here by any specific time. I mean, I could stay on for a while, if it's okay with you."

She could barely breathe, let alone speak. "It's okay with me."

"Just for a while," he added hurriedly. "As long as the kids need me."

"Sure, for as long as they need you." Her heart pounded like wind-driven rain.

The children would always need him. Lydia was certain Powell understood that, and was giving tacit approval for what she planned next.

"Holy smokes, is that meat loaf?"

Batista's eyes nearly popped out of his head while Powell smacked his lips over the fat, meaty sandwich he'd just retrieved from a plain, brown lunch bag without a hint of scrolled writing on it. "Yep. Homemade meat loaf. Nice thick slab of it.'' Hunkered behind the truck as protection from the icy drizzle and frigid wind, he took a giant bite and chewed, groaning with exaggerated pleasure. A small audience of curious co-workers garbed in lemon-yellow rain slickers gathered. ''Umm-m.'' He allowed a bit of barbecue sauce to dribble onto his chin. ''Onions, sausage, mushrooms, hickory-smoked flavoring. Double sauced.''

''Double sauced?'' Sam, the foreman, licked his lips. ''Woo-ie. I sure do love a thick slab of double sauced meat loaf.''

Powell made a production of finishing the sandwich in a few manly bites, then retrieved a fat, chocolate cupcake from the hidden recesses of his lunch bag. ''Well, what do we have here? Fudge frosting, cream filling. Not bad, not bad at all.''

Batista was practically salivating. ''Sure in hell looks better than them leafy-stuffed things she used to pack for you.''

''Took awhile to train her,'' Powell replied. He didn't think it necessary to mention that he'd prepared this luscious repast with his own callused hands. Nor did he feel his cohorts needed to know that Lydia had somehow discovered that he'd been ditching her healthy pita salads and had informed him in no uncertain terms that he could either pack his own lunch or starve, and she didn't much care which.

Things had changed between Powell and Lydia. He wasn't exactly sure how or why, but everything was different than he'd imagined it would be. He was seeing a different side of her now, a softer, more acquiescent behavior that he found oddly appealing. She'd even begun asking his opinion on matters that she'd have previously handled without comment. Powell rather liked that. He liked that she allowed him to do small kindnesses for her

such as bring her a cup of coffee without leaping up to grab
the pot herself, or allowing him to handle a child's question
without interrupting with her own response. And she smiled
more often, too, a dazzling expression of radiance that
made his heart flutter.

Everything was different, from her willingness to consult
with him on routine matters to her new sense of adventure,
a shocking spontaneity that had culminated one rainy afternoon last weekend when she'd blithely dressed the kids
in boots and slickers for a picnic at the lake.

Powell liked the new Lydia. He liked her impetuousness
and the way her eyes sparkled as if she was recalling the
punch line of a joke that only she knew. He liked the way
her melodic laugh sent shivers down his spine.

He even liked the way she'd come to rely on him.

What he didn't like was lying awake at night aching to
make love with her. Memories made it even more difficult,
memories of how sweet she'd once felt in his arms, and
the way her soft, shiny hair had splayed across his pillow.
It was enough to make a man crazy, but he dared not admit
even to himself that she was getting under his skin. Again.

Sam glanced at his watch. "Let's get going, men. A
transformer blew south of the lake. We'll have to bust our
humps to replace it before quitting time."

Batista stood, scratched himself. "Hell, I could use some
time-and-a-half. The wife wants a new dishwasher."

"Yeah?" Sam spit into the rain, wiped his mouth with
the back of his wet hand. "Well, your wife ain't watching
the department budget. Accounting says we've busted our
overtime for the month, so get your bony rumps in gear,
and let's move out."

Groans and mutters accompanied the crinkle of squashed
lunch bags as the sorry crew heaved to its feet as a single
unit. Sam climbed into the truck, reached for the two-way

radio to let dispatch know their location and destination. Batista moved behind the truck to answer a call of nature.

The fourth member of the crew, a quiet young man named Tad, who'd only been on the job a couple of weeks, wandered a few yards up the old logging road, tilting his head and staring up the steep incline of burned-out trees and oozing mud from last night's torrential rain.

Powell called out to him. "C'mon, Tad, when old Sam says no overtime, he means no overtime. Dragging our feet will just cost us extra hours without pay."

Tad glanced over his shoulder, yelled into the wind. "Do you hear that?"

At first Powell heard nothing but the howling of the storm and the pounding of rain on his slicker. He felt it first, a low rumble at his feet, a sinister vibration working its way from his boots to his knees. Then came the sound, a deep, oppressive growl from the bowels of the earth itself. Powell's blood ran cold. "Mudslide!"

Then the earth exploded.

Chapter Twelve

"Accident?" Grasping the telephone receiver until her knuckles whitened, Lydia sagged against the kitchen counter. "What kind of accident?"

Her own voice was raw with terror. The voice on the telephone was crisp, disturbingly detached. "One of the field trucks was apparently damaged by unexpected earth movement. Rescue crews have been dispatched and should be on scene shortly."

"My God." A wave of nausea threatened to choke her. "My husband...has he been hurt?"

"There have been no reports of injury at this time. We understand one of our field employees is in need of extrication. I have no further information." The maddening restraint of the voice wavered briefly. "I'm terribly sorry. I understand your concern, but there's nothing more I can tell you. I was simply asked to inform the families that their loved ones will be delayed, and to assure them that everything possible is being done so news reports won't frighten them.''

"News reports?" Lydia felt faint. "It's serious enough to make the evening news?"

"One of the local stations picked up our dispatch and is sending a filming crew to the location. It's routine for this type of, ah, mishap.'' The dispassionate voice lowered a notch, perhaps because the speaker was embarrassed at using such a tidy understatement.

Lydia was appalled, and she was terrified. Powell could be buried under six tons of mud, and this infuriatingly calm woman dared label it a mishap. A flat tire was a mishap. A stubbed toe was a mishap.

An avalanche of earth large enough to bury a truck was not a mishap.

It was a catastrophe.

Lydia wanted to scream, vent her terror and indignation, but her teeth were suddenly chattering and her wobbling knees threatened to buckle.

Kenny appeared in the doorway, stocking-footed and bouncing frantically. "Aunt Lyddie, Aunt Lyddie, Tami has Sidney's fish food and she won't give it back! She's pouring it out on the floor, Aunt Lyddie, and Sidney isn't gonna have anything to eat!"

Turning away from the wailing youngster, Lydia covered one ear and tried to concentrate on the voice droning over the line. "—As soon as we have further information.''

"Please, wait, where did this happen? Is there somewhere I can go, someone else I can speak with?"

"Sidney is gonna *starve!*''

"As I've said, Mrs. Greer—"

"He's gonna die, Aunt Lyddie! Sidney is gonna *die!*''

"We'll keep you informed.''

"Aunt Lyd-die!''

Lydia's world was spinning out of control. From what seemed a great distance she heard Tami's happy squeal, Kenny's horrified howl and the impersonal voice on the phone offering final reassurance a moment before the line went dead.

She stood immobile, foolishly staring at a kitchen floor that had been painstakingly polished to a high-gloss shine, thereby beckoning Kenny into a sock-skating frenzy, which had allowed his baby sister access to his room, apparently resulting in a two-month supply of fish food being dumped on the recently vacuumed hall carpet.

Just another day of blissful domestic chaos. Oh, and by the way, at this very moment Powell might be fighting for his life.

Lydia's vision blurred. A peculiar buzzing roared through her brain. Eventually she realized it was the dial tone.

She hung up the phone, shaken to the marrow. An accident. Powell had been in an accident.

"Aunt Lyddie!"

Kenny's frightened voice permeated her own fear. She had to be strong. The children needed her. Somehow she managed to cross the room, to take his small hand in hers, to force a reassuring smile. "It's all right, sweetie. We're not going to let anything bad happen to Sidney."

Hours later, after the children were asleep and Sidney had been fed with a few salvaged flakes scooped from the carpet, Lydia sat at the kitchen table, prostrate with relief. A company representative had called only moments ago. All four members of Powell's work crew were safe. Powell would be home soon.

Safe. Home.

Before today those had merely been words, no more or

less important than a thousand others. Now she cherished those words as the most beautiful ever created. Only one other word meant as much to her. *Love.*

Love.

It wasn't just a word anymore, not just a common expression one attributed to everything wonderful, from a warm puppy to a steaming mug of rich hot chocolate. It was an indefinable emotion stronger than an ocean tide, pure as the heart of a child and just as precious. Lydia couldn't deny it anymore. She was in love with Powell. She'd always loved him. She always would.

He was safe. He was coming home.

And she loved him.

It was nearly 10:00 p.m. when Lydia heard Powell's car in the driveway. She met him at the front door and gasped at the sight. He looked as though he'd been dragged backward through a pig wallow. Tired, white-rimmed eyes stared out from a face coated with ocher grime. Red mud crusted in his hair, oozed from his pockets. His skin was nearly obscured by a layer of filth, and his hair was matted on his scalp like muddy roadkill.

"Oh my God." Lydia pressed her knuckles to her lips. Tears sprang to her eyes.

Closing the door behind him, he grimaced, carefully peeled off his clotted jacket. "It's not as bad as it looks. Sam was inside the truck when the mudslide pushed it off the road. It tumbled down a ravine, and the mud rolled over it like a river of slime. The rest of us spent two hours digging through waist-deep muck with our bare hands. We'd still be there if Sam hadn't been on-line with dispatch when the slide hit. He let out a yell right before the radio went dead. It was enough to let headquarters know what happened, but it still took a couple of hours for the rescue

crew to show up with enough equipment to get the truck
out.''

The frightening image made Lydia ill all over again.
What if Powell had been in that truck? ''Is Sam all right?''

''Yeah. Twisted his arm in the steering wheel when the
truck flipped, but nothing that won't heal.'' Clearly exhausted by the ordeal, Powell ran his hand over his mud-
caked hair. ''I know this isn't my scheduled shower time,
but maybe we could make an exception?''

A bubble of foolish laughter burst into her throat. She
swallowed it, but allowed her smile to spring free. ''The
time chart is history. It was a silly idea in the first place.
First thing tomorrow, I'll hammer it into toothpicks and
dump it in the trash.''

He heaved a wistful sigh. ''Can I watch?''

''You can help if you want.'' Lydia took the wet jacket
out of his hands, grasped his elbow and ushered him to the
laundry room. ''First, we're going to get you out of these
filthy clothes.''

''I like the sound of that,'' he murmured, as she struggled
with buttons encrusted in still-damp mud. ''It's been a long
time since you've undressed me.''

A slow heat rose into her cheeks at the memory. It *had*
been a long time. Too long. ''Are you terribly fond of this
shirt?''

''No, why?''

She grasped the lapel, gave a furious yank. Buttons
popped, bounced across the floor. ''The stains will never
come out. No sense wasting time trying to be gentle.'' Ignoring his startled expression, she peeled the garment off
his shoulders. When he'd managed to extricate his arms
from the stiff sleeves, she tossed the foul apparel aside and
busied herself with the hem of the once-white, now grungy

T-shirt, which was tenaciously tucked beneath the belted waistband of his jeans.

Powell gazed from the torn shirt heaped in the corner to her busy fingers wrestling with his belt buckle. "I think I'm getting turned on."

"You like having your clothes torn off, do you?"

"So it seems." He crossed his arms, grasped the splotched cotton hem and pulled the T-shirt off over his head, baring his chest to her hungry gaze.

It was not an unfamiliar sight, yet she was deeply affected by it. Powell had filled out since his college days, adding a sculptured layer of muscle that rippled beneath the grime like the surface of a windswept pond. A scattering of dark hair nested between his nipples, then arrowed down past his navel, pointing the way to his manhood.

As if she needed a map.

Lydia knew exactly what was secreted beneath the telltale denim bulge. The memories trembled inside her like a sweet kiss. A flash of passion, of sweat-slick skin, of murmured words and moist breath. Of sweet fire inside her, flames licking the core of her femininity, singeing the marrow of her soul.

At that moment she wanted him more than she wanted her next breath.

Judging by the turbulent darkening of his stormy gray gaze, he was acutely aware of that. He extended a hand, his eyes hopeful yet wary. "Lydia…?"

She moistened her lips, exhaled with an audible shudder. It took a moment to compose herself. When she was able, she met his questioning gaze, laid her palm against his gritty cheek. He was so dear to her, so precious. She wanted to tell him how the sight of him turned her insides to warm mush and made her heart race like a drumroll. She wanted to tell him how she ached to touch him, to feel his arms around her. She wanted to tell him that she loved him, but she didn't dare.

Love. One word, one syllable with the power of an invading force. Love had driven Powell away six years ago. Her love for him. His lack of love for her. That, and her incessant need for control. She couldn't risk another defeat, couldn't risk driving him away again.

Caressing his roughened cheek, Lydia tenderly traced the strength of his jaw with her fingertips. "Take your shower," she whispered. "I'll warm up dinner."

Beyond the bathroom door, the shower blasted full force. Lydia listened for a moment, her hand poised on the doorknob, her heart pounding in her chest. She caught the inside of her cheek in her teeth, sucked in a fortifying breath and walked in. Steam billowed, shrouding mirrors, clouding the blurred figure moving behind the glass partition.

Closing the door behind her, she unknotted her robe, let it slide to the floor.

A chill whispered against her bare flesh. A nervous shiver wobbled her knees. Inside the shower, nebulous movement caught her eye. She could tell Powell's back was to her. His shoulders rippled beneath the water as he scoured his scalp with his knuckles. Foam lathered white and rich as whipping cream, only to be blasted away as he ducked his head under the steaming spray.

Even through obscuring mist, his magnificence took her breath away. Shoulders strong and sinewy, a muscular back tapering into lean hips, tight buttocks compact enough to fit a woman's hand, firm enough to deflect an affectionate squeeze.

Her palms itched; her fingers twitched. Her flesh tingled with anticipation. She wanted him. She'd always wanted him. Tonight she would have him.

Boldly she stepped forward to grasp the chrome lever. The shower door opened with a snap. Powell's head jerked around, his hand hovering over the clean, wet hair plastered darkly against his scalp.

"Your dinner is warming." Smiling, Lydia stepped inside. "Your appetizer is already hot."

Hot spray bounced from his body, nipping her naked skin. Her thighs quivered; her knees shook; her ankles wiggled like wet noodles. Somehow she remained upright. "Shall I soap your back?" The question was uttered with a sensual purr. "You used to like that."

Powell closed his mouth. His Adam's apple bobbed once. "I still do."

The washcloth hung on a porcelain bar beneath the soap dish. She reached around him to retrieve it. Her breast teased his elbow. He made no effort to step out of her way. Instead he stood there, gazing at her with eyes like a turbulent ocean mist, dark with sensuality, smoldering with promise.

Despite trembling hands, she lathered the washcloth, rubbed soapy circles from his nape to the small of his back. Slow, lazy strokes, sensuous, slick with foam. He responded with tiny twitches, taut shivers that vibrated her body, and reverberated through his.

The feel of him excited her, aroused her, awakened all the sexual fantasies she'd hoarded in the back of her mind since the last time they'd been together. There had been other men in Lydia's life since Powell. None had found their way into her bed. Or into her heart.

Only this man. Only him.

Again and again she circled the washcloth over Powell's body, thrilling to the sharp planes of his shoulder blades, the bars of his ribs, the rounded tautness of his hips, and that gorgeous masculine bottom so perfect it made her drool at the possibilities.

The washcloth lingered there, stroking from the round curve of his hip to the conjunction of his upper thigh, up and down, up and down, right side, left side, right side, left, slower, lower, until he whirled with a ragged gasp and took her wrist in his hand.

His eyes glittered, his lips lush with sexual promise. "Now the front." His voice was a guttural whisper, ripe with carnal nuance.

"Definitely, the front." It came out a breathless murmur, so ragged and husky that she barely recognized the voice as her own. Her arms were suddenly limp, almost too weak to hold the soapy cloth. The sight of his bare chest mere inches away, with rivulets of water sluicing over the swollen muscles and angled planes, was enough to make a less determined woman swoon.

She soaped every inch of him, fought for breath with every sensuous stroke. By the time she'd lathered below his navel, a portion of him surged forth to greet her. She'd have been disappointed if it hadn't.

She took him fully, stroking him with the cloth, but never taking her eyes from his face. His eyelids fluttered. A low groan rumbled inside his chest, but never fully emerged. His shoulders tensed; his jaw quivered. He rolled his head backward, exposing his muscled throat, with thick, corded veins pulsing as wildly as her own pounding heartbeat.

"Enough." He took the washcloth. "My turn."

Without moving his mesmerized gaze from her face, Powell relathered the washcloth, set the soap aside and went to work. Each arm was tenderly tended, then her shoulders, her back, her buttocks. By the time he reached her breasts, Lydia trembled like a sapling in the wind. The cloth was discarded. He lathered her with his hands, circling his flat palms over her nipples until an exquisite electricity tingled from her breasts to the apex of her thighs.

As if by magic he followed the path with his fingers, massaging down to her belly, stroking her honey-blond nest, dipping into the innermost softness of her womanhood. She moaned softly, rolled her head backward, grasping his shoulders to keep from falling. The sensation was too sumptuous for words.

His fingers caressed the slippery flesh, parting the moist folds to touch her deeply, intimately. Every stroke brought a pleasure more intense than the last. He knew her body so well, as if the last time he'd explored it was hours ago rather than years. No one had ever lavished her with such tenderness, raised her body to such rapturous heights.

Only this man. Only him.

Water sprayed her face, her hair. She barely noticed. Her belly burned with insatiable need. Her thoughts blurred into pure sensation, pure arousal, pure desire.

When he pressed the tiny bud of sexuality, she cried out. Arching back, she hooked one leg around his hip, dug her heel into his bottom to press him closer. His erection throbbed against her stomach, hot and urgent. She wanted it, wanted him.

He slipped his hands behind her thighs, lifting her as if she weighed no more than a feather. Both legs encircled him now. She wrapped her arms around his neck, buried her face in the side of his throat. Water spilled from his hair, from her hair, from the steaming shower. Wet skin skated across wet skin; lips blossomed, swollen, warm, enticing. His mouth grasped hers, demanding, insistent, tasting her deeply before moving to test the sweetness of her throat, the silken curve of her jaw, then back to settle upon her plump lips, gently this time, with exquisite care. He swallowed her moan, thrust deeply into her velvety mouth to absorb all of her flavor, all of her sweetness.

Turning around to block the stinging shower spray with his body, he tightened his fingers under her thighs. She broke the kiss, levered herself with her arms on his shoulders. Every breath was a gasp, every gasp a cry of pleasure so exquisite it was almost pain.

Their eyes met; their gazes locked. Then he lowered her slowly, allowing her softness to absorb the sleek, pulsing length of him one shuddering inch at a time. No words were spoken. None were needed. They spoke with their eyes, with their bodies, with the explosive heat of their joining. A deep groan, a desperate cry, a spasm of ecstasy. He filled her with his love.

Sweet fire. Sweet, sweet fire.

Only this man. Only him.

The fragrant aroma of bacon rousted Powell from a sound sleep. He rolled over, reached out as he'd done three times throughout the previous night. This time, his arms returned empty. His sleep-drugged mind cleared. The bacon scent wafted his senses, tempting him into wakefulness.

Had last night been a dream? The ache in his loins was one of overuse, not longing. It had been no dream. What started in the shower had continued in bed. Three times, maybe four, each wetter, wilder than the last. Years of deprivation, weeks of yearning had culminated in a night he'd never forget.

But the best part, the sweetest part, had been in between sexual liaisons, when they'd dozed in each other's arms. He could still feel her sleeping softness nested in his embrace, could still smell her special fragrance on his skin.

It had been a night of ecstasy, of sheer joy and pure bliss. The best was yet to come.

Pivoting his feet to the floor, Powell indulged in a luxurious stretch. Muffled voices filtered from the hallway, Kenny's high-pitched chatter along with Tami's baby grunts. Tiny footsteps, fast-paced and hurried. Children, Powell had learned, never moved from place to place slowly. They dashed, sprinted, darted and galloped. He liked that about them. He liked their energy, their optimism, the instant gratification they sought. Crying one minute, giggling the next, children were incredibly complex creatures with fully integrated personalities and a simplistic manner of twisting life to suit themselves. Powell liked that, too.

At the moment, he liked pretty much everything about life in general, and his life in particular. It was, he decided, a very good day.

Whistling softly, he dressed, then ambled into the hallway just in time to dodge a toddler on a tear. Tami bobbled down the hall grasping a small stuffed toy and grunting madly to herself. She wasn't steady enough on her feet to run effectively, her fat little legs occasionally speeding beyond her ability to keep up. This was one of those occasions when the toddler's torso turned toward the doorway, while her tiny feet forgot to follow. She bounced off the wall, sat down hard, then scuttled sideways with a ferocious baby frown. Only when she saw Powell standing there did she break into tears.

He scooped her up, kissed her chubby cheek. "There, there, peanut. You'll grow up fast enough. Don't rush things."

Sniffing, Tami wiped her face with the back of her hand, then pointed toward the kitchen, babbling madly.

"What's that? Aunt Lyddie's cooking bacon and eggs for breakfast?"

Huge blue eyes widened. The baby gave a vigorous nod.

Grunting, she wiggled to get down. Powell accommodated her, set her back on her unsteady feet and grinned as she wobbled on her merry way.

Yep, he thought, kids were fun to have around. Dan had been right about that. Maybe Dan had been right about other things, too. Like marriage and family, which Dan had made his top priority. At the time Powell hadn't understood that devotion. Perhaps he'd even resented it. The thought saddened him. Thoughts of Dan always saddened him, so he always pushed them aside.

He pushed them aside now, and followed the delicious bacon smell into the kitchen. Lydia was at the stove, poking the sizzling meat strips with a fork. He tiptoed up behind her, slipped his arms around her waist. "Umm, yummy." He nuzzled the side of her throat. "Good enough to eat."

They both understood he wasn't discussing bacon.

Lydia chuckled, turned her face for his kiss. He brushed her mouth with his lips, sweetly at first, then with increasing ardor. "Good morning," he whispered when she finally broke away, breathing heavily. "Turn off the bacon, give me fifteen minutes and I'll make it a wonderful morning."

She actually flushed. "You're insatiable."

"It's your fault. You're too delicious. I can never get enough."

"Well, you'll have to control your urges. The children are awake."

"Those pesky urges, hmm? Controlling them really doesn't seem to be our strong suit."

Her laugh drifted away as Tami toddled in with a hunk of paper clutched in her baby fist. "Da-da-da," she chortled, handing over the scrap, once a part of a magazine page. The baby babbled some more, but the only recognizable part of her conversation was "Da-da," her word for daddy. Powell felt his heart squeeze at the sound of it. He glanced over and saw that Lydia, too, was affected.

Neither noticed Kenny in the doorway until the boy took his sister's hand and led her out of the kitchen without a word. Curious, Powell followed in time to hear him give his sibling a firm lecture. "Uncle Powell isn't our daddy. He isn't really our uncle, either, but I guess it's okay to pretend."

"Da-da," Tami insisted.

"Uh-uh, he doesn't wanna be our daddy." The boy tossed a protective arm around his sister's little shoulders. "Don't worry, Tami, we're gonna find a new mom and dad. I promise."

That was all Powell heard before the siblings disappeared into the living room.

"Did you hear that?"

Startled, Powell spun around, stared into Lydia's sad face. "Yeah."

Her eyes implored him. "Kenny is convinced he's going to wake up someday and discover that we've given him away."

"That's silly."

"Not to Kenny."

Huffing a breath, Powell massaged his eyelids. "No, not to Kenny."

"We have to do something, Powell, something that will give Kenny the security he needs."

For some reason, the conversation troubled Powell enough that he wanted nothing more than to end it. "Yeah, sure, whatever."

"Do you mean it?"

If he'd been more observant and less agitated by what he'd just overheard, Powell might have noticed the hopeful glow in Lydia's eyes. Instead he wrapped the shield more tightly around his heart, covered his turmoil with a lazy shrug. "Sure I do. Hey, is breakfast ready yet? I'm starving."

Chapter Thirteen

"Nana!" Tami twisted on Rose's lap, clutching her grandmother's face between two roughly insistent baby hands. "Joose, Nana, joose!"

Laughing, Rose managed a quick hug before the baby wriggled down to waddle over and slap at the refrigerator. Rose heaved a regretful sigh. "I don't have any juice, precious. Would you like a cookie?"

The toddler jammed both fists against her mouth, nodding with such vigor she almost knocked herself over. "Coo-kee!" she squeaked as her grandmother rose from the kitchen chair. "Joose."

Rose retrieved the cookie box from a cupboard. "No juice, sweetie, unless your aunt Lyddie has some."

A questioning glance brought a chuckle and a nod from Lydia. "As a matter of fact, I'm fully prepared, juicewise. And diaperwise, toywise, snackwise and every other wise." As proof, she pivoted in her chair, pulled a stuffed diaper duffel from under Rose's wobbly kitchen table. Lydia pulled out a small juice bottle, which sent Tami into a flurry of desperate little ''gimme'' grunts.

Still clutching her cookie, the baby clamored into Lydia's lap, snatched the bottle and chug-a-lugged apple juice in a most unladylike fashion. Lydia chuckled, shifted the gulping child more comfortably, then lovingly wrapped a strand of curly blond baby hair around her index finger. ''I've decided that Be Prepared was a parental war cry long before Boy Scouts commandeered it as a motto.''

Rose's smile was slightly sad. ''Parenthood becomes you, Lydia.'' She lowered herself back onto her chair, paused for several breaths before speaking again. ''Susan would be pleased.''

A lump caught in Lydia's throat. ''I could never take Susan's place, Rose. I wouldn't even try.''

Waving away that concern, Rose regarded her thoughtfully, and with a reverence that was touching. ''All my daughter wanted was for her children to be loved and well cared for. She trusted you to do that for her. You have, and I'm grateful.'' The older woman gazed toward the window, smiling at the happy laughter of Powell and her grandson playing outside. ''Thank you, too, for telephoning me so often over the past weeks. You have no idea how it warms an old woman's heart to believe she's wanted.''

''You are wanted, Rose. Your knowledge and advice has been invaluable. Besides, the kids want to talk to you as much as I do. They love you, Rose.'' Lydia brushed wet crumbs from Tami's bibbed overalls, then set the empty juice bottle on the table as the baby squirmed down and wandered into the living room. ''I love you, too.''

A grateful gleam illuminated eyes that still appeared tired enough to be worrisome. ''And I love you, dear. You've been so good to me, and to the children. I'm afraid I don't tell you often enough how much you mean to me. Powell, too, of course. He's such a good man.''

''Yes, he is.'' Looking away, Lydia snatched a paper napkin from a ceramic holder and made a production of dabbing sticky juice dribbles from the table. Powell *was* a good man. He was a good father, too. And a magnificent lover. Lydia was crazy about him. So were the children. They loved Powell dearly, and Lydia was certain he loved them. Deep down, she firmly believed he loved her, too.

Oh, he'd never said as much. He'd only said the *L* word once in her presence, on that fateful night years earlier. Later he'd denied it, told her he hadn't really meant it, pretended it was just one of those things men said in the heat of passion.

Then he'd walked out on her.

Perhaps he hadn't loved her then, but despite his reticence to repeat the word, Lydia was certain that he did love her now. She believed that with all her heart. She had to believe it or she'd go mad.

So she continued to tell herself that love had always been frightening to Powell, that she understood that much about him. Still, there was more she didn't yet understand.

His mood swings, for instance. There was no doubt in her mind that Powell was happy, but there had been moments over the past week or so where he'd also been brooding, tense, even a bit snappish. A couple of days ago, for example, he'd come home with the news that he'd been offered a management position. Lydia had been thrilled for him. Powell, however, had simply shrugged it off, saying that he hadn't decided whether or not to take it.

Something in his eyes had warned her off, so she'd swallowed her questions, offered her brightest smile and changed the subject. He'd been emotionally withdrawn for the rest of the evening.

They hadn't made love that night. But the following morning, he'd reached for her with such smoldering passion that her blood still steamed at the memory.

She shivered, felt a rush of heat stain her cheeks, and slipped a covert glance at Rose to see if the woman had noticed. Apparently she hadn't. Rose was gazing into space with a peculiar look in her eye, and a troubling grayish hue around her pale lips that was more evident as she shifted into a shaft of sunlight.

Fretting over the woman's unhealthy pallor, Lydia reached across the table to touch her arm. The flesh was cool, slightly moist. "How have you been feeling, Rose?"

Thin shoulders shrugged beneath a bulky-knit sweater that hung like a blanket on a scarecrow. "I have good days and bad, but all in all I can't complain."

"What do the doctors say?"

"They want to do a procedure of some kind." Rose chewed her lower lip, frowned into her coffee mug. "Balloons in a person's veins." She shuddered. "Sounds like voodoo to me."

"Oh, Rose." Lydia stroked her friend's bony wrist. "If the doctors think it's best, you should consider it."

"I will, hon." She flashed a nervous smile, patted Lydia's hand. "Now, tell me how marriage is treating you." Her smile widened knowingly. "You look happy."

"I am."

Chuckling, Rose lifted her cooling coffee, peered over the mug rim. "So, maybe things are going to be a bit more permanent than you first thought?"

There was no sense being coy with the woman who understood her better than her own mom. "Powell and I have reached an agreement."

"An agreement, is it?" Her chuckle expanded into a guffaw. She set the mug down and slapped her knee, laughing. "Young folks nowadays even turn affairs of the heart into a business arrangement. Land sakes."

Grinning foolishly, Lydia gave a shrug. Despite her concerns about Powell's occasional mood lapses, the memory of this morning's lovemaking flashed through her mind again, stirring those old, familiar feelings. She recalled his tousled hair, his sleep-dazed eyes, his warm smile as he'd brushed his lips across her brow, whispering, "Good morning, beautiful." Then his fingers had edged underneath the covers to fondle her bare breasts, while hers traveled downward, seeking the aroused flesh below his belly.

They'd made love again, just as they'd done seven hours earlier. Just as they'd done nearly every morning and almost every night for the past two weeks.

To Lydia, the renewed consummation of their relationship signified the permanence of their union. She had no doubt the marriage was as real to Powell as it was to her. Her smile was probably a bit giddy at the moment, but Lydia didn't care. Rose would understand. Rose always understood. "Somehow I suspect Susan knew this would happen."

The older woman's eyes gleamed. "Yes, child, I suspect she did."

Shrill laughter from outside reminded Lydia that Powell and Kenny wouldn't be playing ball forever. There was a reason for their visit today, a reason Powell wasn't completely aware of because Lydia had wanted a private moment with Rose first. This moment was as private as she was likely to have, so she sipped some tepid coffee to clear her throat, took a deep breath and plunged forward. "The guardianship papers were finalized last week."

"Oh? That's good, isn't it?"

"Yes, yes it is." She took another sip of coffee. "The

thing is, I've been discussing the situation with Clementine—''

''Clementine?''

''She's Dan and Susan's lawyer, who has been acting as the children's legal advocate.'' Lydia continued when recognition in the woman's eyes was confirmed by a curt nod. ''Anyway, it seems that there are a few drawbacks we hadn't considered. For example, as guardians, Powell and I don't have the ability to make decisions about the children's future care. As it now stands, our relatives wouldn't have any legal status in regards to the children. If something happened to Powell and me, and you weren't, er, available, the kids would be made wards of the state, and go directly into the foster care system. Also, they wouldn't have the same inheritance rights of biological and—'' she coughed, glanced away ''—adopted children.''

Rose blanched. After a long moment, she said simply, ''I see.''

Lydia fidgeted with her fingers, swallowed hard, laid her clasped hands in her lap. ''Since Dan's parents are deceased, you're the children's closest blood relative. If you have objections...'' Her voice trailed away, returned on a whisper of air. ''We'll respect your wishes, of course.''

Afraid to look at Rose for fear she'd recognize hurt in her eyes, Lydia focused on a peculiar knife scratch in the Formica tabletop. From the corner of her eye she caught movement across the table.

Rose shifted, crossed her legs. ''You want to adopt my grandchildren.''

Stiffening her shoulders, Lydia forced herself to meet the woman's gaze. ''Yes.''

Rose nodded, skittered a glance toward the sparkling window, beyond which Kenny and Powell were still engaged in their touch football game. ''I won't be around

forever," she said finally. "I want to make sure my grandchildren will always have family to love them, cherish
them, keep them safe and secure. If adoption will make that
happen, you'll hear no complaint from me."

Lydia's breath slid out all at once. "This won't change
their relationship with you, Rose."

"I know that." Her smile was genuine. A sparkle of
moisture touched her tired eyes. "Do whatever you have
to do," she whispered. "Just promise me you'll always
take good care of my babies."

"I will, Rose." Lydia seized the woman's hand with a
grateful squeeze. "I will."

A few hours later, the tired but happy family piled into
the car and drove down the mountain to the neat suburban
house they now called home. Lydia was relieved to have
Rose's approval for her plan, although she hadn't seriously
believed the woman would have any objection. Rose was
a smart and savvy lady, clearly convinced that adoption
would provide her beloved grandchildren with the financial
and emotional security they deserved.

Now all Lydia had to do was convince Powell.

The bills were mounting. Powell hunched over the
kitchen table, poking a calculator and muttering under his
breath. A strange invoice caught his attention. "What's
this?"

Stepping away from the kitchen sink, Lydia wiped her
wet hands on a towel as she peered over his shoulder. "Oh,
a pair of shoes for Kenny and a couple of new outfits for
Tami. She's growing so fast she can barely squeeze into
shirts that were roomy on her just a few weeks ago."

"Yeah, but seventy-five dollars?"

"I'll pay for it."

The hurt in her voice pricked at him. "I told you I could handle expenses. I just wondered what the bill was for, that's all."

"Well, that's what it's for."

"Yeah. Okay." Combing his fingers through his hair, he put the receipt aside and went on to the next bill. Home insurance, $350. Powell nearly choked. Fair enough, it covered an entire year, but the only insurance he'd ever budgeted for in the past was on his car. Now there were two cars and a house. Fire, flood, theft, liability. Not to mention the decrease in take-home pay since he'd added the children to his medical insurance policy. By the time he paid to insure every eventuality, he'd be bankrupt.

No wonder Dan had gone gray before he was thirty. Powell could feel those grizzled hairs pop out of his own scalp every time he wrote another check. It was amazing how much money it took to keep two small humans in cookies and jumpsuits. Not to mention visits to the pediatrician, legal bills and household expenses he'd never even thought about before, like the cost of a power mower and the hundred-dollar-per-hour plumber hired last week when Tami flushed a plastic block down the toilet.

As it was, Powell practically needed a skip loader to haul the bills in from the mailbox. Since Lydia's paycheck had gone from eye-popping to petty cash, the lion's share of household expenses fell on Powell's formerly sturdy shoulders. He'd always made more money than he needed. Suddenly, he felt like a financial failure. He felt old. He felt trapped.

He felt like Dan.

Lydia came up behind him to massage his neck. "Powell, why don't you reconsider that fishing trip with your friends this weekend? You could use a couple days of rest and relaxation."

"I've already decided not to go, because I can't afford it," he snapped, regretting both his tone and his words, but unable to stop either. "I can't afford the gas, I can't afford the bait, I can't even afford the damned fishing license."

Dan hadn't been able to afford those things, either.

Frustrated, Powell pushed away from the table, stood so quickly he nearly knocked the chair over. He tried to avoid looking at Lydia's ashen face, but her eyes drew him like a magnet. There was pain in her gaze, and a guilt that gnawed him like a rusty blade. "I have money in the bank," she said quietly. "Not a lot, but certainly enough for you to take a weekend holiday with your friends."

He knew exactly how much money she had in the bank. They'd pooled their finances simply to survive. "We're going to need that soon enough. Christmas is coming, remember?"

Was that bitterness actually emanating from him? Powell couldn't believe it. What was wrong with him? Why did he feel as if there wasn't enough air in the room?

Panic boiled within him, the same panic he'd felt six years ago, when he'd bolted rather than face the nameless fears chewing him up inside. And the look on Lydia's face—he'd seen that six years ago, too. When he'd told her he was leaving.

He'd gone away because she'd gotten under his skin, had burrowed into a secret place in his heart that no one else had ever reached. That had scared him then. It scared him now.

Not only had she found her way back to that same secret place, she'd put up curtains and moved in. Somewhere along the line his relationship with Lydia had taken an irreversible turn. Powerful emotions clogged his mind, overwhelmed his senses, emotions so deep, so gut-wrenching that he dared not even acknowledge their existence.

"What is it, Powell?" Lydia asked softly. "What's really bothering you?"

"Stamps," he blurted. "We're out of stamps. How can I pay bills without stamps?"

She regarded him with wary eyes. "There's a roll of stamps in my desk. Help yourself."

He felt like a fool. "Okay. Thanks."

Leaving the kitchen before his traitorous tongue could spout further inane idiocy, he moved quietly down the hall, pausing briefly to peek in on each of the children. They were both sleeping peacefully. A dull ache began in the center of his chest and spread outward. They meant so much to him. Too much.

Too damned much.

Inside Lydia's office, Powell turned on a lamp, then moved toward a desk layered with faxes, reports and other business documents. Presuming the stamps would be in the shallow center drawer, he yanked it open and found what he was seeking.

He also found something else. An unfamiliar packet of legal documents.

He was studying them when Lydia appeared in the doorway, breathless, her eyes huge. "I just remembered I might have put the stamps—" her gaze was riveted on the bound papers he held "—somewhere else."

Icy calm settled over Powell like a death shroud. He flipped a page, then another, then tossed the package on the desk. It landed with a thump. "Adoption papers." His voice wasn't harsh, but the context was.

Lydia flinched. "Just a draft, for review purposes. Nothing final."

"Nothing final." The repeated phrase rolled roughly off his tongue, hung in midair while they both considered its impact. "Well, as long as it's nothing final I suppose it doesn't matter that I wasn't consulted. After all, it has nothing to do with me. Except, of course, totally alter the course of my life.''

''We've talked about this, Powell. You implied you were willing to consider strengthening our legal bond with the children, to give them the security they crave, and to protect their future.''

''Funny, I don't recall 'I've asked Clementine to draw up adoption papers' being part of any conversation.''

Lydia heaved a sigh, very soft but nonetheless fatalistic. ''You didn't say anything, Powell.''

''You're right, I didn't say anything, so you just did what you wanted. Lease an apartment, file for adoption. I say nothing, so you just do it.''

The life seemed to drain out of her eyes. ''Adoption makes sense, Powell. It's what Kenny wants, what he needs desperately to feel secure. And it's important for us, too.''

''How so?''

''Because as adoptive parents, we'd be empowered with legal authority not granted under guardianship laws, including the right to make decisions about the children's future care. They'd also have inheritance rights. We've discussed this, Powell. I thought you agreed that adoption made sense.''

''I agreed that strengthening our legal status made sense. I never agreed to adoption.''

''It's just a word, Powell, just a legality. Nothing will change.''

''Everything will change, don't you see?'' He hated the desperate croak in his voice, hated the shock reflected in Lydia's eyes, but felt powerless to control either. ''The children's name will change.''

She stared blankly. ''Their name?''

''From Houseman to Greer, right?''

"Well, yes, but I've already discussed this with Rose, and she agrees that it's best for the children—"

"With Rose?" His fist landed on the desk without his permission, and hard enough to vibrate a stapler. "You've discussed our future with Rose before you bothered to discuss it with me?"

The color drained from her face. "Rose is the children's grandmother. Clearly we needed her approval before pursuing the matter."

Powell knew that. Of course he knew it. He just couldn't control the explosion of sheer panic inside his chest.

"I don't understand your concern with the change of their names, but—"

"It's disrespectful. Dan and Susan were our friends. Now we're going to erase their name, eliminate them from the children's lives, pretend they never even existed."

With a sharp breath, she steadied herself on the doorjamb. "You know better than that, Powell."

Yes, he did know better than that, but the hollow argument, the damnable words just kept spewing out, obscuring the real truth, drowning it in a sea of ancient history and utter minutiae that had nothing to do with the honest issue. He knew that.

Lydia knew it, too. He could tell by the look on her face as she drew herself up, clasped her hands together and studied him intently. "Let's get down to it, shall we? Your problem isn't with an apartment three thousand miles away, or a lease negotiated without your permission six years ago, and it isn't with a choice of surname. It's with the permanence of adoption, and what that means for our future as a couple." She waited for him to deny it.

He couldn't.

She took a shaky breath. "I've been deluding myself, haven't I?"

"What do you mean?" Powell asked, although he feared he already knew.

"Somewhere along the line, this marriage became real for me, this family became real. I thought it was real for you, too, but I was wrong, wasn't I?" She waited, her eyes begging him to dispute it, to take her in his arms and promise her forever.

But he couldn't, he just couldn't.

Deeply conflicted, Powell realized he'd reached a crossroads in his life. He had a choice to make, a big one. Either end things now, or be prepared to make a lifetime commitment to Lydia and the children. He wasn't ready for that commitment. It scared the hell out of him. But he wasn't ready to let go, either. His heart screamed out in protest against a life without Lydia, a life without the children who were so dear to him.

Powell, who had always avoided failure by avoiding the attempt, suddenly found himself trapped by his own emotions. He didn't know what to say, so he said nothing.

Lydia made the decision for him. "You'd think I'd have learned my lesson years ago. Apparently not." Her voice was soft, slightly tremulous, but resonant with determination. "I allowed myself to love you all over again. I allowed myself to rely on you. I should have known better because this time children are involved, children who have already been abandoned by one set of parents, and who will certainly suffer even more emotional damage by a second abandonment. If this family is a ruse, Powell, it's better to end it now than later."

"Lydia—"

"No." She held up a hand, stopping him. "This is my fault, not yours. You've lived up to the original agreement. I'm the one who took it further than you were willing to go." There were no tears in her eyes, only exquisite sad ness. "You're entitled to your freedom, Powell, and you shall have it."

The room spun around him. Freedom. It was what he wanted, what he'd cherished most in his life. Or at least, it had been at one time. Suddenly he wasn't certain anymore. He wasn't certain about anything.

The telephone rang, startling him. Lydia answered. She spoke briefly, a few soft, clipped words. Powell wasn't really listening. *Freedom.* The significance sank like a rock into the pit of his stomach. *You're entitled to your freedom...*

And you shall have it.

Lydia hung up the phone, turned back to him, looking pale and wan.

A frisson of fear skittered down his spine. "What is it?"

"It's Rose," she whispered. "She's had a heart attack."

An hour later, two sleepy children were buckled into the back seat of Lydia's car, and Powell was packing the last of the suitcases into the trunk. The car shuddered as Lydia climbed into the driver's seat. A cold drizzle coated his hair, gathering into icy rivulets that slid down his neck, chilling him to the marrow.

Powell closed the trunk, rounded the vehicle and wedged his body in the open car door so she couldn't close it. "At least let me come with you."

She avoided his gaze by selecting the proper key from a fat ring, inserting it into the ignition slot with more care than necessary. "We've discussed this, Powell. The children and I will be gone for several days, perhaps even a few weeks."

"I can drive you up there, even take care of the kids while you go to the hospital, then catch a flight back in a day or so."

"That won't be necessary."

"It's snowing in the mountains."

"I've driven in snow before." She flipped on the ignition, let the engine idle to warm up. "I just called the highway patrol. Highway 80 is open all the way to Nevada, but they recommend carrying tire chains in case the snow builds up over the summit."

"You have chains?"

"Of course."

"But can you install them yourself?"

She rubbed her eyes, heaved a long breath. "There are chain monkeys every hundred yards at the checkpoint areas," she said patiently. "They install chains. It's what they do."

"For a price."

"Yes, for a price." She stopped him as he dug into his wallet. "I don't need your money, Powell. You do, remember?"

His face heated as he remembered how he'd stomped around like a chafed bull complaining about money, just as Dan had done.

No, not like Dan.

Awareness struck like a lightning bolt. That wasn't like Dan at all. Dan had always joked about never having enough money, but the voice that resonated in his memory, the angry man flinging checks across the table and bitterly decrying the cost of raising children, that hadn't been Dan at all.

It had been Powell's own father. The realization was as sudden as it was shocking. Powell remembered himself as a young child, trembling in his bedroom while his father ranted and raved in the other room. It had terrified him, made him feel guilty and worthless. He'd vowed that if he ever had children, he'd never complain about money, about the problems kids caused, about the time and effort it took to raise them.

Powell had broken that promise tonight, just as he'd broken so many other promises. And he'd broken something else, something he cherished beyond all else. He'd broken Lydia's heart. Again. "Lydia, wait—"

"We'll be going straight to the hospital," Lydia said tersely. "I want the children to see their grandmother as soon as possible in case…" Her voice wavered. She swallowed hard, stared out the windshield. "In case tomorrow's procedure doesn't go well. The children and I will be staying at Rose's place. You can reach us there."

She pressed the brake pedal while shifting into gear, a clear warning to Powell that their discussion was over. He stood, his hand hovering on the door latch. He wanted to speak, wanted to say something, anything. As usual, he remained silent.

Lydia turned on the windshield wipers. They swished softly in the darkness. "I'd appreciate you feeding Kenny's fish but… It might be best if you weren't here when we return."

With that, she closed the car door and drove away. Powell stood there watching, with rain in his face and fear in his heart, until the vehicle's taillights disappeared into the night.

Terror settled like a lump of ice in his gut. The freedom he'd so jealously guarded had been returned to him like a precious gift. Now he could relinquish the overwhelming responsibility, the drudgery of wiping grubby little faces, calming childish fears. Could give up the heavy warmth of small, sleepy bodies cradled in his arms, the stifling sensation of pudgy arms wrapped around his neck. Gone now, all gone. He was alone. He was free.

He told himself he was grateful. He told himself he was glad. And he told himself the moisture on his face was only rain. Hot, salty rain.

Chapter Fourteen

Blinking back tears, Lydia steered slowly through a light snowfall. The highway was nearly deserted, more likely due to the lateness of the hour than the dreary weather. It was nearly midnight.

In the back seat, both children slept peacefully. For that, at least, Lydia was grateful. They didn't know their grandmother was gravely ill. They didn't know that the man they'd grown to love as a father was preparing to bow out of their lives. They didn't know that their world was crashing down around their tiny shoulders.

All that would become painfully clear to them soon enough. But tonight they slept soundly, surrounded with sweet dreams and bright hopes.

Fool me once, shame on you.

She should have known better than to let herself need

Powell again, to let herself love him again. She had no one to blame but herself.

Fool me twice, shame on me.

Even worse, she'd allowed the children to love him. She could never forgive herself for that. There was no doubt in Lydia's mind that Powell would be long gone by the time they returned home. The children might never see him again.

She might never see him again.

A pain struck in the center of her ribs, rotated out like a whirling blade. The thought was devastating. Never see Powell again? Nothing terrified her more. It was a nightmare from the past wrapping icy fingers around her heart and squeezing it lifeless.

Lydia would love Powell forever. She knew that now, accepted it with stoic sadness, because it didn't matter anymore. Powell didn't love her, at least not in the way she deserved to be loved. Completely. Irrevocably. Forever.

If Powell wasn't capable of that, it was best to find out now. It was so much worse this time because of the children. They'd be hurt, bewildered, confused. But they were young. They'd get past this sadness and go on with their lives.

Lydia wondered if she could say the same for herself.

Because this wasn't all Powell's fault. In fact, if she was brutally honest, it was Lydia herself who had caused all this misery and pain. She'd caused it six years ago, because she'd kept secrets from Powell for his own good. At least that's what she'd told herself at the time. The truth was that she simply hadn't wanted to relinquish control.

Control. It sounded so crass, so arrogant. And it was, in

a way. But it wasn't control over others that Lydia sought, it was control over her own life, and the fear of losing it.

She'd made excuses for herself, of course, told herself that it was natural to study every eventuality before taking someone else into her confidence. That way she'd be able to respond articulately to every concern, every possible question. It was, after all, the nature of a detail-oriented person like herself to be meticulous. Nothing wrong with that, nothing at all.

Unless it was used as an excuse to excise others from the decision process and prevent them from taking charge of their own destiny.

Lydia now realized that was exactly what she'd done throughout her tumultuous relationship with Powell. Despite the excuse of best-intentions, the bottom line was that she'd consistently usurped unilateral command over issues that affected his life, issues about which he had every right to make his own judgments. Except that she had insisted upon making those judgments for him.

Such personal revelations weren't pleasant, but they were realistic. Lydia was nothing if not realistic. For the first time she understood that the same fear of failure that propelled her to personal perfection also demanded complete control of any situation over which she felt inadequate.

When defeat was not an option, victory was not allowed.

It was a painful lesson, one she'd learned too late.

The snow was falling harder now, coating the windshield as the wipers strained under the weight.

Squinting into a white glare, Lydia thought at first she was being blinded by oncoming traffic. She soon realized that the light from her own headlamps, refracted by the swirling storm, was being flung back into her eyes. All she could see was a curtain of solid white. To her horror, she realized that visibility had dropped to near zero, and she could barely make out the center line of the road.

She touched the brake lightly, slowing the car to a crawl. A glance at the rearview mirror revealed nothing more than she saw out the front. If there was a vehicle behind her, she couldn't see it, nor could she see any trace of the highway center line, or even the highway itself. There was nothing but thick, swirling snow. The car was completely engulfed.

So this was what they called a whiteout.

It was her final thought before the car veered over an embankment and sailed into a snowy ravine.

Powell retrieved a beer from the fridge, popped the top as he wandered from the kitchen to the dining area. The beer tasted flat, but he barely noticed. His eye was drawn toward the wall where Lydia's time chart had once resided. Only a small nail hole remained, along with the construction-paper clock with movable hands that she had created for Kenny.

But something new had been added—several childish drawings taped around the paper clock. He wondered why he hadn't noticed them before, and took pains to study them now. A crayoned yellow blob with something akin to an orange beak was labeled *Sesame Street* in neat, block letters. There was also a sketch of a clock with the big hand at twelve and the small hand at three.

Another drawing reflected what appeared to be a four-legged creature entitled *Wishbone;* the sketched clock reflected a time of three-thirty. There were several other illustrations, childish renditions of favorite cartoon characters, each neatly labeled with a clock specifying time. Obviously the small gallery had been created so that Kenny would know exactly when his favorite programs were on television. The clock drawings aided the child in learning to tell time; the neatly crayoned labels helped him recognize letters and words.

It was a good idea, Powell thought, as clever and creative as Lydia herself. She was good with the children. More than good, actually. She was wonderful. Loving and gentle, firm when necessary, indulgent when she thought he wasn't looking.

But Powell was always looking, always watching her from the corner of his eye while trying to feign indifference. It was a talent of his, feigning indifference. He was good at it. And look what it had gotten him.

His precious freedom.

That was, after all, what he wanted, what he'd always wanted. He should be grateful, but he wasn't. He should be massively relieved. But he wasn't. He was, however, alone. That should have been okay with him.

But it wasn't.

He took another swig of tasteless beer and wandered into the hallway. It was late, but sleep was the last thing on his mind.

He found himself standing over Tami's vacant crib, inhaling the sweet baby smells. Bubble-scented powder, delicate lotions and oils. The tattered blankie was gone, of course. Since the baby refused to sleep without it, Lydia would have taken it with them. In the corner, however, Tami's stuffed dolphin, the beloved "fissy" from their aquarium trip, lay discarded and abandoned. For some reason, that hurt Powell.

His heart felt exquisitely tender at the moment. Raw. Swollen. Bruised.

From the nursery he went to Kenny's room, still cluttered with tiny vehicles and disjointed segments of toy track from a raceway set he particularly enjoyed. On the dresser, Sidney swam in circles, his buggy fish eyes focused on his narrow glass world as if there was nothing of consequence beyond it.

Powell felt a sudden affinity for the creature. He understood the comfort it took from its familiar surroundings, and the terror of looking beyond the glass walls into a world of frightening proportions. Sidney couldn't possibly comprehend the excitement and adventure lurking outside the tiny enclosure; he was only a fish, after all. But Powell understood. Powell was a man. A man craved excitement and adventure. A man craved freedom.

Of course, a man's home was also his castle.

Castle. Freedom.

Freedom. Happiness.

Happiness. Home.

Powell stood there, staring into the fishbowl as if some universal truth had suddenly appeared. *Happiness. Home.* All of his life he'd equated freedom with happiness, but despite having avoided commitment and responsibility, he hadn't been truly happy until Lydia and the children had come into his life.

Until he'd found his home.

Home wasn't simply a place to stack his sports magazines; it was anyplace he shared with those he loved. He loved Lydia and the children, loved them with all of his heart. They were his happiness.

And they were gone.

*   *   *

Rubbing his sleepy eyes, Kenny yawned, shivered, squinted at the frosted car window. "Are we there yet?"

"Not yet, sweetie." Lydia tucked half of the blanket she'd retrieved from the trunk around the youngster, and the other half around his sister, who was fussing quietly, trying to find a comfortable position in her car seat. "Zip up your jacket, Kenny. That's a good boy. Now I have to go outside for a while, but I'll be back soon."

"Where are you going?"

"Just up the hill a little ways."

He frowned. "How come?"

"Because the car is stuck in the snow, and we need someone to call a tow truck for us." Lydia punctuated the benign statement with a bright smile, hoping the child wouldn't notice that the vehicle was solidly jammed against a tree halfway down the mountain and so far from the highway that there was no chance of them being spotted unless she could climb back up the embankment to flag down help. "You can watch your sister for me, can't you? There's a bottle in the diaper bag, and some cookies and apple slices, too. I won't be gone long. I promise."

"Aunt Lyddie?"

She paused with her hand on the door latch. "Yes, sweetie?"

"How come your head is bleeding?"

"It's just a little bump, nothing to worry about."

Clearly the boy was worried. His lip quivered. "I don't want you to go."

"I know you don't." Sighing, Lydia wiped condensation from the window, stared into the storm. She was prepared for an emergency, of course. She was always prepared. Inside the vehicle she had extra food, water, blankets, flares, flashlights—everything necessary for survival. Outside, snow swirled and the wind howled, and the storm blasted the mountain with all of nature's unleashed fury. Lydia couldn't control the storm. Nor, she realized, would she be able to survive it long enough to bring help.

And if she didn't survive, the children wouldn't survive.

Smiling, she reached over the seat back to stroke Kenny's pale face. "All right then, I'll wait until it stops snowing. Would that make you feel better?"

Limp with relief, the child sagged bonelessly against his seat belt. "Uh-huh."

"So, has anyone ever taught you…" she paused to pull a bottle from the diaper bag and hand it to the fussing baby "…the 'Knick-Knack' song?"

Kenny grinned, nodded, took the cookie she offered. "This old man," he sang softly, "he played ten."

Lydia joined him. "He played knick-knack on his shin."

Tami giggled as they sang with increased enthusiasm. "Knick-knack, paddy-whack, give the dog a bone. This old man came rolling home."

"This old man—"

Snow swirled.

"He played nine."

Wind howled.

"He played knick-knack with his mind."

A child laughed.

"Knick-knack, paddy-whack, give the dog a bone."

Lydia sang with all her heart.

"This old man came rolling home."

For the children. Always, for the children.

* * *

"What do you mean they aren't there?" Tightening his grip on the receiver, Powell barked at the hapless desk nurse as if the poor woman had been personally responsible for the advent of a world war. "She should have been there an hour ago."

"I'm terribly sorry, Mr. Greer, your wife hasn't arrived yet."

"She must be there," he blurted stupidly. "She has two small children with her." As if one thing had anything to do with the other.

Panic rose like bitter bile in his throat. On the other end of the line, the nurse soothed him and took his telephone number, promising to contact him the moment Lydia and the children appeared at the hospital. Powell barely heard her. The moment he hung up, he dialed Rose's apartment. There was no answer.

Over the next thirty minutes he called Rose's number three more times, dialed the hospital twice and made several frantic calls to state trooper headquarters in Nevada, along with every California Highway Patrol office between Sacramento and the state line. All he learned was that there had been a few minor accidents reported before Highway 80 had been closed by the storm, but no one matching Lydia's description had been involved.

By 2:00 a.m., Powell was beside himself. Unable to sit still another moment, he grabbed his keys, jumped in his car and floored it. When the highway reopened to traffic, Powell would be there. There wasn't a shred of doubt in his mind that he'd either find his wife and children or die trying.

Bending over the front seat, Lydia tucked the blanket around the dozing children strapped in back. They'd been asleep for nearly an hour, and the snow had lightened to a few stray flakes. A few minutes ago Lydia had heard the hum of traffic back up on the highway.

It was time.

She tucked several flares in her pocket, grabbed her flashlight and went for help.

Traffic was creeping at a snail's pace, bumper-to-bumper vehicles winding ponderously up the hill. Powell had given up pounding his steering wheel. All that did was bruise his hand and make his blood pressure shoot up fifty points. He wouldn't be any good to anyone if he let the panic take over. After being trapped in a parking lot waiting for the highway to open, he should be thankful to be moving at all.

And he would have been, if thoughts of Lydia and the children weren't eating him alive. He had to find her. Dear God, he had to.

After a few miles, the traffic flowed faster, more smoothly. Powell swallowed hard, forced himself not to stomp on the accelerator. He had to pace himself, go slowly enough to keep a sharp eye on the embankments for tire marks or other evidence of an accident.

An accident.

The wave of nausea nearly crippled him. He fought it off, then slammed on his brakes as traffic ahead of him slowed again.

He cursed out loud, slapped the steering wheel with the flat of his hand a moment before bile rose into his throat, nearly choking him. He saw why the traffic had slowed, and was sickened. The right lane was closed up ahead, filled with flashing red-and-blue lights from emergency vehicles.

As he inched closer, he saw flares set up along the shoulder of the road, several Highway Patrol cruisers and a tow truck hauling a crunched vehicle out of a ravine. Powell glimpsed only the rear portion of the dented sedan on the end of the tow hook. A glimpse was all he needed. It was Lydia's car, all right. What was left of it.

A trooper was directing traffic away from the right-hand lane. Powell steered around the startled officer, drove through the line of flares and jerked to a stop beside the humming tow truck.

"Hey!"

He leaped from the car, charged into the snow to examine the vehicle being hauled upward. It was empty.

"Hey, you!" The angry voice was closer now.

Powell spun around. "My wife," he croaked, too distraught to be embarrassed by the emotional crackle of his otherwise manly voice. "My wife and kids were in this car."

The officer's frown melted into an expression of sympathy. Two other law enforcement types appeared from behind the tow truck. One of them spoke. "Mr. Greer?"

Powell spun around, frantic. "My wife...my kids..."

A female trooper stepped forward, smiling gently. "They're fine, Mr. Greer, just fine. They'll be happy to see you."

"Where—?"

"In my cruiser." She touched his elbow, directing him through the powdery snow and around the tow truck, then pointed to two other patrol units parked on the shoulder about fifty yards away.

One of the passenger doors swung open. A woman stepped out, wet, shivering, wrapped in an unfamiliar blanket. One hand held the folds of the blanket at the center of her chest; the other was pressed to her lips.

Powell bolted forward. The blanket fluttered to the snow as she emitted a small cry and rushed into his arms. "Lydia, Lydia." He kissed her icy face, her hair, her eyelids, moist with happy tears. "Oh, God, I was so scared—you're hurt." His fingertip grazed the outer edge of a puffy laceration just above her right brow. Frantic, he called over his shoulder. "She needs medical attention!"

"Powell, no—"

"Ambulance! We need an ambulance—"

She touched his lips, silencing him. "It's nothing, Powell, I'm okay. We're all okay."

The scurry of small feet caught his attention a millisecond before Kenny threw himself at the embracing couple. "Uncle Powell, Uncle Powell, the car drived over a big cliff, and we ate cookies and sang songs, and then Aunt Lyddie went outside and was gone a real long time, and then a whole bunch of real nice policemen carried me and Tami up the hill, and Tami started to cry 'cause she was cold, but I didn't cry because I knew you'd come get us—" the boy refilled his lungs with a noisy wheeze "—and you did, you really did!"

Struck mute by the power of his emotions, Powell freed one arm to encircle the beaming boy and pull him up into the embrace with Lydia, who was laughing and crying at the same time.

"I'm so sorry, Powell," was all she managed to say, but she said it over and over, until he silenced her with a kiss.

The warmth of her lips soothed him to the marrow, and

her sweet shudder left him breathless, gasping for air. "There's nothing to be sorry about," he said when he finally found his voice. "Thank God you're all safe. The car doesn't matter."

She bit her lip, staring into his eyes. "It's not the car, it's what I said to you earlier tonight, it's what I did by not telling you about the adoption papers, it's—"

"Adoption?" Kenny's head sprang from its resting place on Powell's shoulder. "You're gonna adopt us?"

Lydia went white, but Powell just laughed, so loudly that even Kenny was shocked. "You betcha, buddy." His laughter died in a lump of pure emotion. "I love you, Kenny, and I love your sister, more than I could ever have believed possible. I don't want to be Uncle Powell anymore. I want to be your dad. I know I can't take your real dad's place, and I don't want to, but I promise that I'll love you every bit as much, and I'll try very hard to be the kind of father he'd have wanted for you and your sister."

Huge eyes studied him intently. "Forever and ever and ever?"

"Yes, Kenny. Forever and ever and ever."

For a moment the boy sat in the crook of Powell's arm without moving, without speaking, without even acknowledging that he understood what he'd been told. Suddenly he threw his small arms around Powell's neck, hugging him fiercely before squirming down and dashing toward the patrol car, from which a disgruntled baby wail was emanating. "Tami, Tami, guess what! Uncle Powell is gonna be our real dad and Aunt Lyddie is gonna be our real mom, forever and ever and ever!"

Lydia touched Powell's face, turning it toward her. "Is that true, Powell? Am I going to be their real mom?" When he nodded, her gaze bored straight into his soul. "And what about us? Am I going to be your real wife?"

"You already are." He lifted her frigid hand to his lips, kissed each knuckle, then brushed her palm against his cheek. "I really do love you, Lydia. I always have, I always will. I can't tell you that doesn't scare me. It does. But I can tell you that the thought of living without you scares me more."

A single tear slid down her cheek, deflected by the tilt of her smile. "That's all I wanted to hear, my love. That's all I've ever wanted to hear."

Epilogue

Almost a year to the day from their less-than-auspicious Reno wedding, Lydia and Powell renewed their vows in an elegant chapel dripping with white roses, and scented with the sweet fragrance of their love.

Dressed in a white satin gown with an embroidered scoop neck and butterfly sleeves, Lydia wore a lacy wreath of tiny rosebuds in her hair, and the gold starfish necklace that had been Powell's first gift to her glittered at her throat. She felt as bridal as if this had been her very first wedding.

In a sense, it was. Beside her stood the only man she'd ever loved. Confident, beaming, free of doubt, Powell smiled like a man who knew exactly what he wanted out of life and had finally found it. He took her hand, leaned down to whisper in her ear, "This is the wedding you deserve." With a devastating, mischievous grin, he nodded toward the distinguished, immaculately tailored clergyman holding a white Bible instead of a fistful of note cards. "Fully zipped, too."

Lydia stifled a chuckle, felt a tug on her skirt and gazed down into the cherubic face of her beloved little girl. At two, Tami had blossomed into a happy, confident child, filled with curiosity and energy in equal measure. Gussied up in organdy and lace, with flowers in her golden baby hair and cheeks as pink as the petals in the basket she held, Tami blurted with breathless exuberance, "Pretty flowers!"

Smiling, Lydia shifted her own bouquet, freeing a hand to touch her child's precious face. "I know, sweetheart. You sprinkled the flower petals perfectly, but you don't have to pick them up right now."

"Uh-huh." Proving her point, the little girl busied herself by retrieving each of the scattered petals and reverently replacing them in her basket.

Kenny, standing on Powell's right, huffed in frustration, tugged at the tiny, white bow tie adorning his miniature tuxedo. "You're only s'posed to throw them down," he muttered to his sister. "You're not s'posed to pick them back up again."

Feathery blond brows crashed into a familiar frown. "My flowers, *mine!*"

A titter of amusement flickered from the audience of friends and family. Lydia's parents, beaming and proud, across the aisle from Powell's parents, who held hands throughout the ceremony in a display of affection that seemed to surprise Powell as much as it enamored Lydia. Rose was there, too, smiling and dabbing at her moist eyes. After a slow, arduous recovery, Rose was her old self again, with sparkling eyes and a glow of recaptured health that touched Lydia to the core.

In the center of the church was Clementine St. Ives and her assistant, Dierdre. Both women had smiled broadly as Lydia glided down the carpeted aisle. Clementine had given her a knowing wink. Lydia had winked back.

Now the ceremony had begun. The pastor spoke eloquently of love, of commitment, of the sacredness and sanctity of holy matrimony, while Tami picked up flower petals, Kenny tugged at his tie and Powell clutched Lydia's hand as if fearing she'd sprint away.

As if there was any chance of that. She'd gone back to work several months ago, but with a different priority. She still enjoyed her job, was satisfied and fulfilled by the career that had once meant everything to her, but now Powell and the children were the true focus of her life. She loved them with all her heart.

The ceremony was beautiful, dignified, everything their first wedding was not, although Lydia still looked back on that rather undistinguished beginning with fondness. She suspected that Powell did as well.

After the exchange of vows, the pastor presented them to the congregation, then brought Kenny up to stand beside him. A hushed buzz emanated from the audience, dissipating into utter silence as Kenny cleared his throat to speak.

"Dearly beloved people," he piped loudly, then waited until the pastor whispered the next line into his ear. "We are gathered here to celebrate... Huh?" He listened, frowned. "Oh, yeah, to celebrate the union of a brand-new family."

Kenny sucked in a quick breath and began to ad-lib madly, much to the delight of the crowd. "On account of Tami and me got to go see a judge last week, a real nice man in a big black robe, and he signed adoption papers so now we really are a family, and so now I get to…um…"

The boy looked quizzically up at the pastor, who bent to whisper final instructions. Stepping solemnly forward, Kenny extended both of his small hands. Lydia took his right hand; Powell took his left. "By the power 'vested in me as a kid, I now pronounce you Mom and Dad." The pastor whispered, Kenny grinned. "You can hug us if you want to."

"Oh, we want to," Powell murmured, scooping the boy up on the crook of one arm while Lydia gathered up the petal-picking baby.

As a family, they faced the smiling congregation. "Ladies and gentlemen," the pastor intoned. "I present to you Mr. and Mrs. Powell Greer, and their beautiful children, Kenneth and Tami Lynn Houseman-Greer."

Applause isn't customary at the conclusion of a wedding ceremony. This time, it was appropriate. For Powell, for Lydia. And for the children. Always, for the children.

In the lavender-scented parlor, Clementine stroked the old tabby cat in her lap and smiled at her beaming assistant. "'Twas a lovely wedding."

"Yes it was." Dierdre set a platter of cookies and milk on the credenza, handed Clementine a manila folder. "Your next appointment," she explained. "A young boy of about ten, I'd say. He's waiting in the lobby."

"Is he now?" Clementine perused the file without disturbing the snoozing cat. "Well, then, best send him on in."

Ten minutes later, Clementine served milk and cookies to her newest client, a youngster willing to trade his most valued possessions, a used boom box and a piggy bank, to find the father he'd never known.

Every child deserves a father, Clementine thought. *And that's what it's all about, after all. The children.*

It's always about the children.

* * * * *

Don't miss the next heartwarming story
in Diana Whitney's touching miniseries
FOR THE CHILDREN
available September 1999
in the Silhouette Romance,
A DAD OF HIS OWN.

Sometimes families are made in the most unexpected ways!

Don't miss this heartwarming new series from
Silhouette Special Edition®, Silhouette Romance®
and popular author

DIANA WHITNEY

Every time matchmaking lawyer
Clementine Allister St. Ives brings a couple
together, it's for the children...
and sure to bring romance!

August 1999
I NOW PRONOUNCE YOU MOM & DAD
Silhouette Special Edition #1261
Ex-lovers Powell Greer and Lydia Farnsworth knew *nothing*
about babies, but Clementine said they needed to learn—fast!

September 1999
A DAD OF HIS OWN
Silhouette Romance #1392
When Clementine helped little Bobby find his father, Nick Purcell
appeared on the doorstep. Trouble was, Nick wasn't Bobby's dad!

October 1999
THE FATHERHOOD FACTOR
Silhouette Special Edition #1276
Deirdre O'Connor's temporary assignment from Clementine
involved her handsome new neighbor, Ethan Devlin—and
adorable twin toddlers!

Available at your favorite retail outlet.

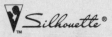

SILHOUETTE BOOKS
is proud to announce the arrival of

THE BABY OF THE MONTH CLUB:

the latest installment of author
Marie Ferrarella's
popular miniseries.

When pregnant Juliette St. Claire met Gabriel Saldana than she discovered he wasn't the struggling artist he claimed to be. An undercover agent, Gabriel had been sent to Juliette's gallery to nab his prime suspect: Juliette herself. But when he discovered her innocence, would he win back Juliette's heart and convince her that he was the daddy her baby needed?

Don't miss Juliette's induction into
THE BABY OF THE MONTH CLUB
in September 1999.
Available at your favorite retail outlet.

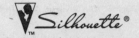

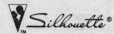

"Fascinating—you'll want to take this home!"
—**Marie Ferrarella**

"Each page is filled with a brand-new surprise."
—**Suzanne Brockmann**

"Makes reading a new and joyous experience all over again."
—**Tara Taylor Quinn**

See what all your favorite authors are talking about.

Coming October 1999 to a retail store near you.

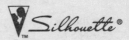

THE
FORTUNES
OF TEXAS™

This BRAND-NEW program includes 12 incredible stories about a wealthy Texas family rocked by scandal and embedded in mystery.

It is based on the tremendously successful *Fortune's Children* continuity.

Membership in this family has its privileges...and its price.

But what a fortune can't buy, a true-bred Texas love is sure to bring!

This exciting program will start in September 1999!

Available at your favorite retail outlet.

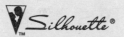

Silhouette ® SPECIAL EDITION ®

presents **THE BRIDAL CIRCLE**, a brand-new miniseries honoring friendship, family and love...

THE BRIDAL CIRCLE

by

Andrea Edwards

They dreamed of marrying and leaving their small town behind—but soon discovered there's no place like home for true love!

IF I ONLY HAD A...HUSBAND (May '99)
Penny Donnelly had tried desperately to forget charming millionaire Brad Corrigan. But her heart had a memory—and a will—of its own. And Penny's heart was set on Brad becoming her husband....

SECRET AGENT GROOM (August '99)
When shy-but-sexy Heather Mahoney bumbles onto secret agent Alex Waterstone's undercover mission, the only way to protect the innocent beauty is to claim her as his lady love. Will Heather carry out her own secret agenda and claim Alex as her groom?

PREGNANT & PRACTICALLY MARRIED (November '99)
Pregnant Karin Spencer had suddenly lost her memory and *gained* a pretend fiancé. Though their match was make-believe, Jed McCarron was her dream man. Could this bronco-bustin' cowboy give up his rodeo days for family ways?

Available at your favorite retail outlet.

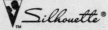

Silhouette ®
TM